THE TWO *Last* MOMENTS

HANNAH SHIELD

Cover Photographer: Wander Aguiar

Cover Design: Angela Haddon

Diana Road Books

Edgewater, Colorado

THE TWO *Last* MOMENTS

PROLOGUE

Lark

*P*lenty of things piss me off in this world. Hiking isn't number one, but it's up there. Why spend hours walking to a destination only to turn around and wind up where you started?

Night has fallen, and the temps have dropped to chilly, but I'm still sweating under my backpack. My feet ache in my thrift store Nikes. I've gone plenty of miles today. Mostly by bus, but my sneakers have done their fair share. At least my current journey is leading me someplace important. And after I get where I'm going, everything will change. That knowledge terrifies and elates me all at once.

I've tried to run before. But this time, there's no going back.

I check the directions on my phone again to make sure I haven't missed a turn, though I've had my route memorized for days now. First, the walk from Travis's house to the bus and into town. Then the longer trip to the main terminal in West Oaks. Now the final couple of miles. No dollars to waste on ride shares.

What will they say when I get there? When I explain where I came from and why I'm here? What if they hate me?

"Stop it, Lark," I whisper to myself. For once in my life, I'm choosing to be brave. Because it's easier to step out of line to help someone else, rather than just yourself.

I pass by rows of cozy looking homes. Flowers blooming, toys scattered on porches. A BMW pulls into a driveway, and the woman in the driver's seat eyes me with suspicion from inside. I walk past with a disarming smile, but I'm not sure she buys it.

Just a skinny, sweaty girl in her twenties hoofing it through your neighborhood. Don't mind my scraggly hair, messy eyeliner, or the tattoos. Please don't call the cops.

In my life, I've learned you can't trust many people, and a uniform is no guarantee. Not everyone is who they claim to be. Most folks are out for themselves, but the few who really care are priceless. They're worth sacrificing for.

That's why I'm doing this, even if it's the scariest choice I've ever made.

As I get deeper into the neighborhood, the green lawns stretch further back, and the houses get larger and fancier. I feel even more out of place. But I'm getting close to the right address.

The chiming of my phone makes me cringe. A text. I shouldn't look, but I can't help myself.

We know what you're doing, it says.

Chills roll through me. "Screw you," I reply out loud. "I'm already gone, and you can't stop me."

About half a mile later, there it is, with the numbers of the address decorating the mailbox. The property is even prettier than it looked on Google, full of shady trees. I can see pale stone and the edge of a white porch.

I've been imagining a willow growing in the backyard. If there is one, I bet it's beautiful, all swaying branches and tiny flowers. A little slice of heaven, probably too pure for the likes of me. But a girl can hope.

I'm trying to earn it. To make up for all the times I wasn't strong enough before. I'm so close that it seems like I could reach out, and I'd be there. I'll tell them the truth, and maybe they won't turn me away. They'll believe me.

Please.

My phone rings, and I flinch, the moment broken.

It's him. *Again.* I don't answer, but he leaves a voicemail. Against my better judgment, I listen.

"Lark, you'd better turn around right fucking now or you know what'll happen."

I doubt he's bluffing, but I no longer care.

It feels so good when I start to cross the street toward my destination. Such a simple act of defiance, but it means everything.

Then I hear an engine accelerate. My head turns sharply to follow the sound. Dread floods my body like poison. Headlights fill my vision.

He's already found me.

1

Danny

I step through the doorway holding a tray. "Madame, your dinner is served."

"Oh, really? Didn't know this place offered fine dining."

"For you, we're making it happen."

Nina does her best to sit up, while Jess, the night nurse, adjusts the tilt of the hospital-style bed. It's an odd contrast to the more familiar decor in her room, a new presence I'm still getting used to.

"This evening, we have filet mignon in a red wine sauce with truffle mashed potatoes." With a flourish, I point at the plate, which actually holds white rice and diced chicken breast. One of the few meals Nina can keep down the last few days.

I set the tray over my grandmother's lap, ignoring the scents of ointment and antiseptic. Then I pull up the stool that I keep by the bed.

Nina gives me a tired smile and picks up the fork in her shaky grip. "You tired of this yet? 'Cause I sure am. If I were you, I'd be back on shift tomorrow."

"Nope. This is where I want to be. I think the better question is, are you tired of me yet?"

Her sardonic expression turns serious. "You think that's possible?"

"I'm just checking," I say lightly.

Nina's never been a traditional grandma. She's an adventurous badass with wild stories of traveling the world in her younger days. Yet through all the ebbs and flows of my life, Nina has been my constant.

She and my grandpa were sipping margaritas on a beach in Panama when the news came: my parents were selling my dad's company for big bucks and moving to London—without *me*, their inconvenient seventh-grade son. Mom and Dad would've shipped me off to an impersonal boarding school, away from my friends and everything I knew.

So Nina and Grandpa stepped up. They moved back to West Oaks, our seaside town about seventy-five miles west of Los Angeles, to raise me. That was over twenty years ago. Since then, Nina has pushed me to seek out my own adventures. And I have. I joined the Army after college. When I returned to West Oaks, I became a firefighter, a job that didn't leave me with a ton of time to see her. But never once did Nina guilt trip me, even when I deserved it.

When Nina got her diagnosis, everything changed once again for the both of us. Ovarian cancer has metastasized to her bones. Her prognosis is bad enough that she's decided she doesn't want further treatment. *Fuck*, that news laid me right out on my ass. Shook up my whole world.

It was my turn to step up for *her*.

I took a leave of absence from work. Moved in. It's not a question of Nina having adequate care. We've got nurses trained in hospice care at the house every single day. My father's money covers that. We're lucky, because plenty of family caregivers have little to no backup given the expense.

But who better to stand by Nina through this than a grandson who loves her?

Now is when she needs me. The *only* thing that would make me go back to work tomorrow is if Nina didn't want me here.

She sighs, pushing chicken with her fork. "I hope you'll go out and do something fun for yourself tonight?"

"I was in the garage earlier during your nap. That was plenty fun."

"I don't mean working on that car all alone. When's the last time you saw Matteo?"

He's my closest friend, a fellow WOFD firefighter. "Matteo's busy these days. Angela's six months along now. They're in full baby-prep mode."

Nina's smile brightens. "No wonder he's occupied. I'm not one to lecture you about settling down, but you should have the kind of love your grandfather and I had. It takes the sting out of life. I'd...like to see that."

I brush a stray hair away from her face and swallow the lump in my throat. "I know. But I'm not in a hurry for things to change." I've got all the change that I can handle at the moment.

"I'm just thinking if you had a girlfriend to distract you, you wouldn't be bugging me so much."

"Is that right? Am I 'cramping your style'?" I add air quotes. "Did I say that right? I wouldn't want to use your old-timey slang wrong, *Grandma*."

"Oh, now you've done it. Go find something to occupy yourself, *Junior*."

"Oof. That's a low blow." I stand up, tucking the stool into its place against the wall. "I actually do have exciting plans. I'm going for a run." My second one of the day, actually. But I need it. Seeing Nina in that bed...damn, it gets heavy.

I push out an exhale.

Her eyes tell me she understands. And she feels the exact same thing. "Then get out there," she says. "Maybe you'll find somebody else to bother instead of me."

I give her a kiss on the cheek, check in with the night nurse on my way out, and hit the pavement.

I take my usual lap around the neighborhood. It's quiet tonight. Hardly anybody out. The air is cool, with a hint of marine humidity.

The houses around here are sprawling, each positioned on a generous plot of land. We're not in the West Oaks Hills, which is the wealthiest part of town, but this is still a nicer neighborhood than Nina could ever have afforded on her own. My dad bought the house for her when she retired. Of course, being my father, he didn't ask for her input. Just presented the key and the deed like a king bestowing a gift. And my grandmother accepted that gift gratefully, because unlike me, she's not one to complain about a windfall.

I'm probably not giving my dad enough credit. If I had to guess what kind of house Nina would love most, regardless of cost, it would be that one. Rustic style. Plenty of guestrooms, where she hosted exchange students before her illness. Big leafy trees and tall palms, manicured flower beds. Score one for Dad.

But while I share my father's full name, he goes by Chris instead of Danny. And we've rarely seen eye to eye.

Dad always wanted me to be a doctor. That was never my plan. I worked my ass off to become a line medic, then once I left the military, that experience transferred naturally to EMT training. For the past several years, my schedule as a firefighter has been demanding but predictable. Twenty-four hours on shift, then forty-eight off. It can be hectic, but I like the rhythm of it. Spending time with my teammates. Getting that adrenaline rush when a callout comes.

The best part, what truly fulfills me, is healing people during their worst moments. I'm a temporary presence in their lives, but I do everything I can to make a difference.

When I'm off duty, I go out with my friends, usually finding a hookup for the night. There are plenty of sweet girls in West Oaks and the surrounding towns, and a never-ending supply of tourists passing through. I like all shapes and sizes. If they could leave a review the morning after, I'm confident I'd have a rating well above four stars. I happen to take pride in a job well done.

But when it comes to women, I don't do the long-term thing. I'd rather stay nimble. People change their minds too easily. Leave when you least expect.

If you trust someone with your whole heart, you're just giving them all they need to break you. Nina's the only person who has that much of me. And now, with her in hospice…

But I'm taking this run to get my mind *off* the heavy shit. Doesn't seem like it's working.

When I'm almost back to Nina's house, I hear an engine rev. The sound is aggressive. *Angry.* Out of place on a quiet night. The hairs on my arms raise like a lightning storm is brewing in the air.

I turn the final corner, and that's when I see her. There's a woman standing frozen in the middle of the street. A backpack dangles from her hand.

And a car is bearing down on her, her silhouette glowing in the headlights.

Holy shit. It's going to hit her.

"Hey! *Look out!*"

I sprint toward her, but it's too late. There's a sickening thud. She goes flying, her body landing on the sidewalk.

I reach her and skid to a stop. My knees hit the ground

beside her. Behind me, the car's brakes squeal. I figure the guy's getting out to help. He must not have seen her.

"Call 911!" I shout. I'm an EMT, but I don't have my equipment with me. She needs a hospital.

But when I look over my shoulder, the car is moving again. The engine whines as it reverses at high speed. Then the guy puts it back into gear.

The car accelerates, steering directly at us.

What the hell?

Understanding spreads through me, along with a hefty dose of rage. Hitting the woman was no accident. This fucker is trying to kill her. And maybe me while he's at it.

I don't have a choice. I have to move her, *now*.

I scoop the woman into my arms, trying to keep her stabilized. She could have head or spinal injuries, and I'm jostling her, but if this madman hits her again, she'll be far worse off. I have to take the risk.

I take off just as the car jumps the curb.

Tires grind into the damp lawn behind us. The sound of metal on metal blasts through the air, and I glance back. The car just took out the neighbor's mailbox, and it's still coming.

I need cover.

There's a huge walnut tree in front of the nearest house, so I dart behind it, trying to put something solid in between us and that death machine. He veers toward us again, but then seems to think better of it. He steers the car in a wide arc, tires spinning in the grass.

The car rocks as he bumps over the curb again, retreating. And after a brief pause, he speeds away down the street.

My lungs start to work again. Just barely.

I lay the woman on the ground. She's young, maybe early to mid-twenties. Blood streaks from cuts on her forehead and cheek. Dark hair splays around her head. Her eyelids flutter, her panicked gaze fixing on my face.

"Hey, talk to me," I say. "What's your name?"

"Please…please…" Her attempt to speak ends in a groan.

"Don't try to move. You need to go to the hospital. I'll help you, okay?"

A door opens behind me, and there are shouts. Footsteps. The neighbor must have heard the noise. I hold up a hand to keep him back. While I'm checking her airways and vitals, running through the protocols, I hear the neighbor on his phone. Calling 911. Good.

But the woman's eyes are rolling back. She's losing consciousness.

"Police and paramedics on their way," the neighbor says. "Who is she?"

I'm still looking for signs of trauma and Cushing's Triad so I'll be ready when the ambulance gets here, but I don't even have my jump bag. I'm working blind. "I don't know," I reply. All I know is that someone tried to kill her. And I can't get her pleading voice out of my head.

Please.

2

———————

Lark

*H*arsh florescent lights shine in my eyes. Strange faces surround me, and hands grab at me.

No. No, stop.

I thrash my arms and legs. I have to get away. I have to run.

"Shit, Bradley, get back in here," someone shouts. "She's flipping out again!" There are footsteps. More voices.

Then, I see him. Blue eyes. Eyes that I know.

Safe, they tell me. *You're safe.*

I open my mouth, trying to speak. "I… I'm…"

"You're okay," he says, leaning over me. "If you don't stop fighting, you're going to hurt yourself."

There's a prick in my arm. Darkness descends over me again.

~

MY EYES BLINK OPEN. I hear moaning.

It takes a moment to realize that the moaning is coming from me.

I close my mouth and try to concentrate. I'm breathing. In and out. I'm in a bed. Something's beeping nearby. A machine. When I look down at myself, dark hair sweeps past my shoulder.

My head feels heavy. Fuzzy.

"Hi," says a deep voice. "How're you feeling?"

There's a man sitting beside me. His long-sleeved T-shirt is snug against a muscular frame.

I try to move, but I can't. Anxiety seizes me, makes my throat close up.

"Whoa, don't start that again." He touches my arm. "Everything's going to be fine."

Somehow, when I look at the man next to me, the terror recedes. Dark blond hair falls across his forehead, the kind of blond that looks brown when he leans his head at an angle. His eyes are blue. The placid blue of a lake on a calm morning.

I know those eyes.

I feel like I should know his name, but I can't remember it.

"Why...can't I move?"

A woman in chunky red glasses and medical scrubs walks into the room as I ask the question. "Ah, you're up. Welcome back. You were getting feisty earlier, so we had to sedate and restrain you." She's holding a tablet computer. "This guy's the only one who could calm you down."

Blue Eyes smiles tentatively at me. "You're at West Oaks County Hospital. You were in an accident. Do you remember?"

"Not really." An accident. What kind of accident? Am I hurt? I can't tell. Sedated must mean drugs, and that could explain the swimmy feeling in my head. Not the fun kind of swimmy though. This feeling is crap.

"I want off this ride." My voice slurs.

"I don't blame you. Give it a few minutes."

"Your eyes…"

"Yes?" he asks.

"Are nice. You're nice to…look at."

Wow. I have zero filter apparently.

He chuckles, a breathy sound that runs over me like a caress. "Relax a bit. Have some water." He holds up a glass for me to drink. When I'm done, he sets the glass aside, then rests his elbows on his knees, peering at me. "I'm Danny. Danny Bradley."

"Hi, Danny."

"What about you?"

"Me?"

I get lost trying to figure that one out. What *about* me?

A few minutes later, the nurse is finished checking my vitals and who knows what else. I'm feeling more awake and in control, though my arms and legs are strapped to the bed like a cannibal on a true crime show. I plan out what I'm going to say.

"Sorry…if I was being weird." I clear my throat. "I'm very chill now."

Danny smiles. The nurse crosses her arms over the tablet, lips quirking like she's hiding her own grin.

Sure, drug me and laugh at me when I'm a hot mess. That seems fair.

"Promise I'm better. You can untie me, right?"

"Not just yet, hon. I'm Julie. What's your name? You didn't come in with any ID." She poises her finger over her computer.

I speak without thinking. "Lark."

"Last name?"

"I…" I wait for another answer to come. But there's nothing.

And it's not just that. There's *nothing* where I can feel

there's supposed to be *something*. Like I'm groping in a dark room, and I can't find the light. "I don't know my last name."

The machine by my bed beeps faster.

"That's okay," Danny says. "Take your time."

I turn to him. "Your name is Danny, but do I *know* you?"

He and Nurse Julie exchange a glance. They're talking silently about me, and I don't like it. There's a lot about this situation I don't like.

"I remember…"

"You remember?" Danny prompts.

I trail off, not sure where I was going with that. Just that I remember *him*, though I have no idea from where.

His eyes. I remember his nice eyes.

And I remember bright lights coming toward me. But other than that, I don't remember how I got here. Where *here* is, aside from West Oaks County Hospital.

West Oaks. Where is West Oaks? Am I still in California?

What is happening?

"Please untie me."

Danny's hand touches my arm. The contact is too brief before he lifts away.

Nurse Julie gives me a long look. "Maybe in a bit. You're due for another dose of pain meds."

"I don't want any. I won't go anywhere. *Please*? I don't want to be tied down."

Danny lifts his eyebrows, looking at Julie like he's asking the same question. Pleading for it, even. He doesn't like this either.

"Not yet," she says. "Why don't you close your eyes, Lark. Rest a bit longer, and then we'll see?"

"I'm not…" I'm going to say *tired*, but the moment my eyelids close, I lose the remainder of that thought. But one thing follows me into the dark. Or should I say, two.

Danny Bradley's ocean-blue eyes.

3

Danny

ina answers my FaceTime call right away. "How is she?" my grandmother asks.

I lean against the wall of the hallway. "It's mixed. No major injuries, so that's good. Her name is Lark. But that's all she remembers about herself."

"That's it? Really?"

"Yep. It's like one of those TV shows where somebody forgets their entire identity."

Nina's lying in her bed, more animated than she usually is at this time of day. But today has been eventful to say the least. We've been messaging off and on since I arrived twelve hours ago.

Some people might ask why I've spent half a day at the hospital with a woman I don't know. Helping people in emergencies is my job, when I'm not on leave anyway. I usually hand the injured off to other professionals when my part is done. Yet for some reason, Lark has latched onto me. I'd be an asshole if I just left her here alone. Though maybe it's more than that. I can't stop thinking of how small and delicate she felt in my arms. The desperate plea in her voice after the car hit her.

Please.

Damn, that's going to haunt me.

"Is Matteo still there?" I ask. When I took off, Nina's evening nurse Jess was at the house. But she doesn't stay all night. I had to arrange for more people to fill in the gaps. "He's sent a million texts and I haven't caught up on them all."

"Of course I'm here, asshole," my friend's voice chimes in, though I don't see him in the video. "Where else would I be?"

I snort. "Hi to you, too."

Nina's eyebrow arches. "You heard the man. Matteo's been here all day, and Starla is here too." Starla is the daytime nurse. "But *updates*, Danny. I need updates."

"Shouldn't you be napping?"

"How could I sleep at a time like this?" She frowns at me, but she's also pausing to take a few breaths. Nina's tired. I can see it. Mentally, she's as sharp as ever. It's her body that's slowing her down.

I glance around, making sure there's no one within hearing distance. "Lark had no ID, so we've got no idea who to call for her. She acts like she knows *me* though. Well, she doesn't know who I am exactly, but she seems to recognize me. She gets upset when I leave the room."

"Are you with her now?"

"I'm just in the hall. She's sleeping."

"And you *don't* know her, Danny? You're sure?"

"I've never seen her in my life."

"Sounds like Lark has some sort of amnesia," Matteo says. "That's common. A lot of people who've suffered trauma don't remember the event until later."

"But she doesn't remember anything else, either. Not her

last name, where she's from or how she got here. I've heard of things like this, but I've never seen it before."

"What are they doing for her?" Nina asks. "The doctors?"

"I'm not sure. She just woke up again a little while ago."

When we first brought her in, Lark was unconscious. The main focus was on her physical injuries. I'd been able to tag along in the ambulance because I knew the paramedics who responded. I just needed to be there, needed to make absolutely certain that she was getting what she needed.

Please. That word kept repeating in my head. The way she clung to me. *Please*.

Of course, she went straight to the emergency department and out of my hands. While she was being treated, I called West Oaks PD. They'd already sent units to the accident scene after the 911 call.

My friend and roommate Cliff Easton was on patrol duty, and he came to the hospital to interview me about the incident. I gave him a description of the car, though I didn't see any plates. I couldn't make out the driver either. It wasn't much to go on, but Cliff got started on putting out a bulletin on the vehicle's description. *Wanted for questioning. Hit and run.*

But I'm convinced it wasn't just an accident. The guy was going for a second round. Aiming at her.

It was attempted murder.

And then there was the backpack. She'd been holding it when I first spotted her. But when I went back to look just before the ambulance left, the bag was gone. Probably where her ID went. I think the guy who attacked her took it from the street.

Why?

I was halfway through Cliff's questions when there was a commotion in the ED. Shouting. Someone came out and grabbed me because they knew I'd come in with Lark. Apparently she was awake and freaking the fuck out.

Screaming, trying to fight her way free. She was so difficult they were afraid they'd hurt her more in the process of subduing her.

Yet somehow, the moment she saw me walk into the room, she calmed down enough for them to sedate her. She reached out for me and clung to my hand until she passed out from the drugs. I think she's scared and feels connected to me because I helped her.

When I was a line medic, my guys trusted me. But I'm not so sure I warrant the kind of faith she's instinctually placing in me.

"What about the man who hit her?" Nina asks. "Have they found him yet?"

"Not that I know of. Cliff was here taking my statement. He said West Oaks PD would send more officers today to canvas our neighborhood for witnesses."

"Yeah, patrol was here," Matteo says.

"Was the case assigned to Angela?" I ask. She's Matteo's girlfriend and a West Oaks PD detective.

"No, it's someone else. But she was going to stop by and see Nina anyway. She'll keep us updated on the search for the suspect."

Nina adds, "I hope the cops track down that fucker and paste his ugly mug all over the news!" She takes a shaky breath, and I worry she's getting too worked up. An attempted murder on our quiet street is too much excitement.

Once, my grandmother was the toughest person I knew, more ornery than some drill sergeants. But that's not her reality anymore. My head goes to places I don't like when I think too much about it. But it's true.

"Why don't you take that rest," I say. "I'll get out of here as soon as I can."

"Don't you baby me." She points a finger at the screen.

"That poor girl in the hospital is the one who needs a knight in shining armor, not me."

I huff. I'm a first responder, and I'm proud of that. But a knight in shining armor? Hardly. More of a hired gun, just with a med kit instead of a weapon.

"I'll see what I can do," I say.

"I agree with Nina," Matteo chimes in. "You can't take off if the girl needs you."

My friend's tone irks me. "Didn't say I was going to."

"Somebody's testy." He laughs. "And it's not me."

"I'm not testy. Just a little tired. I'm not taking off yet. But I *do* have my own responsibilities. And you've got yours."

Matteo's got a big personality, both funny and as loyal as any guy I know. He's also never met a damsel in distress he didn't want to rescue.

"Just saying, if you need any advice on being a real American hero who received a commendation from the mayor…"

Ugh, not with *that* again. I roll my eyes. "Then I'll call Angela."

"Go on," Nina says. "Keep making yourself useful. But keep in mind, when I said you should find yourself a distraction, I didn't mean it *this* literally."

"Now you tell me."

4

Lark

When I wake up again, Danny is sitting in a chair looking at his phone. So I take the opportunity to look at him.

While his hair is somewhere between brown and blond, the scruff on his chin is darker. He's wearing a necklace on a black silk cord, and sometimes he touches the pendant, rolling it between his fingers. Like an absentminded habit. He purses his full lips.

Where do I know him from? Why can't I remember?

He must feel me looking, because he glances up and smiles, tucking away his phone. "Feeling any better?"

"Some. I think. Do I know you?" I asked before, but I don't think he answered.

His brow creases. "Honestly, I'm not sure. That's why it's confusing."

"What is?"

"Why you're so attached to me."

I feel my face heat up. "Sorry."

"I'm not complaining." His phone buzzes with a call, and

he glances at it before sticking it into his pocket with a pensive expression.

"You're not going to get that?" I ask.

"It's okay. I'll handle it later. Right now, I'm here with you."

I have no idea why—I guess we've established I know almost nothing at the moment—but my throat swells and tears suddenly burn in my eyes. I blink them away, hoping he doesn't see. But something tells me he does. I feel like he sees *everything*. Looks straight through me. I shouldn't like that. I seem to be missing certain facts about myself, but I know I don't like being scrutinized. Yet I don't mind it from him.

I guess that's fair, because I was just watching *him* like a creeper. Which he noticed. And that's after telling him he's "nice to look at," which I'm sure he knew already.

I claimed to be chill earlier, but I may have spoken too soon.

Nurse Julie comes in to check on me again. Asking about my pain levels, if I've remembered anything else. And once again, she makes an excuse when I ask her to take off my restraints.

As soon as she leaves, I pepper Danny with questions of my own. "Okay, what the hell is going on? What was this accident? Why am I tied down like I tried to bite someone's face off?"

He just stares at me, lips pressed together.

"I *didn't*, right?"

He exhales and smiles. Danny smiles a lot, though he doesn't always look happy. Hmm. That's an observation I file away to consider more later.

"Not that, no," he says. "You didn't bite anyone."

"Could you untie me, then? I won't tell Nurse Julie it was you."

"Are you planning an escape?"

"I'll go with *no*. I do promise not to bite anyone's face. Especially not yours."

His laugh is louder this time. Richer. Yet still gentle. Looking at him, all big and muscular, I wouldn't expect anything about him to be soft.

"You got a little too specific there at the end. But I'll take my chances." He loosens the straps at my wrists and ankles. Then he winks. "Our secret. Don't snitch on me to Julie."

"I would never. You can buy my silence with a cheeseburger. And fries."

He presses a hand to his broad chest. "Now I feel taken advantage of."

I try to sit up, and that's a mistake, because my head pounds and the room spins. "*Oh.* That's not good." Lightning fast, Danny's hands are gripping my shoulders and propping me up. His touch is warm, and his ocean-blue eyes are *right there*, inches from mine.

"Careful. No escape attempts yet. You're not well enough for that." He eases me back against the pillows. He's sitting on the mattress now.

He's bigger than I even realized. Big enough to dwarf me. But his touch is so gentle, it's like a whisper.

"I wish you would tell me what happened," I murmur.

His thumbs caress up and down my skin before he sits back and lets me go. "Like I said, you're in the hospital. You've been here since last night. It's…" He checks his phone. "Wow. Past lunch time. No wonder you're asking about cheeseburgers."

"But what happened last night? The accident?"

"To be honest, I'm not sure how much I'm supposed to tell you. This kind of thing isn't my specialty." He stands up to stretch, revealing a stripe of golden stomach and more dark-blond hair. He tugs his shirt down over a pair of running pants, muscles flexing beneath the fabric as he moves.

"What *is* your specialty?"

"I'm a medic and a firefighter."

"Is that why you were there when I got hurt? You responded to the accident?"

"You remember?"

"Just…" Two moments swim up again from the darkness in my mind. "There were lights. Bright lights. And then…" *I'm going to help you, okay?* "You." My eyes dart up to meet his. "You saved my life. Maybe that's why I'm attached to you."

"But that doesn't happen with most people I save."

"Oh." Yep, I've officially entered creeper territory.

He chews the inside of his lip. "I wasn't on duty. I'm on an extended leave from work, actually, for family reasons. I live near where it happened. I was out for a run, saw what was going down. Tried to stop it, but I couldn't. I'm sorry."

"What was going down?"

He tilts his head. Doesn't answer.

"Come on. Tell me *something*. Did I have a phone? Or a purse or anything?"

"You did have a backpack. I looked for it after I called the ambulance, but it had disappeared."

"Did somebody take it?"

"I don't know for sure."

"But there's a lot more you're not saying. Right? Do you think I can't handle it?"

He's still contemplating his response when a doctor walks in.

"I'm going to return that phone call from a few minutes ago," Danny says to me. "I'll be right outside, okay? You can call for me if you need me."

I nod, not wanting him to go, but also determined to

prove my levels of chill. I'm not the weirdo who's got an insta-obsession with her savior. So not me.

The doctor does a lot of the same checks Nurse Julie did, humming and nodding his head as he questions and examines me. "We're going to run more tests, but it seems you got very lucky, Lark. No broken bones or other internal injuries. You've got a nasty lump on your head, and a CT scan is next, but I'm not seeing indications of serious head trauma."

"But I don't even remember my last name or anything else about me. Isn't that stuff I should know?"

He jots something down on his tablet. "More doctors will be evaluating you. But there's something else." He pauses, frowning. "On the X-ray, I noticed healed fractures in your metacarpals. The bones in your fingers. And one in the ulna of your left arm. Do you remember those injuries?"

"No."

"I also noticed fading bruises on your legs and torso. They appear to be older, not from the car accident. Along with the healed fractures, they're consistent with injuries in abuse victims."

Abuse? "I told you. I don't remember." My voice shakes.

It takes a long time for him to answer. "All right. But if you do, we have resources for you. I'll grab some pamphlets."

Danny, please come back. But I don't call for him. Instead, I shove down those fearful feelings. The doctor leaves, and I muster up all my strength and will to stand up. I totter into the bathroom without ending up on the floor, my IV cart tagging along with me.

I pee. Wash my hands. My reflection catches my attention. The woman in the mirror is familiar. I don't exactly know her, even though I know that she's *me*.

This woman is young, but she's got fine lines near her eyes and around her mouth when she frowns, as if she does that a lot. Her hair is dark, almost midnight black, trailing to her elbows. Bright green irises. Tattoos of vines, leaves, and flowers run up and down her arms.

Small bandages dot my reflection's face, with bruises cascading along one side of my head.

Carefully, I reach down and tug up my hospital gown. More bruises mar the skin of my legs and stomach. Most are from the car accident, I assume. But others are mostly faded, just outlines. Older. Like the doctor said.

Someone gave me those bruises. I know it like I knew my name before, although I still can't remember how the bruises happened. Or what they mean.

They're clues to a mystery I can't begin to solve.

And I'm standing right here at the center of it, alone. Except for Danny.

5

Danny

I'm in the hallway again, and the doctor is still with Lark. It was Matteo who called me, following up with a text asking to chat alone, away from the prying ears of Nina.

"Hey, man. What's up?"

He gives me an update on how Nina is *really* doing, and I'm thankful she decided to take her afternoon pain pills and a nap. Each day is a little different for her. Some days, she's up and walking around, chatting and laughing. Other times, the pain in her bones gets so bad she can't leave her bed. She gets short of breath and needs oxygen, or she'll feel too tired or sorrowful to speak. Balancing the right amount of pain meds is always a juggling act. Too little is excruciating, but too much dulls her to the world. The risk of overdose is terrifying and ever-present. But right now she's resting peacefully, and for that I'm grateful.

After I say goodbye to Matteo, I check on the DoorDash order I placed a little while ago. It's almost here. By the time the doctor leaves Lark's room, I've got a bag of In-N-Out in my hand. I knock on her door.

"It's me," then I add, "Danny."

"Come in."

I push open the door. "Hey, still hungry for that cheeseburger?"

Lark is climbing back into bed. She must've been using the restroom. "Are you kidding? *Thank you.* You really are a lifesaver." Once she's settled in bed, she grabs the bag and digs right in.

I ordered plenty for both of us, unless she has some kind of superhuman appetite. But I'm happy to be the bearer of cheeseburgers and reassurance, whatever I'm able to give her. Contrary to Nina and Matteo's assumptions, I'm not going to abandon this girl. Even if I do have to get back on track soon.

But when will that be? Looking at her, that's not a question I can answer.

Lark polishes off her burger and starts on her fries, pounding them like she hasn't eaten for a week. With her skinny frame, I'd believe it. I'm not saying she isn't pretty, though. With her creamy skin, pink mouth, and long lashes, Lark is plenty easy on the eyes.

Enough noticing, I tell myself.

She hands the second burger to me, and I unwrap it. "Sure you don't want this one too?"

"Nah, I'm good," she says with her mouth full. "I heard your stomach growling."

"My stomach thanks you." I lift my burger like I'm toasting her, then take a bite.

We eat in silence for a bit before she speaks again.

"You said you had to make a call?"

I wipe my mouth with a paper napkin. "To update my friend Matteo. He's taking care of my grandmother while I'm here. She's not well, and I moved in with her and took time off work recently to help out."

"Oh." Lark frowns, picking at her fries. "Does she need you? Do you have to go?"

"She's covered for now. She's got nurses, and some more friends of mine are heading over in a bit."

"You seem like someone with a lot of friends."

"I guess so. I've never had trouble making them. I must not be intimidating. Some have even said I have nice eyes." I wink, and she studies me with an amused glimmer in her green ones. Then she glances down and pops another fry into her mouth.

"Thank you for being here. It really *is* nice of you, and I think that's rare. Most people don't give a shit."

"Are you thinking of something specific?"

"I'm light on specifics at the moment."

"Of course, my mistake. I guess I'm just a nice guy. But if you'd rather I not stay, say the word."

"Don't go," she says quickly, and then her cheeks darken like she's embarrassed. "Unless you have to."

I slouch in my chair, all casual. "I'm happy to stick around. This is like a vacation for me, actually. Cheeseburgers and conversation. All right by me."

Lark gives me a hesitant smile. She eats another fry. "You don't make this a habit? Sitting at the bedside of every stranger you save?"

"If they asked me to, I would." *Probably*, I add silently. *Maybe.*

"So you're the selfless type?"

Ha, no. "That's overstating my qualities. What type are you?"

She hums like she's thinking. "I suspect I'm the cynical and broody type. With a heavy dash of sarcasm."

I laugh again. "You don't remember your last name, but you remember that much?"

She shrugs. "Guess so."

We talk a bit more, until Lark's eyelids are heavy, staying closed for longer and longer each time she blinks. Before long, she's asleep.

Minutes tick by, and I squirm in my seat, wondering what the heck I'm doing.

Lark asked me to stay, but I was sticking around even before she said those words. *Would I make this a habit?* No. Hell, no. It would be nice if I could sit at the bedside of every injured person I help on the job, but that's not how things go. When I treat people at the scene of a fire or some other emergency, I'm a fleeting presence in their lives. There and gone.

Nina's an exception because she's my grandma. And because she's earned it.

But with Lark I feel this urge, beyond all reasoning and logic, to hover. Check on her. Make her feel safe. Maybe it's because she got hurt on Nina's street. Or because she screamed for me in the ED like I was the only person in the world who could calm her.

Or the way my chest swells and my pulse thumps when her green eyes lock on mine.

Or it could be the memory of that car bearing down on her. The thud of her body when it hit. The horror inside me when I realized the driver was coming back around for another go at her, and the fragile weight of her in my arms.

That must be it. I'm worried the guy will figure out where she is and try to hurt her again. Now *that* makes sense.

I'll call up Cliff and make sure West Oaks PD sends someone here to watch over her.

But after that, I'll have to say goodbye. Lark is already doing much better. Tomorrow, I need to be back home with Nina. And that's just the way it is.

∽

THE NEXT DAY, I bring In-N-Out for lunch again. Lark digs right in. "You're back," she says after her first bite. "Wasn't sure if you would be."

"I wasn't sure either." And yet, here I am. Even after I resolved yesterday to return to my own life and stop inserting myself into Lark's. I just…couldn't stay away. "Is that okay with you?" I ask.

She swallows another bite of cheeseburger. "If you bring greasy food, you're welcome anytime."

I grin and pull up the chair by her hospital bed. "Did you sleep well overnight?"

"Like shit. It can be noisy around here. I don't like things beeping at me."

I nod sympathetically. In the Army, I learned to sleep anywhere, but it does take some practice.

Lark's looking better today. More color in her cheeks, not such dark circles under her eyes. She doesn't have the IV anymore. It will take her time to fully recover, but I suspect she would've been discharged already if not for her memory issue. Plus her lack of any friends or family offering to care for a woman who doesn't know her own last name.

She's still alone. *Really* alone. Fuck, it's not okay.

And that, right there, is why I'm back at her bedside. I had to check in on her. I'd be an asshole if I didn't.

"How's your grandmother?" Lark asks.

"Nina's having a good day. She's usually best in the mornings. Afternoons can be tougher."

"You should bring her In-N-Out. That would cheer up anybody."

"Trust me, I do, when it's not too rough on her stomach. Providing comfort food is one of my top tactics to make people like me."

"So this is a sneaky plan of yours? I thought you were

doing it out of the goodness of your heart. Like some kind of hero."

"Nah, I'm just a guy trying to do what he can."

"Sounds heroic to me."

I just shrug. "Do the doctors know yet why you lost your memory?"

"If they do, they haven't shared. Some different people have come to talk to me. I lost track of them all. They only ask questions. Not so great with the answers."

"Anyone from West Oaks PD? The police?"

"Yeah, but I told them to come back later. I'm not a fan of cops. Firefighters are okay."

That gets another smile out of me. "Why not cops?"

"Just a feeling. Like knowing that In-N-Out is one of my favorite burger places, even if I can't remember going there. I think cops make me nervous because they don't always help when people need it." She frowns and turns her eyes to the food wrappers in her lap.

I reach over and gather up her trash. "I'm sorry to hear that. But I guarantee the cops trying to help you now are good people. One is even my roommate. When I'm not living with Nina, anyway."

"Do you think there's anyone out there looking for me?" she suddenly asks. "Friends or family, wondering where I am?"

I drop the remnants of our lunch into the trash can. "I'm sure there are. They're probably frantic not knowing. But they'll find you."

And what about the guy driving the car? The guy she doesn't know about yet, or at least doesn't remember. What about *that* guy? I've been worried about that piece of work since we got here. I've been in touch with Cliff, and he said they placed a discreet unit near Lark's room to keep an eye on things, as I requested yesterday. Nobody has tried to come near her. But the police haven't made any arrests either, nor identified the car that tried to run her down.

The investigation is ongoing. That's what Cliff keeps telling me.

"I liked talking to you yesterday," Lark says. "Could you stay for a while again today? Unless your grandmother needs you. Or...a girlfriend." Her lips twist. "I was trying to be subtle about prying for info, but I don't think it worked."

I bark a laugh. "No girlfriend. Or any significant other." My pulse kicks as I say that.

I wonder if Lark has got anybody in her life who would put *her* first, the way Nina has always chosen me. I really hope Lark has somebody like that, because everybody deserves it.

I cross my arms. "If I have to take off, I'll call one of those many friends of mine to take my place keeping you company. In fact, you might prefer I do that now. Some of my friends are a lot more interesting than me."

"I doubt that." She returns my smile, and it hits me smack dab in the chest. She's laughed and smirked a few times around me, but that's the first time I've seen her truly smile. It's...*damn*. Really beautiful. The smile of a woman who has no idea how gorgeous she is.

Or what kind of affect that smile has on a red-blooded hetero male.

Behave, Danny-boy, Nina scolds in my head. That's not why I'm here. It's *not*.

"Either way," I say, "you won't be alone. I can give you my number, and you can call me later if you want. Using the hospital phone, or after. Wherever you end up. Your other friends haven't found you yet, but you've got one right here."

"Thank you." She blinks tears away and puts on a stoic face. "Really."

Most of the time, when people thank me, I just shoot

back an easygoing *no worries* or *no problem*. But this time, that doesn't feel like enough. I want to say more.

What I end up saying is something *really* stupid.

"We're going to find your people and get you home safe and sound. I promise."

The instant the words are out of my mouth, I want to pull them back. When it comes to helping someone get their life in order after a trauma, there are no guarantees. I can't promise someone will walk again, that their loved one will survive, or that they'll recover family heirlooms after a fire.

But for some reason, with this woman, I want to do the impossible.

Fuck me, but when I said *I promise*, I meant it.

6

Danny

"Knock, knock." A woman in a lab coat is at the door, her thick hair in a braid over her shoulder. "Lark, can I come in?"

We both look up from the nature documentary we were watching on my phone. The doctor walks inside and shakes Lark's hand. "I'm Dr. Cruz from the psychiatry department."

"I remember. You were here yesterday."

"Good to know your short-term memory is intact," Dr. Cruz responds. Doctor humor, I guess.

I stand up from the chair where I was sitting. "I can step out and give you some privacy."

Lark's eyes go wide with a hint of panic. "I'd rather you stay."

The doctor glances between us. "It's up to Lark, of course. You're a friend of hers?"

"I am. I'm Danny Bradley. I was there when Lark was hurt the other night."

"He saved me," Lark adds. "Danny hasn't told me exactly what happened that night. I'm sure it's because he's trying to protect me, but I don't need that."

I shrug sheepishly. *Busted.*

"I need to know what's going on," Lark insists.

Dr. Cruz settles into the chair that I vacated, while I remain standing. They talk for a while, and the doctor examines her. Finally, she sits back down and runs a finger along her chin thoughtfully.

"Are you going to tell me what's wrong with me?" Lark's fingers twitch against the blanket. I feel the urge to reach out, but I don't move because it seems like something a closer friend would do. Not a guy she just met.

But are any of her close friends nearby?

I go closer and hold out my hand. She takes it with a tiny, grateful smile.

"Lark, you've described a generalized loss of almost every aspect of your identity," Dr. Cruz says. "You still remember how to talk, walk. You remember the latest pop music hits and who's president. Yet you can't connect to specific memories of your life. I believe you have dissociative amnesia."

"Does that mean I have a brain injury?"

"No. Your CT scan was clear. The root cause of most dissociative amnesia is psychological. The fact that you've lost your memories means you've gone through something emotionally traumatic, and it's probably not the physical injuries alone. Most people who are hit by a car don't experience dissociation of this kind. It's rare."

Lark squeezes my fingers.

"A lot of trauma victims have trouble remembering the event at first," I point out.

"True. But Lark did hold on to a few recollections about the triggering event, which is curious. She remembers the headlights from the car. And she remembers *you*, Danny, though that was the first moment she met you. Right? She remembers *you*, yet Lark has dissociated from nearly everything else."

"I don't have a clue why that would be." If the doctor is suggesting I'm keeping important info back, she's wrong.

"But how do I get my memory *back?*" Lark asks.

"There isn't one agreed-upon treatment in these cases. Some people with dissociative amnesia aren't bothered by it at all. They simply go on with their lives until their memories return, believe it or not."

"That's not me. I'm definitely bothered."

"Understandably. Most likely, your memories will come back on their own. Perhaps in response to certain triggers, like seeing familiar things from your life before. Or being faced with the events that caused you to block your memories in the first place. At the same time, we don't want to re-traumatize you. We should take this slow and steady." She stands up. "I'll come by again to see you tomorrow morning. Does that sound all right?"

"I guess."

"We'll work through this together." We watch Dr. Cruz leave the room.

As soon as she's gone, Lark fixes me with a glare. "You heard her. I need something to trigger my memory. Tell me what happened the night of the accident."

"She was talking about easing into it." I'm still hung up on the word *re-traumatize*. That's exactly what I've been afraid of doing.

"That's bullshit," Lark spits out. "You know more than you've told me. I want to know what you know *now*."

"Is this about Dr. Cruz's suggestion that I know you from somewhere else? I swear to you, I don't." I run a hand over the stubble at my jaw. "And I'm not going to mess around with your psyche in the hopes that it doesn't hurt you."

She narrows her eyes at me. "Shouldn't that be my choice?"

"It's my choice too. Now that we're friends, you should know I can be stubborn when I want to be."

"You're not the only one." Lark kicks off her blanket and lowers her feet to the floor. Her hospital gown has ridden up, revealing a long stretch of slender leg and pale, creamy thigh, mottled with bruises. There's a flare of heat in my chest and my stomach, and I glance away. *No perving on the injured girl.*

I'm too busy chastising myself to realize what she's doing until a few seconds have passed. In that time, Lark has walked on unsteady legs to grab her street clothes from a cubby.

"Where do you think you're going?" I ask.

"You're the only friend I have. If *you're* not going to tell me what I need to know, I have no choice but to find out for myself."

"Hold on. What does that mean?"

Angry green eyes turn toward me. "I'm going to the scene of the crash."

She heads for the bathroom, holding the back of her gown closed, and stumbles. *Shit.* I swoop in just before she falls, my arms closing around her. She's so small that she's practically weightless against me. I could probably circle her waist between my two hands.

My cock jumps, because as close as she is, I want her even closer.

I clear my throat, edging backward to gain a little distance. "Let's get this straight. You told me no escape attempts, and here you are, making a break for it?"

"Yesterday, I promised not to bite anyone, not that I wouldn't escape."

"You're not well enough to go. You can barely stand up on your own."

"That's just because I've barely stood at all for the last couple days. They can't force me to stay here, and I doubt they'll fight too hard to keep me anyway. My hospital bill is on the county dime unless they figure out who I really am. I'm just doing them a favor."

"Those are...all good points," I admit.

"I lost my memory, but my brain is still working just fine." She taps her temple. "Now either help me get dressed or get the hell out of the bathroom."

Before I can prepare myself, Lark drops her gown onto the floor at our feet.

Oh, fuck.

Do not look.

With my eyes on the off-white ceiling, I help Lark with her jeans and T-shirt. Every time my fingers graze bare skin, I feel another jolt of liquid heat in my veins.

I'd been trying all damn day not to focus on how stunning she is. The grassy green of her eyes, the striking contrast between her pale skin and black hair. And the tattoos on her arms, which are *definitely* my taste. No, I wasn't noticing any of that. Didn't seem right with her bruised and afraid. Not to mention the fact that she could be a mature-looking eighteen-year-old for all I know, while I'm thirty-three.

She could have a boyfriend who's waiting for her. A husband. No ring, though...

Nope. Not happening.

It's over within a couple of minutes, and I can't decide if that's too soon. She steps away from me, and I finally let myself exhale. I might have lost an IQ point with how intensely I was focused on not getting hard.

Lark turns around, and her wide-eyed look is back. She seems to transition between devilish one moment, innocent the next.

And apparently, it's my kryptonite.

"I'll take a bus to the crash site if I have to," she says. "Or hitchhike. I'd Uber, except for the *no phone* issue. Unless you want to save me a lot of time and take me there yourself."

She's bruised and bandaged. Her entire body was slammed by three thousand pounds of steel less than two days ago. But I believe her when she says she'll go without me if she has to. Lark isn't going to let anyone, least of all me, keep her locked up.

This woman is a fighter. Damned if I would want her to change.

"You're going to be a handful, aren't you?"

She grins and loops her arm through mine. "Took you until now to figure that out?"

7

Lark

*W*e're only in the parking lot, and Danny's already having second thoughts. "This is a bad idea. I should take you back."

"Too late. You already aided and abetted my escape."

Although my entire body aches, and I'm a swirl of conflicting emotions, I'm relieved to be outside. *Free*. I hate being cooped up. I have no idea why I would hate it, if I have a specific reason or not. All I know is that I *do*. It's not as bad when Danny's with me, but still, being stuck in my hospital bed made my skin crawl.

I inhale deeply, tipping my head back to let the sun shine on my face. The movement makes my brain hurt, but I don't care. Danny's arm goes around me on our way to his car, and I lean into him.

"If there's any sign you're in distress," he says, "I'm taking you back to the hospital. No arguments."

"Oh, there will be arguments. But if you pick me up and carry me, I probably couldn't stop you."

His eyes move over me, assessing. The attention makes my skin prickle with heat. Like when I dropped my gown in the hospital bathroom, naked as the day I was born underneath. I was trying to provoke a reaction, prove a point. But really, what the hell was I thinking?

Maybe I was testing him. If so, he passed it. He avoided looking at me. But part of me had wanted him to sneak a peak. Just a little one.

"You don't know your own strength," he says. "It took multiple orderlies and nurses to sedate and restrain you in the ED."

"That's one of the things I can't remember." Like those fading bruises on the rest of me. That thought extinguishes any flicker of desire.

I know Danny wouldn't hurt me. That's why I felt brave enough to undress in front of him. But what if he'd seen the bruises too, and had realized what they meant? He'd pity me more than he does already.

"Trust me, you're plenty strong."

I shrug, not quite believing him.

There's a classic Dodge Charger up ahead. Candy apple red, white racing stripes. "Oh my God. Please tell me that's your car."

He nods. "Yep. It was my grandfather's. He restored her, and I helped a little." He's trying to be modest, but I see the pride in his face.

"I think I just fell in love." I have to take a moment to drag my fingers along the frame, admiring its sleek lines and perfect condition. "She's gorgeous."

"You like cars?"

"Who doesn't love a 1968 Charger? It's legendary. What's she got under the hood?"

"Seven liter Hemi V8."

"Four-speed manual?"

"You guessed it."

I whistle and then look up at him, feeling a smile dawn on

my face. "That's something else about me. I like cars." And it's a *good* something. Not old bruises or a fear of being trapped. A giddy laugh bubbles up from my chest.

Danny is smiling too. "At least we've confirmed you have good taste." He opens the passenger door for me and helps me inside. When I'm nestled into the leather seat, I'm even happier as I examine the dashboard. "Can I drive?"

He's just lowered himself into the driver's seat. "Do you think *I'm* the one who hit my head? Hell no, you may not."

"Just testing you." I'm pretty sure I know how to drive though. It's probably one of those muscle memory things. Like riding a bike.

I wonder what other muscle memories I've held on to.

I'm less happy when Danny drives way too slow to his neighborhood. "The suspension is tight," he says when I complain. "I don't want to hurt you."

"You're hurting this car's feelings. She's not meant to go slow."

"And yet she will. Because I'm making her."

I grumble at the unfairness of it. But I'm impressed with his patience.

And the way he wants to take care of me is nice, too. Must be a firefighter EMT thing. Even though he claims not to be heroic.

It doesn't take long for Danny to turn off the main roads and into a neighborhood. "Does anything look familiar?" he asks.

"No. Not yet. Do you think it's possible I live around here? Or I have friends and family who do?"

"Maybe," Danny says. "I've been in touch with West Oaks PD. I have some friends on the force, including a guy named Cliff, who's my roommate. He's the one I mentioned before. He and the other officers have been interviewing neighbors. Showing around your photo."

It's been less than two days since my accident. It makes sense that the police are looking into it, but I'm just one girl. Aside from my lost memories, I'm not even that badly injured. How many resources would they devote to me?

"Maybe I have a car parked around here somewhere. And the police just haven't found it yet."

"That's possible."

He pulls up to a curb and puts the car in park. I see skid marks on the asphalt from tires braking or accelerating hard.

I open the door and plant my feet on the ground. Before I can even stand up, Danny's out and around the side, offering me his arm. I take it and stand up. Together, we walk out into the middle of the street.

"This is where it happened," Danny says.

I stare at the road, at the marks on the neighbor's lawn. *Come on. Remember something. You were here.*

I don't feel…anything.

"I thought there'd be police tape or something."

"They usually wrap up scenes pretty fast, especially for a public street like this."

Someone drives by, looking at us curiously, and we have to stand off to the side to let them pass. But then we go back out and stand near the black skid marks.

"Tell me what you saw that night," I say. "How did it happen?"

"I was out for a jog. Coming around for my second lap. That's Nina's place over there."

He points at a mailbox a few doors down. There are too many trees and hedges in the way to see much of the house. But there's the corner of a porch. Pale stone.

I feel a tingle of recognition. Then it's gone.

"You doing okay?" Danny's got one arm around me, another on my wrist, and I realize he's taking my pulse. I can feel it thrumming against his skin, fast but not out of control.

His chest moves against my back when he exhales. His warm breath tickles my ear and neck.

"I'm fine, doc," I say. "Not freaking out."

"Okay. Good. So, I'd just turned the corner and—"

"You can skip the boring parts."

His breath is soft again on my neck. "Do you want me to tell the story?"

I glance up at him. He still got his hand on my pulse. His eyes are more like the sky than the ocean right now. Cloudy but endless. "I'll zip it." I draw the finger of my free hand across my lips.

The corner of his mouth twitches up. "I saw you in the road. The car was heading for you, and you turned and faced the headlights. You were frozen like that. Which is normal, by the way. A lot of people freeze."

"Okay." I still don't like hearing it. Why wouldn't I run?

"I realized the car was going to hit you. I ran toward you. Shouted. It all happened pretty fast." He guides me toward the marks on the neighbor's lawn. "Still doing all right? Your pulse is up a bit."

"That's because a sexy firefighter has his muscles all up against me," I say matter-of-factly.

He makes a choked cough. "You really don't hold back, do you?"

"Guess I'm not shy."

"Oh, we've established that."

"Anyway. Keep going."

He takes a breath. "You landed here on the sidewalk. Then I heard the engine of the car, and I realized the car had reversed. It was…"

My pulse is racing now, and I know he feels it. "Spit it out, Danny. Please."

"The car came at you again."

"He was trying to kill me," I whisper.

"Or put you out of commission."

Then he succeeded. My knees go weak, and I sag. Luckily, Danny's already got me by the waist. He holds me up.

"I lifted you into my arms. Ran toward that tree there, the big one. The car jumped the curb and tore up the grass. But he gave up pretty quick. Backed up and took off. I think he may have grabbed your backpack at some point too, because it was gone when I looked. After that, I was in medic mode. Did what I could to make sure you were stable until the ambulance arrived."

Once I'm steady, I take a few steps away from Danny. Studying the scene. I imagine a girl who looks like me on the ground. Danny carries her to safety. She would've gazed up into his eyes, though it was a little too dark to see the richness of their color. I can remember staring into those eyes, but I'm also detached from it. Like that girl wasn't really me.

Aside from the headlights of the car getting larger as it accelerated, I can't picture anything else. Nothing except Danny. His face as he looked down at me, moonlight and streetlights picking up the blonder strands in his hair. I remember that much. I was here that night, and though it's awful, I cling to that knowledge. It makes me feel real.

"You said it was a *he*. Did you see him?"

"Not in any detail," Danny says. "The person had broad shoulders, so I assumed he was a man. But I can't say for sure."

I swallow around the thickness in my throat. "So that's why you didn't want to tell me. The guy did it on purpose. Why? Was it random? Or was he there for *me*? Will he try again?"

"We'll make sure he can't get to you. I've got a lot of friends, remember? We're going to help you."

I believe he means that. Danny's done nothing but help me since the moment he saw me in the street that night. But

I can't expect this man I've just met to take care of me. Where will I stay? How will I find the loved ones who are—I hope—out there looking for me, while avoiding that psychopath who wants to hurt me?

But for all those questions, there's another one that keeps returning to my thoughts. What was *I* doing here that night? I must have come here for a reason.

Suddenly, the hairs on the back of my neck raise. My skin prickles, and my heart takes off at a sprint like I'm already running.

Someone's watching me.

I spin around in place, scanning the dark recesses of the street and the windows of the houses, which show only reflections. It's daylight, but there are still shadowed spaces that the sun doesn't touch. Behind bushes and under cars.

He could be anywhere.

"What's wrong? What is it?" Danny closes the distance between us, his face drawn with concern.

"There's someone else here. Someone watching. It's…" It's a feeling of déjà vu. An instinct telling me *danger*. It doesn't subside until Danny pulls me close to him, swiveling his head as he looks around for the source of my anxiety.

My protector. My only friend in the whole world. I'm safe in his arms.

But for how long?

8

Lark

*D*espite my fear, I'm not ready to leave the scene of the accident yet. So Danny locks me in the car and stalks around like he's my own personal sentinel, checking the perimeter.

I gasp when there's movement, but it's only a cat darting out from beneath a Lexus in a driveway.

Slowly, the freaked-out feeling subsides, and my heart rate calms. Nobody else jumps out. No threats. No bad guys.

I must've been remembering something about the accident. That has to explain that sense of déjà vu, but there's clearly nothing out there. Just a quiet street. The man who ran his car into me is long gone by now.

He must be. The guy would be an idiot to stick around the scene of the crime, right?

I relax against the seat, admiring the interior of Danny's car. The soft leather, the cool retro gauges in the dashboard. And the chrome. The *chrome*. What if this is my career? Selling fancy cars? Or maybe I'm a mechanic.

I gaze at my hands, noticing the calluses and old scars.

But trying to guess things about my life is just going to

lead to disappointment. It's another one of those instincts I keep getting. Disappointment feels like a well-worn path in my brain. I'm probably a light bulb saleswoman or something random and unsexy like that. If I even have a job.

Danny knocks on the car window, and I get out.

"It's all clear out here," he says.

"Guess I was imagining it. Sorry."

"I'd rather be safe than do nothing. How're you doing?"

"You're always asking me that."

"Because I want to know."

"I'm staying calm. Mostly."

"No urges to bite any faces?"

"Come closer and we'll see," I deadpan.

He smiles slowly. I bet I could write a whole book on Danny's different smiles. Or at least a Wikipedia article. "Want to go to Nina's house and meet her?"

"Wait, for real?"

He shrugs like this is no big deal. Like he didn't just invite me into his grandma's home. *His* home. *Me*, the rescue he picked up on the street who had to be restrained at the hospital.

"We're friends, remember?" he says. "Nina's been hearing about you since yesterday. She can't wait to meet you in person. You're the talk of the neighborhood."

"Oh, *great*. I'm gossip fodder."

"Hard not to be when you lose your memory like a soap opera character. You're famous around here." He winks. "Unless you're too tired?"

I am tired. I'm a little all over the place. But I'm also curious about Danny and his family, and I'm not all that excited to head back to the hospital yet. Especially not if more psych evaluations are ahead of me. I want to get better, but I don't like being prodded and studied.

"Let's go meet Nina," I say.

But I'm less excited when Danny mentions, as we're strolling down the sidewalk, who else will be there.

"There's a detective from West Oaks PD at the house right now, and you can talk to her as well. She wants to get your statement."

"A cop?" I stop walking. "Is that necessary?"

"Very necessary." He turns back to face me. Trees create a background of green behind him, setting off the contrasting strands in his hair. "Lark, you were a victim of a crime. I've been dealing with West Oaks PD so far, since you've had a lot going on, but they need to interview you. They're trying to figure out who hurt you. Plus, they're going to need more info to find your identity."

"Okay, fine," I grumble. "That does make sense."

He takes my hand and pulls me along. "Don't be nervous. This detective is a friend of mine. It'll be casual."

When I think about cops, I don't get the warm-and-fuzzies. But these are Danny's friends. So they can't be all that bad. "You'll be there the whole time?" I ask, feeling weak but needing to say it anyway.

"I've got you." Danny's deep blue eyes promise that he means it.

If I'm not careful, I might follow those eyes anywhere.

The house is two stories with a wraparound porch. It looks like a place that could belong out in the country and not in an upper middle-class neighborhood near the beach. Danny jogs up the porch steps, tugging a key ring from his pocket. He unlocks the door and steps inside, waiting for me to follow.

"Hey, I'm home."

We pass through a large foyer and then a living room. There's an eclectic mix of furniture, different styles and eras. It's warm and inviting. A house that's lived in.

We walk down a wide hallway that has windows all along

the right side and doorways on the left. There's laughter and voices up ahead.

A tall, burly man steps out of a doorway. He grins when he sees Danny and me. "Hey! We were just talking about you. Both of you." His voice echoes off the hard surfaces of the hallway.

"Lark, this is Matteo De Luca," Danny says. "He's my closest friend at West Oaks FD."

"You mean your coolest friend. The most fun at a party."

"We just let him think that," Danny mutters to me. "Gotta give the poor guy *something*. He doesn't have much self-esteem."

Danny is tall, but Matteo is huge. Thick dark hair, a matching beard, and intense eyes. "So you're the mystery girl?" Matteo holds out his hand, which dwarfs mine when we shake.

"I'm a mystery even to me."

He laughs. "Come on," Matteo says, waving me into the room. "There are seats in here. You're injured, so you should sit down and rest."

Danny nods. "Just what I was about to say."

"Uh oh, *two* overprotective firefighters? Not sure I can handle that."

A woman with dark curly hair appears in the doorway. "You have no idea. These two are a lot when they get together." She's wearing a long sundress, which curves around her pregnant belly. Matteo swings an arm around her shoulders, bending to kiss her on the cheek.

"I'm Angela," she says. Her eyes dart to where Danny's holding my hand, though her expression doesn't change.

"Lark."

"*Do* you need to sit down?" Angela asks. "I'm sure you can speak for yourself, but you were in an accident, and there's no shame in taking time to heal."

"I was lucky. No broken bones or major injuries, thanks to Danny."

"The hero of the day." Matteo grins.

"It can't just be *you* all the time, De Luca," Danny responds. "As much as you'd love to hog the attention."

Angela pats her man on the chest. "So true."

Danny leads me further into the room. He makes the rest of the introductions. There's a blond guy named Cliff Easton, the roommate Danny mentioned.

Cliff waves at me. "Nice to meet you, Lark." He's a little younger than Danny and obviously a cop. The West Oaks PD polo gives it away, but even if that guy was in a tux and top hat, I think he'd scream cop. A goofy, friendly one. But still a cop.

"That's Starla," Danny says, gesturing to a petite, middle-aged woman. "She's our daytime nurse."

I shake her hand, and her grip is firm. "Good to see you looking well," she says. "We've heard all about you."

"And this is Nina. My grandmother."

Nina's lying in the hospital bed that dominates the room. Her blond and gray hair is neatly styled, and she's wearing red lipstick. She has the aura of a matriarch, someone who's used to being in charge, but her smile is kind.

Nina reaches out for my hand, and I go over to her. "From what Danny has told me, you have a dramatic story. Can't wait to hear more of it."

"Neither can I."

Nina's laugh is quieter and hoarser than Danny's, but equally gentle. "Keep that sense of humor, girl. It'll serve you well. My Danny-boy's taking care of you?"

He huffs. "Nina, you're ruining my tough-guy image." Everyone else in the room cracks up.

"You hold your own," Matteo says. "But *tough guy* is over-selling, and I doubt Lark is buying it."

"You're one to talk," Angela counters. "Biggest softie I know."

"So is Danny!"

"Quit telling my secrets. I had Lark thinking I was her hero." Danny flexes a bicep, and I'm *definitely* buying that. Everyone laughs again. Nina smirks at us both, and I feel my cheeks burn.

"He's been great," I assure his grandmother. "Heroic is right."

I look over at him. He smiles back at me as he plays with the pendant at his neck. There are a lot of people in here, yet that smile feels like it's just for me. And suddenly, I'm facing even more danger than I realized.

Some psycho tried to run me over, and he might still be after me. But I'm also in danger of getting more than just a little attached to my savior. A man whose literal job description is saving lives. He swoops in to help, but that doesn't mean he'll stick around.

Danny lives in a fancy house, surrounded by these laughing, kind people who obviously love each other. I'm a scrawny, bruised-up girl with no backstory and an endless list of problems.

I don't need all my memories to know that I don't belong in his world.

9

Danny

*L*ark pulls up the stool to Nina's bedside and sits to chat. Seems like they're already getting along well. But that's no surprise. My grandmother has always been easy to talk to, free with her attention, and ready with her advice too—whether you want it or not. She's that way even with strangers. That's just who she is.

Lark joked before that I have a lot of friends, and it's true in some ways. But for a woman who can get downright cranky, Nina is the queen of making friends. She could walk through the grocery store and come out with a new guest for dinner. That's why hosting exchange students was such a great fit for her. She loves nothing more than making a new person feel comfortable. But not through syrupy-sweet niceness. Nina puts people at ease by being real and treating them like family, bossiness and all.

She's forgiving, too. Maybe too forgiving if you ask me.

My heart pangs to see Nina's fiery energy diminished. But Nina doesn't want anyone's pity. Much like Lark. The two of them have a lot in common.

Matteo's girlfriend Angela taps on my arm, pulling me

into the hall. "Is this a good time for me to take Lark's statement?"

As Matteo told me yesterday, Angela hasn't been technically assigned to Lark's case, and normally a patrol officer like Cliff would handle an initial victim statement on his own. But I hoped Lark might be more comfortable with Angela. Especially considering how reluctant she is to speak with anyone from the police.

"Yeah. She's nervous, and I didn't want to push it first thing. Give me five minutes? We'll meet you in the living room."

I go back to Nina's bedroom. She and Lark are talking quietly, heads together, and Lark is laughing. Warmth blooms in my chest, seeing that. I hate that I'm about to spoil the mood. "Sorry to interrupt, ladies. Lark, Angela needs to get your statement. She's the detective I mentioned."

Her mouth drops open. "*She's* the detective?"

Nina pats Lark's hand. "Angela's a sweetheart. Go on. We'll talk later, all right?"

Lark nods, though I can tell she's unsure. I understand her surprise about Angela. I've known the detective for less than a year, but from what I've heard, Angela was more straight-laced before she met Matteo and went through a bunch of upheaval in her life.

Sometimes, the only way to face a problem is to change. Adapt. Matteo has said that Angela is far happier now than ever. And I'm sure she is.

But most of the time when shit goes down, people want to erase it. To go back to the life they had before. That's what I've always strived to do for the people I've helped, either as a medic or a firefighter. To pick up their pieces and help put them together again during the brief time I'm in their lives.

That's what I want for Lark.

Because when *you know* a major change is coming for you,

and you can't do anything to stop it or reverse it? Or when you lose something and can never get it back? That's pretty much the shittiest feeling in the world. I wouldn't wish it on anyone.

WE SIT down in the living room. Angela takes the seat across from Lark, while I'm sitting next to her. Cliff has his phone on his knee, a notes app visible on the screen.

"Lark, Cliff works with me at West Oaks PD," Angela says. "He's going to take notes on our interview, and he'll use his body cam to record it. Danny thought you'd be more comfortable here than at the station."

Lark squirms on the couch cushion. "This is fine. But I've already told the doctors and Danny what happened. Danny was there himself."

"I understand how difficult this is. I've been a victim of a crime too, and it's hard to keep talking about it. It's totally up to you how this goes, but it does need to happen. Is there anything else you need before we get started?"

"No. I just wanna get it over with."

I put my hand, palm up, on the cushion close enough that she'll see it. Lark laces our fingers together.

Everyone else is quiet while she tells Angela what she knows. There isn't much. But there is something she didn't mention to me before.

Knots form in my stomach as I listen.

"I have some other bruises on my legs and stomach." Lark's eyes are on the rug. "Older ones. A doctor at the hospital noticed them, as well as some broken bones that had healed. He thought...maybe I'm an abuse victim."

"*Fuck*," I mutter. I shouldn't, but I can't help myself.

"I'm so sorry," Angela says. "That must've been frightening to realize."

"Not like I remember it." Lark's voice has dropped to a whisper.

I force myself to sit there and hold her hand, not moving. Not even breathing. But inside, I want to scream. I want to go out and find the asshole who did these things to her. What the fuck is wrong with people?

She was running from something when I first saw her. Someone. Maybe she was trying to get away from her abuser, and he wouldn't let her go.

Lark's hand feels so small inside of mine.

Angela asks a few more questions, and then Cliff takes over. "We've interviewed the neighbors up and down the street, as well as in the nearby vicinity. Several mentioned seeing a young woman matching your description walking through the neighborhood, coming from the direction of the main boulevard."

Lark doesn't say anything, so I ask, "Walking the whole time? She didn't get out of a car or anything?"

"Not that we've found." Cliff turns back to Lark. "It seems like you made a straight path here, to this street."

As if she was heading this direction for some purpose. "But none of the neighbors recognized her?" I ask.

Cliff shakes his head. "We'll also try circulating her photo in the local media to check a wider pool of people."

"Could she have been heading to someone's house, but they didn't expect her? Or they didn't know what she looked like? She could've been…making a delivery?" I'm grasping at anything I can come up with.

"We haven't found any indication of that," Cliff says. "We tried a Geo-fence, which is where we pull the cell numbers from the towers for anyone in the close vicinity of the accident. Danny, we saw yours. But the others nearby either belonged to neighbors or were anonymous. Unregistered. Lark, if you had a phone nearby, we couldn't locate it, and the cell tower dump didn't lead us to the driver of the car, either. But we've also been collecting doorbell cam footage. There was, ah…" He taps his finger against his phone screen, clearly stalling. "This might be tough to hear."

"Say it." Lark's jaw is tight, teeth clenched.

"We've got a video from the homeowner directly across the street from where the accident occurred," Cliff says.

I didn't think Lark could get much paler, but she does. "It recorded when the car hit me?"

"Yes. And it recorded Danny arriving on-scene within seconds. Then the car accelerating toward both of you."

"I don't want to watch it," Lark says.

"You don't need to," Angela rushes to say. "We've asked the homeowner for all copies as part of the investigation. We're going to keep it strictly confidential, and you don't need to worry about anyone else watching it for now. But that will change once we've found a suspect and brought charges. I don't want that to upset you, but you need to be aware of it."

Lark doesn't respond, but I feel a tremor go through her. A lock of dark hair falls across her cheek. I fight the urge to brush it back. But that's a losing battle.

Lark has her eyes on the carpet, and she looks up when my finger tucks the errant lock of hair behind her ear. That small point of contact, the slide of my skin against hers, is electric. I swear I can see it in her eyes. The way the green deepens in intensity.

I know it then, down to my bones.

I'm going to do absolutely anything I can to help this girl. Fuck what I normally would do. Because the shit Lark is dealing with? It's nowhere near normal.

Cliff is still talking. He hasn't noticed the silent exchange between me and Lark. But Angela? She's got an eyebrow slightly arched, and I'm sure she's missing nothing.

I rest my hand on Lark's shoulder and squeeze. "Did the doorbell cam get a picture of the driver?" I ask Cliff.

"No, man. The video shows him stopping to open the car door and pick up Lark's backpack, but his face is blocked from view. The car had tinted windows. No plates either. You were right about that."

"But we've got an APB out on the make and model of the vehicle," Angela adds. "It'll have damage to the front end. We've got the tire tread imprints. Something may turn up."

Lark's eyes have gone dark. Like a forest at night. "What about finding my identity? If the guy who went after me is someone I knew, maybe my friends or family would know him too. Even if I can't remember him."

"Exactly what I was thinking." Angela smiles, and the aggressive shine in her eyes matches Lark's.

Angela reviews everything they'll do to find Lark's identity. There's a national fingerprint database run by the FBI, and they'll run Lark's prints to check for matches. They'll also check her DNA in a similar database.

"Even if the DNA match is with a family member, it'll turn up," Angela says. "We're also keeping tabs on NamUs. It's a national clearinghouse for missing persons cases. As soon as your friends and family realize you're gone, they'll contact local police wherever they are. They may have already done so. It's just a matter of time until we connect with them."

"You make it sound easy," Lark says.

"It's legwork. In can take time, but we'll do our utmost to make it happen."

"See?" I lean in and whisper. "You've got a lot of people on your team."

She smiles, but it doesn't reach her eyes.

"Officer Easton," Angela says to Cliff, "write up what we have so far and meet me back at the station."

"Yes, detective." He says goodbye, then heads for the front door like a man with a mission.

Angela gets up and sits on the other side of Lark, reaching for her other hand. "The county provides services for all crime victims, including therapy. I'd like to make an appointment for you to meet with one of our resource officers, and she'll go over your options."

"The psychiatrist at the hospital already talked to me. But I don't know if sitting and talking in an office is going to help me get my memory back."

"It could help in other ways. Will you consider it?"

Lark hesitates, subtly leaning into me. "I'll think about it."

"That's all I ask." Angela rubs her belly. "So you're heading back to the hospital?"

Lark glances at me, but all I do is raise my eyebrows, putting the question back at her.

"Not excited about it, but yeah. I'm supposed to be staying for observation. Maybe they'll write research papers about me and my dissociative amnesia." She smirks. "I'm a rare case, apparently."

"I'll be right back," I whisper to her. "I won't go far. That okay?"

I excuse myself while she and Angela continue to talk.

I want to do more for Lark. I just have to figure out how to make it happen.

∽

I'M NOT sure if Nina will be awake. Usually she naps in the afternoon. But she and Starla are watching an old episode of

Gray's Anatomy on Nina's iPad. She hits pause when she sees me.

"How is Lark?"

"Doing all right. Angela's been great with her."

"But what's the plan?"

I don't need any more explanation to know what Nina means. My grandmother doesn't screw around when there's a problem. She might not always *tell me* there's a problem, but she'll be doing her damnedest to handle it.

"I'm supposed to take Lark back to the hospital. We might have left without permission."

"My Danny-boy, misbehaving? Who would've thought." Nina eyes me sardonically.

"What? I usually follow the rules."

"And you'll also bend them to within an inch of your life."

"But bending isn't breaking," I point out.

Nina's nurse, Starla, clucks her tongue. "Danny, you need to take Lark back. The hospital is the best place for her. That way, once they release her, it'll be an easy transition to an in- or out-patient facility."

My body goes rigid. Dammit. I should've realized this was how it would go.

"A *mental hospital?*" Nina asks. "Is that what you're talking about?"

"Or a group home," Starla says. "It's nothing to be afraid of. They'll take good care of her. And with no idea who she is and with no one to take charge of her, what else can the county do? They'd be irresponsible to just turn her loose on her own. The girl would be homeless."

My grandmother fixes me with a glare. "Daniel Christopher Bradley the Second, you're not letting that girl be sent all alone to a mental hospital or turned out on the street."

I hold up my hands. "That's the last thing I want. Actually, I—"

"It's one thing if she truly needed full-time psychiatric care. But she's more than capable of managing herself. She just needs a little help. A roof over her head and some sound advice. She'll stay *here*."

"My first priority is you, though. I intend to help Lark, but I could make other arrangements for her."

My grandmother scowls at me like I've just said something patently offensive. "What is your daddy's damned money for, if not this? Helping someone in need? I want to pay Lark's hospital bill, for starters. I'll trust you to handle that. But we've got this big house just sitting here."

"I was thinking that too. But—"

"But *nothing*. If you leave that girl to fend for herself with no friends and no memory, I'll never forgive you." Her nostrils flare. "Why are you smiling?" she spits out.

I perch my hands on my hips. "Because you're preaching a fiery sermon to the choir."

"Don't patronize me, boy. In fact, I'll write you out of the will."

I cover a laugh. We both know she's kidding. I don't care about inheritances, and besides, the money is my father's. Nina has access to a large trust fund that my dad set up for her, but it's not something she can pass on.

"Ouch. You're playing hard ball."

"Honey, that's the only way I play."

"And I wouldn't change that." I drop a kiss on Nina's cheek. "You're a good soul, Nina."

"So are you, when you listen to me. Now get out of here and help that girl. That speech wore me out."

I head back to the living room.

A few days ago, this was the last thing I ever would've expected to find myself doing—inviting a woman I barely know to live with me. But if Nina agrees this is the best move, who am I to argue?

Lark deserves someone to look out for her. If she hasn't got anyone else, then it'll have to be us. Nina and me.

Lark is standing with Angela, and Matteo has joined them. All three are talking quietly. The moment I step into the room, Lark's head lifts, and her shoulders visibly relax.

"Danny."

I ignore the shiver that runs through me when she says my name. "Could I talk to Lark a second?" I ask my friends.

"Sure," Angela says. "We were just finishing up."

"Did you need me to stay here longer?" Matteo asks.

"No, thanks. You've both been great. I appreciate it." I give Angela a gentle hug and a rougher one to Matteo, who claps me on the back.

"You're doing the right thing," Matteo says into my ear. It's probably his highest compliment. Aside from, *this pasta is even better than what I could make.* Which he has never said to me, ever.

"Which part?" I ask. Because he doesn't know yet about the decision Nina and I just made.

"All of it. Whatever it is you're planning, I've got faith in you." He's said this quietly enough that the women didn't hear. "You'll know what to do." Matteo claps me on the shoulder, then takes his girlfriend's hand. We say a last goodbye, and then they head for the door.

Lark and I are alone again.

She's still got her arms crossed over her stomach, eyes on the rug. She looks like she's putting on a brave face, but inside, she's bracing herself. "Guess it's back to my hospital room. I feel like I've been playing hooky from school."

"Yeah, I'm sure we've caused some sort of paperwork nightmare for the hospital admins."

"What is life, except a paperwork nightmare?" Lark throws me an offhand smile and walks toward the front door, following after Matteo and Angela.

I catch her by the arm. "Hey. Wait."

She turns back.

"What if, instead of the hospital, you stay here with me and Nina? I'm no psychologist, but if you need emergency care, I'm your guy."

Lark's eyes are wide. Grassy green and innocent. Equal parts hope and fear.

Gah, what that look does to me.

But when she smiles, it's all wicked humor. "You do seem pretty strong. You could handle me if I flip out again."

"Do you think that's likely?" I tease. "If so, maybe I *will* need Matteo's help. Two firefighters might be enough to handle you."

"I'll take it easy on you."

"I would appreciate that. I haven't been doing my usual weightlifting since I moved in here."

"But you *are* serious?" she asks. *"Really?* If this is some kind of test, and I'm supposed to refuse to be a burden…"

"I wouldn't ask if I didn't mean it. I was just talking to Nina about it. In fact, she insisted. Apparently I'll be disowned if I don't get you to stick around so she can make sure you're all right."

"What about what you want?" Lark asks softly.

"I want you here."

Heat flares in my stomach. Maybe I should've chosen different wording. She glances around the foyer as a blush moves up her neck, as if she's having the same thought.

"And I want to say yes. No, I *am* saying yes, because I don't have many alternatives. But you would just do that for me? Some woman you don't even know?"

I don't want Lark to think… Fuck, that I would expect some kind of payment in exchange for helping her.

"We're friends now, so I'm helping out a friend. It's a big house. Plenty of space. You'd have your own room and bathroom." Just in case she had any hesitation about sleeping arrangements. Any fleeting attraction I feel toward her is just that. Fleeting.

Some other man hurt this woman, and I'd never want to contribute to that. Even inadvertently.

She hesitates, then says, "Okay. Thank you. I want to contribute, though. I'm not sure if I can cook, but I can try. Or I could clean. Put me to work."

"Your first priority is to heal. It'll probably just be a day or two, anyway. We'll find your people. I bet they're looking for you as we speak."

"And what about the guy in the car who ran into me?" Her eyes lift. "It happened just down the street from here. What if he comes back?"

Then I'll fucking deal with him.

"Then it's all the better that you're staying here," I say. "We have a strong security system on the house. I don't like bullies, and Nina certainly has no patience for them. Think of me as a protective big brother. I'll look out for you."

Even as I say this, it strikes a wrong note within me. I don't have brotherly feelings about her. But I should. I shouldn't be having any other kinds of...urges. Not with an injured woman who needs a true friend more than anything else.

She's off limits. *Way* off limits.

There's a hint of reluctance in her face, but it's gone in an instant. "Until I find my people," Lark says.

"Until then."

10

Lark

It turns out moving in with Danny and his grandmother is easier than I would've expected. For a day and a half straight, pretty much all I do is sleep. My sleep had been uneven at the hospital, and I must've been running on adrenaline and fumes.

Talking to Angela—Detective Murphy—took a lot out of me, too.

But my second morning here, I wake up feeling almost normal. Normal as far as I know, anyway. I have less than a week of memories to base that on.

I kick off the covers and scoot out of bed. In the bathroom, I brush my teeth and study my face in the mirror, my mind sifting through the knowledge in my head like I'm taking inventory.

My name is Lark. *Check.* I'm staying with the Bradleys in West Oaks, California. *Check.*

And no, nothing else has miraculously cleared up inside my brain.

But the aches and pains in my body are getting better. My

bruises are starting to turn garish colors, which means they're healing.

As Danny promised, I have my own suite here. A queen-size bed, a small desk along one wall. An attached bathroom with soft linens and modern tile. But homey touches keep the room from being sterile. Like the framed cross-stitch designs on the walls, and the mismatched blankets and pillow covers.

The decor in here reminds me of the rest of the house. Like someone chose items one by one without a bigger plan in mind. Seems like the way that I would probably decorate. A bit of this, a little of that.

My favorite part about this room is the view from my window. A tall privacy fence surrounds the garden. Flowers grow everywhere out there, in pots and on bushes and on vines on trellises. The trees along the fences are heavy with lemons and oranges. I can practically smell the fruit blossoms through the window, and I can feel the pruning shears in my hands, carefully trimming each plant so it'll learn to grow.

Who knows? Maybe I'm a plant expert in my regular life. Or at least a plant enthusiast. Maybe I have a garden of my own.

The best part of the backyard is the weeping willow tree. I've found myself staring at it whenever I haven't been napping. There's something about the swaying branches that calms me. It feels comfortable and familiar to me. The same way it feels to be around Danny.

And Danny Bradley has the most tranquil blue eyes ever displayed on a human—*Check*.

Just one of those things I know.

Aside from a final visit to the hospital, where I explained to a very annoyed Nurse Julie that I was checking out, Danny and I haven't been on any more field trips.

The last time I checked in with Angela, she didn't have any news about finding my family or my real identity. I don't have a cell, but there's an actual landline in my room. I assume if she has updates, she'll call.

After a quick shower, I dress in some of Nina's old clothes and venture out into the kitchen. There's no one here, but there's a pot of coffee brewing and a plate of pastries. As if a breakfast fairy has come through recently and waved a magic wand. That would explain some things, because the Bradley household is a little too wonderful to be real. Except for Nina's illness, obviously. That part is a smack of reality, and it sucks.

I gulp down coffee and eat two croissants slathered in jam and butter, then go to Nina's room. "Hello?" I say quietly.

She's awake, lying in bed and working on a crossword puzzle with the help of her nurse Starla. But there's a man here too, wearing scrubs, someone I haven't met before. He's probably in his thirties, with a stocky build. His eyes sharpen when he sees me, moving down my body so quick I almost miss it.

"Look who's up and at 'em," Nina says. "Come have a seat and chat. This is Ryan." She nods at the male nurse.

"Hi." He smiles shyly and shakes my hand, the touch lingering. "I'm training with Starla today. You must be Lark."

"I am."

Starla purses her lips. I'm guessing she saw Ryan giving me the once-over. He seems like he's just eager for gossip, but I'm not interested in being his entertainment.

Starla is our mother hen. From what I can tell, she spends a few hours here on most days, while Danny takes care of Nina the rest of the time until it's night. That's when Jess arrives for a shift. I guess Ryan will be picking up a few as well, helping to fill in if the other nurses aren't available.

"So Lark," Ryan says, "it is true you have amnesia? You can't remember *anything*?"

Starla clears her throat. "Ryan, we need to go over a few more things. We're not off the clock just yet."

He smiles apologetically, as if he expects me to be disappointed, then crosses the room. While the nurses murmur off to one side, looking over a cabinet filled with medical supplies, I sit on the upholstered chair in the corner.

Nina's smothering a laugh. "A lot of new faces around here. Better to keep things interesting."

I'm not going to say this out loud, because I'm not a jerk, but Nina looks tired today. Like she's sinking into the bed. I wonder if it's a bad day, or if she just had extra energy on the day I arrived. Pumped up on adrenaline the way I was.

"How are you feeling?" I ask her.

"You'll catch on fast that I don't like answering that question."

"No problem. I don't either."

"Well, that won't work. I do want to hear how *you're* doing. Know your last name yet?"

I laugh louder than I meant to. I like this lady, I really do. Somehow, her curiosity is endearing because it's wrapped up in sarcasm. That might be my love language. "Nope. The hospital put me down as Lark D-o-e. What's with that, anyway? *Doe* as a substitute last name?"

"I'm sure Danny could tell us, given that he was a college boy. Just as well he's not here because I've got enough facts in my brain."

I almost ask where Danny is, but I don't want Nina to think I'm not interested in talking to her. That couldn't be further from the truth.

"Starla," Nina goes on, "what do you think Lark's last name could be?"

"Hmm." The nurse scrutinizes me, though she's still sorting through supplies. "Looks like she could have Irish heritage."

"Lark O'Malley?" Ryan supplies.

Nina scoffs. "You're not getting the point of this game. Give us some more interesting options. How about Lark Van Stiltskenhammer?"

My nose wrinkles. "That's a terrible name."

"Exactly. Memorable, though. Which would be ironic."

"Ha, I see what you did there. Ironic because I forgot it?"

"I knew you'd catch on quick."

For a while, Starla, Ryan, and I come up with increasingly ridiculous last names for me. Nina chuckles along with us, closing her eyes for longer intervals. She's wearing out.

We're entertaining her so that she can relax, and I'm happy to oblige. Nina and Danny are doing a ton for me, so I want to pay them back in any way I can. But besides that, this is fun.

Starla leaves the room to show Ryan the laundry, and then it's just Nina and me. "You slept well yesterday," Nina says. "You must've needed it. Has Danny given you a tour of the house? Shown you where everything is?"

"Kind of, the night I got here. He gave me some clothes of yours to wear. I hope that was okay." I didn't see her yesterday, between my own exhaustion and Nina's frequent naps.

"That was more than okay. That was *my* idea. I expect the credit. And I ordered a bunch of bath stuff too. Hope you've got what you need?"

"More than enough. Thank you." I wondered where all the shampoo, deodorant, and tampons in the bathroom had come from. I'd assumed they already had it stocked for other hypothetical guests. "You have such a big house. Do you have people staying here a lot?"

"I did. Before, you know, *this* mess." She gestures at the bed, the equipment, herself. The whole shebang. "I boarded high school exchange students from overseas."

"Really? That sounds...like a lot of work."

She laughs. "It was the kind of work I enjoyed. I'm retired, but I needed something to keep me on my toes. I always loved traveling and meeting people. This way, I could stay close to Danny and have the travelers come to me. You're providing me with the same service, so thank you."

"I don't have many interesting stories, though."

"Then make shit up, I don't care." She shrugs. "Fact or fiction, all the same to me."

I mirror her grin.

"If you have food preferences," she says, "just speak up. We use a meal delivery service and it's easy to make adjustments."

Ah. The breakfast fairy. I noticed that someone dropped off meals in my room while I was sleeping yesterday, too, but does she mean *every meal* is delivered? I didn't know that was a thing. How rich are these people? "I'm easy. If there's anything I don't like, I can't remember it. Guess we'll find out."

"Sounds good. Also, you'll need the security code from Danny so you can come and go as needed. We've had some break-ins here in the past."

"Did they take much?

"Cash, mostly. Loose valuables. Now, I keep the security system set at night. We've got cameras too."

I'm glad to hear it. I feel safe here, but it's nerve-racking to think that such a nice neighborhood would still have crime.

Well, I already knew that, didn't I? I was the victim of a crime not far from Nina's door a few nights ago. It's surreal to think about it.

I make a slow circuit of the room, glancing around. Nina doesn't seem to mind. There are pictures on the walls of the Bradley family. I see Danny at various ages, which feels strange. Like I'm seeing something personal without his permission.

But do I keep looking? Yep.

"Your house is beautiful."

"I appreciate the compliment, but it's not mine exactly. My son owns it. Danny's father. He bought this place as an investment and lets me live here. He and Danny don't get along."

"No?" I'm trying to act like this topic mildly interests me at most. Like I'm not desperate to know everything about the man who saved me and took me in. I don't know how I got lucky enough for a guy like him to find me. Not just nice and funny and panty-dropping hot, but good to his grandma too?

When he's working as a firefighter, he must get chased after constantly by women he's saved. The adoration must get old. Perhaps that's why he doesn't have a girlfriend.

It would be so obnoxiously predictable for me to fall for him. Embarrassing, really.

Nina settles back against the pillows. "Danny's always had an adventurous streak. Took after his grandma that way. Me, I could never stay put in one place when I was younger. My parents told me I could choose between being a nurse and a teacher. Acceptable careers for a girl. But I wasn't having any of that. I came out here to the West Coast and rambled around for a while. Met the man who would become the love of my life, Danny's grandpa. The two of us wanted to see as much of the country as possible, so we decided to become long-haul truckers."

"For real?" I never would've guessed. I don't imagine that many women were truckers decades ago when Nina was young.

"Oh, sure. Why not? My man and I got to be together, see the sights when we weren't on a deadline. Visited every road-side attraction and national park you could think of. I loved it. Absolutely loved it. My husband had a dual Canadian citizenship, and we drove up in Canada for a while. After we had our boys, we couldn't wander quite as much as we wanted. We still tried to get out on the road every summer. But our sons had their own likes and dislikes, as children do. They wanted to spend their summers at home hanging out with their friends instead of road-tripping with Mom and Dad. Could you hand me that water glass?"

I help her take a sip. Then she goes on with her story as if she hadn't stopped. "Danny's father, Chris, he was the first in our family to earn a college degree. Then he went on to business school. Started his own company. I was proud as hell, but I didn't understand him. So it figures Chris didn't understand Danny, either, when his son turned out to have a mind of his own."

Now, we're getting to the good stuff. "What was Danny interested in?"

"All kinds of things. How things worked, especially people. But also engines, cars. He and his grandpa used to spend hours in the garage, tinkering. Chris thought that was a waste of time. Danny went to college, but he didn't do a single other thing his dad wanted. Enlisted in the Army instead of applying to medical school."

I want to ask more about Danny. I want to know everything. But Nina doesn't volunteer more, and I'm not supposed to be pumping Nina for details on her grandson. I'm supposed to be learning about *her*.

"You said boys. How many do you have?" I ask.

Immediately, I know I shouldn't have asked. Her expression shuts down. It takes a long time for her to speak the next words. "Just one other. But he left. He's gone."

"Oh, I'm sorry."

"Don't be sorry. I stumbled right into your question. I wasn't thinking."

"Why did he leave? What happened to him?"

Another pause. Maybe I shouldn't have asked that either, but keeping my mouth shut doesn't seem to be one of my core characteristics.

"Life happened," Nina says. "It's not always pretty, is it? You're young, but I'll bet you know that in your guts. Like I do."

"Yeah. I think that's true." It's that sinking feeling in my stomach. The bruises and scrapes fading from my skin.

Starla and Ryan come back in. "About ready for lunch?" Starla asks.

Nina gives a single nod, though her eyes are shuttered. Not lively like they were before. "Lunch is when I take my pain meds, Lark. I won't be much company after that."

"No problem. Could we talk more later? Or tomorrow?"

"If I'm not too tired. But I might be."

I leave feeling like I screwed up. Like I made a friend and then already lost her. It's bad enough that Nina is sick. Whatever happened with her other son, it hurt her enough that the wound still smarts.

I guess even a home that looks perfect on the outside can conceal pain beneath.

11

Danny

"Son," my dad says, "how's your grandmother? Faring any better?"

I'm out in the backyard, scowling at the cloudless blue sky. There's a nip of fall in the air. I didn't want to make this phone call, but I'm doing it for Nina. She has no idea I called Dad, of course, but I know she'd approve. I like being a good grandson to her. Least I can do.

"It's day by day. Same thing I told you before. She's in hospice, Dad."

"Believe me, I know. I've seen the bills."

I close my eyes, clenching my jaw. *Do not scream. Do not curse.* I don't know how I share DNA with my dad, much less my name. "Are you going to get out here soon? Nina wants to see you."

"I'm trying to work out my schedule. The end of the quarter's coming up. You know how hectic that gets. Well, you probably don't know. But trust me. I can't just take a leave of absence on a whim."

It doesn't go much better from there. I wrap up the call as

quickly as possible, then head into the garage, where I drop my phone onto the workbench and let out a massive sigh.

My father works for a mega conglomerate in London. The same company that bought his start-up back when I was a middle-schooler. My parents love it there, and they rarely return to the states.

Especially not to see Nina or me.

When I was a teenager, my grandpa's garage was my refuge. It was at a different house back then, but the smells were the same. Motor oil, sweat, degreaser and metal. I used to help Grandpa with his '68 Charger, the car I drive now. That car was his pride and joy. His second love after Nina.

A few months after I got my discharge, I was driving around West Oaks and saw a rare '71 for sale. I couldn't believe it. Its paint was riddled with rust, and the engine was shot. But right when I spotted it, I wanted it.

I wanted to believe I could put it back together. Make it just like new.

I can already visualize how this car will look when it's done. Split grill, ducktail spoiler, all the original features. It'll be shiny, midnight black. I still have a long way to go. I remember a lot of what Grandpa taught me, but I'm far from a mechanic. I'm better at treating people than machines.

I've relied on YouTube videos for the really hard stuff, and even then, I'm winging it. So it's been a slow process, slowed even further by my firefighter schedule. I'm talking *years* since I bought this baby, and it's still not done. Sometimes I go weeks without touching it once.

Working on the car is a little like meditation. It's good for me, healing for my soul, yet I'm not always in the mood for it. Even if I might need it.

But I'll get there. I'll fix it.

The side door to the garage opens, and Lark walks in. "I brought sandwiches. If you're hungry."

I grab a rag and wipe off my hands. "I'd love one, yeah. I didn't know you were up and moving today."

"Feeling slightly more human. Not so achy."

"Sounds like progress."

I was up around dawn. I went for a quick run, then had my usual coffee with Nina. It's one of our rituals, though sometimes I sub in chamomile tea for her. Nights are often hit and miss for her, but something about the early morning light gives her a dose of energy. At least, that's what she says. I feel the same way.

Yesterday, I alternated between time with Nina and checking on Lark in the guest room. I also kept a close eye on the cameras around our property, watching for anything suspicious. And I've kept in touch with Cliff, but there's been no word yet from West Oaks PD about a suspect in her attack.

She slept nearly all day. When I saw her lying in that bed, unconscious to the world, she looked so fragile. At one point yesterday afternoon, she was under so deep that I crossed the room and put a hand beneath her nose to make sure she was breathing, like new parents do with babies.

I know that in her waking hours, she's strong. Resilient. But now that she's here, Lark is my responsibility. I don't take that lightly.

She has a bite to her personality, and that draws me in. Whatever else she's lost, she's held on to that. Which must mean that it's an essential part of her. Ingrained into who she is. She's a victim, but she doesn't cower like someone who's accepted it. She's not going to let the world keep her down.

"Remember anything new?" I unwrap the sandwich Lark just handed me and take a bite. Chicken salad. Not bad.

"Just the fact that I hate mayonnaise." She lifts up her sandwich, which is nibbled along one edge. I hold out my hand, and Lark gives me the offending chicken salad.

"Thanks. I'm hungry enough to eat two anyway. There's more stuff in the fridge. Mayo free."

"That's okay. I'll grab another croissant from the breakfast spread. But who is *this* gorgeous girl?" She circles the car and flicks her hair over her shoulder. It moves in a wave, catching the light, and I realize that's the exact finish I want on the car when it's done. That same inky shade of black. And I can't explain why, but that thought makes my dick all kinds of interested.

"How many classic Chargers do you have around here?"

I finish off my first sandwich in three bites, setting the other on my workbench for later. "Just the two. The red one my grandpa restored, which you saw before, and this one's my work in progress. I wouldn't call myself a mechanic. An enthusiastic amateur."

"Enthusiasm makes up for a lot." She glances over the tools on my workbench. "Your piston ring installer is broken, by the way."

"Yeah, I ordered a new one. You know your stuff."

"I'm as surprised as you are," she says with a shrug.

"Want to give me a hand?"

Lark narrows her eyes like this is a trick of some kind. "You'd trust me?"

"Sure." Besides, this car's already been through hell and back. If she screws it up, I'll fix it.

"You're just thinking you'll fix it if I mess up. Aren't you?"

Shit. "How'd you know that?"

"Because I can tell when a guy is humoring me. I don't like it. Or need it."

Damn. Feisty thing, isn't she? "Then I apologize. Hands off my baby. Don't even think about trying to help."

"Thank you."

Laughing, I brush my sweaty hair from my forehead.

Lark points at me. "You just..."

"What?"

"You left an engine grease smudge. Right there."

"Oh." I lift the edge of my shirt to wipe my skin. "Did I get it?"

"No, you just made it worse. And got your shirt dirty."

"It was already dirty." I whip it off. It's a long-sleeved tee, which was perfect this morning since it's getting chilly at night these days. But after a couple hours out here in Nina's garage, I'm starting to bake. I scrub the shirt over my face. "Better now?"

Her eyes are tracing over my bare torso. "Better." Her voice cracked a little, and she clears her throat. "Nice tats."

"Thanks." Like her, I have sleeve tattoos, plus some larger designs on my chest. While Lark's are all botanical, mine are more of a mishmash. References to my life at the time I got them, images that called to me. On my arms, my artist filled in some of the empty spaces with geometric patterns.

"You don't have to show off for me, though," she says. "I already told you that you were sexy. No need to go flaunting it."

I snort. This girl, I swear. "I wasn't showing off. It's warm in here."

"Well *now* it is." She smirks as she peruses my workbench. "I was chatting with Nina earlier. She told me about your dad. How he owns the house, but you don't get along."

My back stiffens. "Yep, that's all true."

"Is it okay that she told me? Do you mind that we were talking about you?"

"Not at all." I'm not an open book necessarily, but I don't have a problem with Lark knowing things about me. If anything, I like that she's interested. That's what friends do, right? They get to know one another. "If you want to know anything else, you can ask me."

"What about your uncle? Nina mentioned him, but when I asked her about him, she clammed up pretty fast."

"She doesn't talk about him much. Travis is my dad's younger brother."

"He left? That's what she said."

"Travis left when I was fourteen, not long after my grandpa died. He'd had some argument with Nina and my dad over money, stole some of my grandpa's stuff, then took off and never came back." Almost twenty years ago now. "He could've come home if he'd wanted to. Nina would've forgiven him. Actually, I'm surprised she mentioned anything about him to you at all."

"Why? She was reminiscing about when her kids were young. It was natural to mention him."

"Yeah, but Nina can keep certain subjects quiet if she wants to. She didn't even tell me she was sick until months had passed. She didn't want my input."

And now, there's something *I* don't like to talk about.

Lark doesn't need to know about the arguments Nina and I had about her care decisions. Hospice certainly isn't a death sentence. It's not a guarantee that she's going to die. We need to be realistic. That's why I've been urging my dad to come see her. But am I giving up on her? Fuck, no. I'm not.

While I want to focus on ways to help her live as long as possible with a good quality of life, Nina seems more resigned. It makes no sense to me. If you can keep fighting, then why the hell wouldn't you? And Nina's more of a fighter than anyone I know.

"But you told Nina what you felt about it?" she asks.

"Sure." I give her an easy smile and take a deep breath to get my pulse to calm down. "I'm like you. I usually say what I'm thinking. With a slightly better filter than yours."

Lark rolls her eyes. "What fun is that?"

We work quietly on the car for a while. I get into a groove.

That meditative space where my mind is wandering, yet not sticking to any particular thing.

"So, you think we're alike?" Lark asks.

"Hmm?"

"You said you're like me. Because we both say what we're thinking."

"We have things in common," I say carefully. "But I'm probably a lot older than you."

"How old is that?"

"Thirty-three."

She's looking down at the engine instead of at me. Her lips and cheeks are pale pink. Probably soft. And she's giving off that innocent, vulnerable energy that really seems to get me going when I'm around her. That's not usually my thing. I don't go for much-younger women or virgins or anything like that. In fact, I'd feel like a pervert if I did.

But the way my blood is trying to flow straight to my cock makes me feel pretty pervy right damn now. Imagining her bent over that car...

Fuck. I need to stop.

I train my eyes on the engine so I'll stop noticing the subtle curves beneath her baggy T-shirt.

Now, I feel her eyes on me. "How old do you think I am?"

"Young," I say automatically, and she huffs.

"That's not helpful. I'm being serious. I've been trying to figure this out. It bugs me that I don't know."

I set down the tool I was holding and focus on her. This is really bothering her, and I was being a dick about it, thinking only of my newly discovered perverted tendencies.

"Come here. Let me see you."

I'm sitting on a stool. Lark walks over to me, stopping when she's just between my knees. If I reached out, I could pull her into my lap. I bet her legs would fit perfectly around my waist.

Nope, not thinking any more about that.

"Unless you went to a disreputable shop, you would've gotten your tattoos after you turned eighteen. But they don't look brand new." I delicately take one of her wrists in my fingers and turn her arm. "Could be several years old."

"I've got fine lines on my face too."

"Not that I've seen."

She scrunches up her face. "Around my eyes and my mouth."

"Anybody has wrinkles when they make that face."

"Danny, I'm serious." She leans in closer to me. Her long hair falls forward, brushing my arm, and a shudder of desire moves through me and throbs in my balls.

Oh, damn.

Without my permission, my hand reaches up, my thumb caressing down her cheek. Her pupils dilate, the rest of her going still.

Since the moment I met Lark, I've been touching her. In the hospital, I held her hand. Put my arm around her shoulders to help her stay calm. But now, touching her somehow has more gravity to it. Like it means something else now that she's standing steadier on her own two feet.

Shit, what were we talking about?

How old she is. Right.

"You're no older than fifty-five," I say.

"You're a dork."

"You disagree? You're *older* than fifty-five?"

"Fine, you can joke about it. But how am I supposed to get an ID or a driver's license if I don't know how old I am? If I try to order a drink at a bar, I can't even prove I'm over twenty-one. Maybe I'm a lot younger, but I've lived a really hard life."

So that's what she's worried about. "If that's true, it means you're a survivor. That's something to be proud of.

But we're going to find your family, and when we do, we'll find out. I don't have a single doubt about it."

I have to keep reminding myself of those facts. I have no right to lay a claim to this girl, even inside my own head.

"Then I wish they'd hurry up. It's been almost four days since the accident. I don't want to stay so long that you get sick of me."

"I doubt that will happen, but I get what you mean. Nothing worse than being the idiot who sticks around when you're not wanted." I'm speaking offhand, thinking about my own crap. But when I look up, Lark is frowning, her eyes cast down and to the side. "Oh shit, I didn't mean you. You could never be—"

My phone rings. It's over on the workbench, closer to Lark. She glances at the screen. "Angela's calling. You should probably answer."

I'm feeling like an asshole for what I said. But she's right.

I stand up and grab the phone. "Hey, Angela. What's up?"

"Danny. I tried calling your landline, but the nurse said Lark wasn't inside. Is she with you?"

"Yeah. She's right here. I can put the phone on speaker."

"Do that."

I hit the button. "Lark can hear you now."

"Hi, Angela. What is it?" Lark asks.

"I just got off the phone with your aunt. We've found your family. We know who you are."

12

Lark

"Her name is Kathy Sullivan," Angela says. "She's your aunt by marriage."

"So she claims," Danny cuts in. He's standing behind me, one hand gripping the back of the chair that I'm sitting in.

I look at the picture of an auburn-haired woman. She's got feathered bangs, a friendly smile. She makes me think of a middle school teacher. Or a mother-hen nurse like Starla.

We're in Angela's office at West Oaks PD headquarters. Angela has on another dress, empire-waisted to allow room for her baby bump, but she's paired it with a gray blazer. She was so low key when I met her a few days ago, but here, where we're surrounded by cops and guns and handcuffs, she seems far more intimidating.

Or maybe it's just the situation. The police make me nervous anyway, even when they're trying to help me. I'm a problem to be handled. A lost person in search of her family.

Is that who Kathy Sullivan is? My family?

Angela rests her arms over her belly. "Ms. Sullivan lives in Eureka."

"Up in NorCal?"

"Yep. She contacted Eureka Police and filed a missing person's report about you. That's what popped up in NamUS. We asked to speak with Ms. Sullivan, and she sent us this to corroborate." Angela puts an ID card on the desk surface and pushes it over to me. It's from a school called Northern California College. And it's got my picture on it, along with the name Lark Richards.

That's my name. Lark Richards.

My first thought is that Nina will be disappointed. It's nowhere near as interesting as the ones we were coming up with this morning.

"We confirmed with the school's records. You attended a semester there a couple years ago before withdrawing. They had your date of birth and address." Angela hands me a sheet of paper with the info. The street name, the numbers... It still means nothing to me. "You're twenty-four years old."

I set down the paper and wrap my arms around my stomach, just trying to take this all in. Danny's hand rests on my shoulder, solid and comforting. I think of how Danny and I were discussing my age just a couple hours ago in his garage. The way he touched my arms and then my face. My body reacted, an electric tingle running through me when his bare skin met mine.

I won't stick around long enough for Danny or Nina to want me gone. Shouldn't I be relieved? Happy?

I don't know what to feel.

"Did you find Lark's driver's license or social security records?" Danny asks. "Anything to fill in the gaps of her identity?"

Angela tilts her head, speaking patiently. "We didn't, which is unusual, but not unheard of if she grew up off the grid and never learned to drive. In fact, one of the first things we did was run Lark's photo through facial recognition, which we can use to match with DMV records. Nothing came up." She looks back to me. "Ms. Sullivan said your parents were modern-day hippies living in a commune."

Which would explain why I feel uncomfortable around cops. My parents were anti-establishment types. That idea rings true for me.

"As far as fingerprints and DNA," Angela goes on, "we didn't find any matches. That means you don't have a criminal record, and your relatives aren't in the government databases either. Again, if they stayed off the grid, that makes sense."

"What kinds of people have their DNA on file?" I ask.

"Convicted felons. Those who've served in the military, like Danny."

So I'm not related to Danny, at least. Probably good to know.

"Police nationwide also upload DNA samples of unidentified crime victims," Angela says.

I bite my lip.

"Finding a match that way was always less likely. I figured your family would report you missing, and I'm glad that was right. I spoke to your aunt on the phone, and she cried, she was so relieved you're safe. Kathy is related to you through marriage, rather than blood. Her husband, your uncle, is working as a roughneck in Alaska right now on an oil rig. Apparently, he's not easy to reach."

I pick up the ID and close my hand around it. "I want to talk to her."

"As you should. I'll give you her number." Angela smiles. "Who knows? Maybe in just a few days, you'll be back home."

Home. Which is apparently Eureka, California, way up north from here. Maybe my aunt Kathy can explain what I was doing in Southern California in the first place.

∾

I HAVE my first conversation with Kathy Sullivan that night.

"Lark! My God, I've been so worried about you!" We're on FaceTime. She has her hair in a ponytail, but otherwise, she looks just like her photo. "You were in an accident?"

I'm sitting in the living room of Danny's home, using his cell phone. He's in the chair across from me, shoulders broad in his T-shirt as he hunches over and twists his necklace in his fingers. He offered to give me some privacy to talk to my aunt, but I asked him to stay. And of course, he said yes. He always says yes, nice guy that he is, but that doesn't mean he wants to.

"Tell me what happened," Kathy says. "Tell me everything."

I tell her what I know about the incident four nights ago. The car racing toward me, trying to run me over. Losing almost all of my memories of who I am.

Kathy touches the base of her throat. "Oh, that's awful, Lark. I'm so sorry."

"I just wish I knew who did it and why I was in West Oaks at all."

"You don't remember anything? *Truly?*"

I shake my head. I already explained about the dissociative amnesia, but it's hard for people to understand, including me.

Her expression darkens. "I don't know why you went to West Oaks. But if I had to guess? I'd say it was the fault of that boyfriend of yours."

Danny looks up sharply.

"Boyfriend?" I choke out.

"I only ever knew him as Cam. You and I..." Kathy sighs. "Well, it's a long story, sweetheart. We had our ups and downs, as all families do. But then, *he* came into the picture. I thought Cam was bad news from the moment you brought him around. He was older. Controlling. You'd been living with me and Ned, but within weeks, you up and moved out. Went to live with him. Ned and I were, well, upset. You and I fought over it. You don't know how I regret that."

I feel Danny watching me. But I can't look at him.

"I didn't hear from you for months, and I'm sure it was my fault. But then you reappeared on our doorstep. You had...bruises."

My shoulders slump.

"Ned and I were overjoyed to see you, thinking it was all over with you and that man. But it became a cycle. You and Cam would break up, then get back together. After a while, we stopped hearing from you at all, and I think Cam wasn't letting you contact us." Her voice waivers. "If you were in trouble and wanted out, I wish you had come to us. All we've ever wanted is to be there for you."

I think about those old bruises. The healed fractures the doctor saw on the X-ray. Bile rises in my throat.

"You think that's why I came to West Oaks? I was running away from him?"

"Has to be. I don't know the exact details. But we can figure it all out if you just come home, Lark. Please. We just want you home."

"What about my parents? Where are they? You told the detective they live on a commune."

She sighs. "Oh, honey, they passed in a car accident when you were eighteen. That's why you've lived with me and Ned since then. I can explain it all later, but just know that we miss you. You have so many friends here who miss you, too. We just want you back."

We don't talk long that first night. I'm too overwhelmed. I can't even talk to Danny about it. After he heard Kathy say that stuff about my abusive boyfriend? It's too much. It's just *surreal*. Like I'm hearing stories about someone else's life.

The next day, Kathy and I talk alone, without Danny. I ask her, "Will you tell me more about my life? Do I have a job?"

"You tried out a few semesters of college, but it wasn't for you." We're video-calling again, and she smiles sadly. "You work for a florist now. Technically, I think it's off the books. But that's how I knew you were missing. Because I would drive by your work most days to check on you, and suddenly you weren't there. The second day, I went inside to ask, and they said you'd disappeared."

I'm a florist. No wonder my tats are all botanical, and I love looking at the plants in Nina's backyard. That's not so bad, is it? Working with flowers all day?

"Do you want to see your bedroom?" she asks. "We kept it just the same, in case you decided to come home again."

Everything is brightly colored, and there are pictures of me tacked to a bulletin board. There are none with me and Kathy together, but I'm smiling with people I assume are friends. My chest aches when I see that.

"Who are those people I'm with in the pictures?"

"High school classmates," Kathy says. "You lost touch with them, and I don't know your current friend group. You never brought them to meet me. But when you come home, we'll be able to start fresh."

It's starting to sink in. I really do have people who love me. They want me back.

I was only supposed to stay in West Oaks until I found my family. That just happened faster than I expected.

ON THE DAY I LEAVE, Danny takes my bag out to the Charger. "You sure about this?" he murmurs. "Completely sure?"

"Yes. She's got a whole plan. Kathy's going to find a psychologist for me to work on getting my memories back."

"What about keeping you safe? That boyfriend she mentioned?"

Ugh, not something I want to discuss with him.

Danny already urged me to tell West Oaks PD about Cam, and he was there when I made the call to Angela. But Kathy doesn't know Cam's last name—he's more of a mystery than *I* am, apparently—and I don't remember him at all, obviously.

Kathy said we'll try to file a restraining order in Eureka. If my ex-boyfriend shows his face and comes near me, he'll be arrested. If he's the one who attacked me here in West Oaks, then he'll go to prison.

"Protecting me isn't your problem anymore," I remind Danny.

And he said it best. *Nothing worse than being the idiot who sticks around when you're not wanted.*

The Bradleys don't feel that way about me now, but they will. It's inevitable, even if they would never admit it. Danny and Nina are good people who make sacrifices for each other. I'm… I'm someone who would choose an asshole named Cam over the aunt who loves me. I'm trying not to judge my past self. But if I keep staying in West Oaks, doesn't that hurt my aunt even more?

"I just need to say goodbye to Nina, and then we can go."

Danny frowns like he intends to argue. But he's silent as I head to Nina's room. I've been keeping her posted on everything Kathy has told me.

I knock on her doorframe. "Hey, I'm ready to go. Can I come in?"

"Of course." I go to her, and Nina holds my wrist in a surprisingly strong grip. "You call us when you arrive in Eureka. Tell us everything that's going on. And if there's even a hint of your ex sniffing around, call the police and call Danny, too."

"I'll be fine. Thank you so much for everything. But you don't have to worry about me."

"That's a load of bull, and you know it. You're a friend, and that's as good as family. You always have a place to stay in West Oaks. Now give me a hug."

I hug her, and suddenly all my insides are bunched up in my throat, choking me. Tears sting in my eyes. I can't believe I've only known her and Danny for a week. But considering how little I remember from before, it's kinda like my whole life.

And now, this part of my life is over.

It's a solid nine hours up to Eureka, so Kathy drives down to meet us halfway. We're supposed to connect with her at a travel stop near Fresno. She says she has friends there, and we'll stay overnight before driving up to Eureka the next day. Danny doesn't say much on the drive, which makes for a long four hours. He drums his fingers against the steering wheel, and the radio fills the silence between us.

Finally, we pull into the travel stop. There are gas pumps for cars and trucks along one side, and a store and restaurant on the other. Danny parks in the lot. A glare rises up from all the concrete, making me squint.

An ache builds between my eyes. In my heart.

He reaches into his pocket and fishes out a piece of paper. "This is my cell. Text when you get wherever you're going, all right? I want to hear how Eureka is. I've never been."

"Guess I'll find out."

We watch the entrance to the travel shop until a woman with auburn hair and feathered bangs arrives. Kathy Sullivan. She's looking all around anxiously, wringing her hands as she scans the passing faces.

A brief moment of panic seizes me. *I'm not ready.*

But I push out of the car anyway.

We head over, and Danny is the first to introduce himself. His face is stoic, gestures stiff as he shakes Kathy's hand. Then Kathy dives toward me for a hug. She squeezes me a little too hard, as if she's afraid I'll disappear again.

"Do you have any other bags?" she asks me.

"Just this." I shrug one shoulder, which is holding the backpack that Danny gave me. It's stamped WOFD. There's not much inside, just a change of clothes and some cash that Nina insisted I take with me.

"Thanks for driving her," Kathy says to Danny. "And taking care of her. I'm so grateful. I thought we'd grab some lunch. Did you want to join us, Danny?"

"If Lark wants me to."

They both look to me. Panic is clawing at me again.

Don't go, I want to say. *Please*. But if we drag this out, it's just going to hurt more later. "We should say goodbye. Kathy, could you grab us a table and give me and Danny a minute?"

She nods and pushes through the glass door into the building.

"So this is it," he says when Kathy is gone.

"Yeah."

"I'd hoped we would have more time working on the '71 Charger together. I could use the help." He smiles, but I can tell it's forced. I know him well enough to see the signs.

"Maybe the next time I'm here." Whenever that is.

"Hope so." His fake smile slips. Danny's fingertips touch my cheek, and the contact makes my nerve endings sing like he's the conductor of my own personal orchestra. I close my eyes and bask in the feeling. It might be the last time. We were just talking about seeing each other again, but when? We live hundreds of miles apart. It's probably not going to happen.

When I open my eyes, Danny is staring at me intently.

"What?" I whisper.

"This is happening too fast. I don't think you should do it."

At first, those words don't compute. *"What?* What do you mean?"

"Come back to West Oaks with me."

I gawk at him. He waits until *now* to drop that bomb? "I... I can't..."

"There's too much we don't know. Let's put the brakes on. It would give us more time to look into Kathy and the rest of your family. And find Cam."

More time for him to be my hero, he means. More time for me to get attached.

Danny Bradley goes around saving women's lives, making them feel safe when they're scared. Asking them to move in with him like those are normal things to do. Being so sexy and kind and *perfect,* all the while asking for nothing in return. Except maybe for some help hanging out with his awesome grandma or working on his gorgeous classic car.

That's *not my life.* It never was, and it never will be.

The longer I stick around and pretend I belong in Danny's world, the more it's going to hurt when I inevitably have to leave.

"I have to go home. And you know it."

He takes my chin in his hand. His eyes move over my face, lingering. Like he's trying to memorize me. Like he's trying to convey all the words he doesn't know how to voice. Takes a step closer. I feel his exhale on my forehead.

"You gonna forget me?" he asks.

"That's not possible." I go onto my tiptoes to kiss him on the cheek. Just to say goodbye. But at the last moment, I change direction.

Without letting myself think about it, I press my lips to his.

Our mouths are closed, and it's barely even a kiss, yet my heart is pounding. My tongue sneaks out and swipes over his lower lip. I just want one taste of this man I can never have.

Then I pull away from him, and Danny looks stunned. The hand that was holding my chin is still raised in the air. "*Lark*," he whispers, his voice rough.

I'm already backing away toward the glass door. "Goodbye, Danny. Thank you for saving my life. And for everything else too. I'll miss you."

I spin around and go inside, fighting back tears.

13

Danny

I can't believe I'm driving away from her. But I can't believe I asked her to ditch her aunt, either.

Come back to West Oaks with me? When her aunt had driven four-plus hours and was standing just inside, waiting for her?

Fuck, I'm a mess.

I drive one-handed, my fingers twisting my necklace into a tight spiral. The radio's off, so I switch it on. But the music grates on me, so I switch it off. The leather squeaks as I adjust my weight in the seat, unable to get comfortable.

Since the moment Angela told us about Kathy, I've had my doubts. I was ready to demand DNA tests to prove she was related to Lark. But the related-by-marriage thing defeated that idea. She did have Lark's school ID, and the photos in Lark's bedroom at her home, which Lark described to me after their call. Kathy had an answer to every question we asked.

I could've had a private background check done on Kathy, which is something the police don't have the resources or time for. But that would've taken days longer. Lark didn't want to wait.

Of *course* she wants to go home.

But if Lark had said yes just now, I would've run off with her, not even stopping to give word to her aunt. Bundled her up in this car and fucking gotten out of town. That would've made *me* look like the criminal. I can just imagine Nina's face if the cops showed up at our door, Kathy Sullivan accusing me of kidnapping her niece.

That would've been a turnabout that none of my friends and family saw coming.

The thing is, I don't just feel responsible for Lark. I *like* her. I'm going to miss her friendship, her presence at the house. Her smile that feels like a prize I've earned. Is that what this is? Just me being a selfish asshole, wanting to keep her around?

As I drive away, I press my fingers to my lips, remembering that kiss. Except for the brush of tongue, which I was way into, it could've been a platonic kiss between friends. Yet I felt it through my entire body like a bolt of lightning, filling me with this white-hot longing. And then I stood there like a fool, frozen in place as she walked away from me.

It was just a goodbye kiss. But I still feel it fucking *everywhere*.

It's possible I'm a little hung up on her. A woman I'll probably never see again.

Using the bluetooth settings on my phone, I call Matteo.

"Hey!" he says cheerfully. "Is Lark with her aunt?"

I swallow, trying to get my vocal cords going. "She is. Yeah. I'm heading back. Everything good at home?"

"Nina kicked my ass at Scrabble. It was brutal. Aside from those wounds, we're solid. Oh, some of the B shift guys were going to stop by here later when I head in. They wanted to hang with Nina for a bit."

"Really? They don't have to do that."

"We've all been meaning to do more since we heard Nina

was sick. I'd worry about whether she can handle five fire-fighters showing up at her house for a visit, but it's probably the other way around. Not sure they can handle the intense grandma energy she's giving today."

I chuckle. "Thanks, man. Tell everyone thank you. It means a lot."

I don't know what I'd do without Matteo and my team-mates. I really don't. Same thing with Cliff and my old room-mates. I'm lucky to have so many friends.

Which makes me think of Lark again. Will she have friends to help her out in Eureka? Friends she can count on? I almost say something about all these doubts swirling in my head. Matteo would probably tell me to turn around and chase after her.

But I can't do that. *Don't be that guy.*

We talk a few more minutes, and I manage to end the call without admitting how much I already miss Lark. But my heart gets heavier with every mile that I put between her and me. I keep glancing at my rearview mirror, though the travel stop disappeared a while ago.

Dammit, I didn't want to leave her. And I still don't.

This might feel better if I could check in with Lark right now. Why didn't I buy her a damn phone so she could text me directly? The convenience store probably had pay-as-you-go models for purchase, and I could've bought one and acti-vated it so she could text me and let me know she's okay and…

Listen to me.

I used to give Matteo shit for trying to save every woman in his life, whether she wanted it or not. Then here I am, dreaming up reasons that Lark still needs me even though she's made it clear she's ready to move on. I have no legiti-mate reason to suspect Kathy Sullivan isn't what she says she is. Lark is ready to get back to her family and her life, as she should, and I should get back to mine.

Enough, I tell myself. *Get your shit together.* Don't be the guy who can't let go of someone who doesn't want you anymore.

I turn up the radio and step on the gas, determined to put Lark Richards behind me.

14

Lark

When I'm sure I won't cry, I go find my aunt. Kathy's sitting in a booth in the restaurant. She almost stands up when she sees me coming, then sits down again. Like she can't keep still.

I slide in across from her.

"He's gone?"

I ignore the way my insides flinch at hearing that. "Yeah. Danny's gone. It was hard to say goodbye."

"He seemed like a nice guy."

"He is." I don't like that she used the past tense.

And is *nice* even the right word? I've called him nice a lot, but he's generous. *Kind*, even when he's frustrating. Wonderful even.

Sexy. Can't forget that.

The brush of our lips together was like a spark ready to ignite a flame. And then it was gone. Extinguished. I wish I'd had more than just that brief taste. What if we'd let those flames catch and burn? Danny's tattooed chest pressing up against me, his long fingers twisting in my hair as his tongue claims my mouth...

"Lark?"

I glance up. "Sorry, what was that?"

Kathy nods at the menu on the table. "I said, you should order something."

"I'm not that hungry."

"You still need to eat. We'll be here a while longer." There's a new sharpness to her voice that wasn't there before.

"All right." I order a club sandwich, no mayo, and pick at it when it arrives.

I do my best to keep the conversation going, but it feels stilted. It doesn't help that Kathy seems even more nervous than before I arrived, not less. Neither of us is eating. I'm not even sure why we're sitting here.

"What's my uncle like?" I ask.

"Who?"

"My uncle Ned. Your husband? My mom's brother?"

"Of course. Sorry, I'm just distracted."

"It's okay. I get it. This is a lot to deal with."

"It is." She clears her throat and pushes away her tomato soup.

Kathy keeps glancing around the restaurant, and I look behind me, trying to follow her gaze. "Are you expecting anyone else?" I ask.

Her mouth stretches in a stiff smile. "No. Not at all."

She's acting weird, but I'm trying to give her the benefit of the doubt. This can't be easy for her. Driving across the state to pick up her estranged niece who's lost her memory.

I finger the piece of paper with Danny's phone number in my pocket. *You're just missing him.* Nothing is wrong.

Kathy folds her hands on the table. "You asked about Ned, didn't you? Actually, I've got some great news. You'll see him later on today. He'll be in Fresno to meet us."

Wait, what?

"I thought you said he was in Alaska. Working on an oil rig."

"I know, but he was able to get back in time for this. He couldn't wait to see you," she says too brightly. "Wonderful news, isn't it?"

Now I'm officially creeped out. I lost my memory, but I didn't lose all of my common sense.

Kathy gets her phone out and checks it. My brain is churning through too many fears and possibilities.

But I can't freak out and panic. Danny isn't here to calm me down, so that means I need to figure this out for myself.

"You said I've lived with you and Ned off and on for a couple years now?" I ask. "Ever since my parents were in that car accident when I was...seventeen?"

"That's right. When you were seventeen. You're like a daughter to us." She says this in a monotone, still staring at her screen. But my stomach just dropped like an elevator when the cord has snapped.

Before, Kathy told me I was *eighteen* when I lost my parents. And that would've been *six* years ago, not two.

It's one thing for her to tell me stories for a few hours during some FaceTime conversations. Another to keep it all straight.

Sweat pricks along my arms. A cold bead runs down my side. "Could I use your phone?" I ask. "I just realized I left something at Danny's house. I need to let him know before I forget."

Her jaw clenches. She's still got her eyes on her screen. "Maybe later. Stay here and finish your lunch, all right? I need to go make a phone call." Without waiting for a response, she scoots out of the booth and walks toward the hallway where the bathrooms are located.

I watch her go, my insides turning to sludge. What the hell is going on here?

On second thought, maybe I shouldn't wait to find out.

I dig into my backpack, grab a twenty, and toss it on the table. Then I get up and walk calmly toward the front exit, keeping the bathroom hallway in my peripheral vision. I don't see Kathy on my way.

Once I'm outside in the parking lot, I'm not sure what my next step should be. I have to tell Danny to come back and get me. It's either that or call the police—not high on my list anyway—but all I can say is that my aunt is acting suspicious.

I don't actually know if she *is* my aunt.

If she's not, then she's been lying to me. Lying since the minute that she filed that missing person's report in Eureka saying her niece was gone.

But why would she do that? It sounds crazy.

What does your gut tell you? That's what Nina would probably ask.

I know the answer.

I go around the side of the building, trying to think this through. Maybe I'm wrong, and Kathy is just nervous. And somehow my uncle Ned made it back from a remote Alaskan oil rig in two days flat…

Yeah, still not buying it.

Danny was suspicious from the moment we learned Kathy's name. I should've listened to him. I should never have told him to leave me here. But I believed everything Kathy told me. Let her convince me with a few photos and a bunch of convenient stories.

If Kathy lied, she must've had a reason for it. She wanted to lure me out here. Why?

I'm behind the building now, resting my back against the stucco facade. Then I freeze when I hear Kathy's voice. "She's asking a lot of questions. No, she doesn't remember anything. But—"

I don't see her, but there's a dumpster near the back door

of the restaurant. She must be on the other side of it. I try to edge closer, fitting myself into a gap between the dumpster and the brick wall of the building. That's one benefit of being scrawny.

I can barely make out Kathy standing by the rear exit of the restaurant, her phone to her ear.

"She's inside eating lunch. *Yes*, I left her. She's not going anywhere. Your bigger concern is me." Kathy pauses. "I don't know how much longer I can keep this going. I'm the one who gave my name and ID to the police. They know who I am. If anyone finds out, I'm the one they'll go after."

Another pause. Meanwhile, I'm silently having a heart attack over here.

Kathy is obviously talking about *me*. But what is she afraid someone will find out? Who's on the other side of that conversation?

"If you want me to deliver her, I want more money."

My hand flies to my mouth as I cover a gasp.

"A thousand more. Not a cent less."

The person on the other end of the line yells. It's so loud I can hear it from where I'm standing, though I can't make out the exact words.

"No, don't come here," Kathy says. "That wasn't the plan! I'm—" She curses, dropping her phone to her side. The other person must've hung up.

I hear the rear door to the restaurant open. She's going back inside. Any moment, she'll realize I left. And whoever she was talking to is on their way here.

I need to be gone by then.

I walk as fast as I can back to the parking lot, careful to watch my surroundings. I'm scanning every face, every car, but there are too many. And my heart is beating too fast. Panic rises like dirty water in my veins.

Find a phone. Call Danny.

I head for the semi parking lot. I'll have more cover there between the trailers. Kathy won't spot me as easily.

A trucker steps down from his cab, and I think of Nina. How she was a trucker once too. This man is older, white hair sticking out from beneath a newsboy-style cap. He gives me a polite smile and a head nod.

"Excuse me, sir." My pulse flutters at my throat. "Could I use your phone? Mine's dead. I just need to call my ride. He's nearby, but…he got lost."

The man's brow wrinkles like he doesn't believe me. And why would he? This place isn't that hard to find. It's just off the freeway, and there's not much else around.

But he digs into his pocket and pulls out his device. "You can use it here. Don't go running off with it, now. I wouldn't appreciate that."

"I won't. Thanks." I take the phone, my hands shaking as I pull out the piece of paper Danny gave me.

Then instinct makes me look up.

The entrance to the convenience store is barely visible around the edge of the truck's cab, and Kathy has just come out. She looks furious. Her head swivels left and right.

Looking for *me*.

I shove the phone back into the man's hands. "Never mind. I need to go."

"But…" He says something more as I walk away, but I'm hurrying around the side of the next eighteen wheeler to get out of sight. I pause there behind the back wheels, my breaths coming short and fast.

Stay calm. Think of a plan.

I'll wait until Kathy goes in the opposite direction, and then I'll ask that trucker to use his phone again, even if I probably seem like a crazy person. I'll call Danny like I meant to. Or if he's too far away, I'll call a taxi. I'll head into Fresno and find a busy place to wait and figure out what to do next.

It's not much of a plan, but it's enough. I can handle this.

Then I notice another driver leaning up against the cab of the next truck over, smoking a cigarette. His body is still and relaxed, but his eyes are narrowed.

"Hey, you need something, sweetheart? Need a ride?"

Yes is right there on the tip of my tongue. I could hide in his truck. He could get me out of here.

But he's watching me like a coyote salivating over a meal, and I don't want anything to do with that.

I set my shoulders. "No, thanks. I'm fine."

The man saunters over. "If you need somethin', I can help."

"I *don't*." I turn to go, but he grabs my wrist in his bony hand.

"I think that you do."

15

Danny

*M*y resolve lasts all of five minutes.

Then I find myself taking the next exit, pulling a U-turn, and heading back toward the travel stop.

The Charger's engine growls as I pull into the lot. I park behind a camper, then head for the building. And there's Lark, visible in the window of the restaurant. She's sitting in a booth picking at a sandwich. Kathy isn't there.

Do I have a clue what I'm doing? Nope. I just didn't feel right leaving the way I did. Until I'm sure she's safe, Lark is still my responsibility. The least I could do is see her off with Kathy.

Maybe I should go into Fresno with them, meet the other people Lark will be staying with. Make sure they seem okay...

"Um, could you move?" someone says.

I glance over and find that I'm blocking the door to the convenience store. I step aside, and as I do, I catch a glimpse of my own reflection in the glass. My shoulders are tense, arms hanging at my sides. I look like a stalker. In fact, this is *nuts*. Lark isn't my responsibility anymore, and I need to let her go. That's what she expected me to do. Not to slink around spying on her.

I blame Matteo. My best friend is the pushiest asshole I've ever met when it comes to heroics, and he's got me acting just like him.

I head into the convenience store, doing my best to act like a normal guy and not some kind of obsessive weirdo. The shop is busy with people grabbing snacks and trailing in and out of the restrooms.

I spot pay-as-you-go phones behind the counter, and boom—there's a sensible excuse for being here. I'll buy one, give it to Lark, then go on my way.

It takes a couple minutes to reach the front of the line. "One of those phones, please?" I point at the clamshell package behind the register.

As I pay, I glance across at the restaurant, which is connected to the store through an open archway. But Lark and her aunt aren't sitting at their booth anymore.

Shit, did I miss them already?

Maybe I can head them off in the parking lot. New phone in hand, I'm about to turn toward the exit when someone charges into the restaurant, coming from the back hallway.

It's Kathy Sullivan.

She grabs one of the waitresses by the arm. "Did you see my niece? The girl with the black hair?"

The waitress shrugs. "Maybe she's in the bathroom?"

"I already checked. She's not there."

On instinct, I take a step behind a display of ball caps so she won't see me. Kathy races to the front door and pushes outside without looking my way.

Where the hell is Lark? She must've left the restaurant in the last few minutes. But I doubt she'd go quietly if someone was forcing her, which means she decided to take off on her own.

I don't know what's up, but I do not like it.

I go outside after Kathy. She's pacing in front of the building like she doesn't know what to do. I slip past her, jogging toward the main parking lot and trying to guess where Lark would go.

The semis. If she wanted to stay out of sight, that's where she'd go. I check my phone, hoping she's somehow managed to text me, but I have no notifications.

Then a scream rings out across the concrete.

I break into a run.

Within seconds, I've found her. Lark is in the shadows between two trailers, and some piece of shit is holding her by the wrist.

"Hey!" I shout.

Before I can reach them, Lark knees him hard in the crotch. The guy collapses onto the ground. She took care of that all by herself, and I want to cheer, I'm so proud of her.

But too quick, the guy is struggling up to standing. I step in and shove him up against the trailer. "Who the hell are you? Did you follow her?"

At the same time, Lark turns and sees me. *"Danny?"*

The trucker guy is quaking in my grip. "I've never seen her before! Jesus, I didn't mean any harm!"

"He's nobody," Lark says.

I let him go, and the guy scampers off.

"You're here." The look on Lark's face just about tears my heart out.

I close the distance between us and wrap her in my arms. Her arms cinch around me, her face at my chest.

"You came back. I can't believe you're *here*. But Kathy's looking for me. We have to go."

"Why?"

"I'll explain later. Come *on*."

People are starting to gather, drawn by the shouts. "I'm

parked this way." I dropped the pay-as-you-go phone some-where, but it doesn't matter. I take her hand and we dash across the parking lot.

"Hey!" a woman yells. "Stop!"

I glance back. It's Kathy. She's running after us. I sprint faster, pulling Lark along with me.

We reach my car, and I take the keys out of my pocket. "Let's go." We jump in. I stomp on the brake and work the clutch, throwing the car in gear.

"Seatbelt," I command.

Lark puts hers on. "What about yours?"

"Later," I mutter.

We tear out of the parking lot, swerving to miss a dark SUV that's just pulling in.

I glance into the rearview mirror. Kathy is slowing at the edge of the parking lot, giving up on chasing us. It doesn't look like anyone else is following either. But that dark SUV I passed has stopped, one door thrown wide open. The driver gets out, his silhouette blurred by waves of heat.

He's staring after us. Staring like I just took something he thinks is his.

The Charger's V-8 engine roars as we eat up the asphalt, heading back south toward West Oaks. Lark has her hands against the dashboard. She's breathing hard. Shaking. Her hair hangs into her face.

"You came back for me." There's awe in her tone and expression.

"I never should've left."

16

Danny

$\mathcal{I}$ put about thirty miles between us and the travel stop. Then I exit and double back a bit, just to make sure that nobody's following. It looks like we're clear.

The tires roll over gravel as I pull us onto a quiet road and park beneath a shady tree. Lark has barely spoken, and I need to make sure she's all right before we keep going.

I need to know what the hell just happened.

A twist of my key shuts off the engine. I unbuckle my seatbelt, which I managed to fasten as I was driving. Lark doesn't make a move to unbuckle hers.

"Hey. Talk to me." My hand cradles the back of her neck, the other brushing the hair from her face. She startles, and her eyes meet mine. The green is even richer, brought out by the tree we're parked beneath. "What happened back there?"

Suddenly, she's moving. Unbuckling her seatbelt. Leaning across the center console into my space.

I'm leaning in, too, pulled by the invisible yet undeniable gravity between us.

And *oh fuck*, her lips are on mine. Mine part over hers.

Unlike our kiss at the travel stop earlier, it's impossible to say who started this one first. But it's not chaste. Not even close.

Lark fists my shirt over my chest, and I hold her head, angling her so I can deepen our kiss. My tongue slides into her soft, yielding mouth. The scent of her is fresh and flowery. Her long hair flows through my fingers.

I'm here. I feel like I'm saying it with every move of my mouth over hers. *I'm not letting you go.*

She whimpers as my tongue strokes. The rest of her melts against me, as if she's just hanging on. Every other thought has vanished from my brain. You could ask me my last name right now, and I wouldn't remember any better than Lark did when she woke up in the hospital.

I could stay here and kiss her until the world stops turning.

Lark moans, and somehow that sound forces rationality back to the front of my mind. I pull my mouth away from hers.

Her pupils are blown wide. Her lips are pink, shiny from my tongue, and that sight makes the blood in my head rush downward, going straight to my cock. I make a growly sound in my chest.

"One more?" she begs.

We dive at each other again, even wilder than before. Tongues tangling, teeth clicking. Lark's hands dive beneath my shirt, ghosting over my stomach. I feel her heartbeat everywhere I'm touching her. Like her whole body is one trembling pulsepoint.

Somehow, she manages to climb into my lap. I hiss as her ass presses the aching bulge in my jeans. My shirt goes over my head. Ends up flying to the back seat. Lark's is next. Her small breasts are covered by a cotton bra, but I feel her nipples against my chest through the fabric. I don't know if this is one kiss anymore, or a hundred. I've lost track.

My hands run up and down her back, while Lark strokes my pecs and my stomach. Her fingers keep moving down, popping the button of my jeans. Tugging down my zipper. She goes to reach inside, and *fuck*, I want her hand on my cock. Jerking me, guiding me inside her dripping wet heat.

"We can't," I hear myself saying. "Oh, *fuck*. We can't do this."

We break apart, and I almost reach for her again immediately, even though I know it's wrong. "Lark." Words. I need words. I need to use my brain right now and figure this out.

But more than anything, I can't hurt her. That's the last thing in the world that I would want. I'll sink my fists into anyone who hurts this girl. And that includes me.

I turn her so she's cradled sideways in my lap, and I turn to push my forehead against hers. "I need to know what happened," I say. "Can you tell me?"

I feel her throat move as she swallows. "I'll try. But... maybe we should get dressed."

"True." If highway patrol wanders by, we shouldn't be sitting here half naked. I grab our shirts from the backseat and we put them on, sheepishly avoiding each other's eyes. But I pull her back into my lap again. Holding her so she knows I'm here and she's safe. She tucks her head under my chin.

"After you left, things were okay at first. We sat down for lunch. But Kathy seemed different from how she was on the phone. More tense and nervous. I figured she was just feeling awkward seeing me again, kind of like how I felt. But then, she told me that my uncle Ned, who's supposed to be in Alaska, would be meeting us later today."

"How did the guy get all the way here from remote Alaska with no notice?"

"Exactly. It made no sense. Then I asked her another question, getting my facts wrong on purpose. She didn't correct me. Like she was forgetting her own story. She got up to make a phone call, and I decided to leave. I wanted to find a phone so I could call you. I knew if I could reach you, you'd help me."

My heart lurches. I hold her tighter against me. "I'm sorry."

Lark takes a heavy breath. "Why are you sorry? You were skeptical of her, and I should've believed you. I never should've gone with her. I'm so stupid."

I lift her chin so she'll look at me. "You're not stupid for believing a convincing lie. That's on Kathy, not you. You did nothing wrong."

She blinks, and I can tell she wants to disagree. But she goes on instead. "After I left the restaurant, I tried to stay out of sight because I figured Kathy would be looking for me. I went around to the back of the building. Kathy was already out there talking to someone on her phone. And she said..." Lark's voice cracks. "She said, *'She doesn't remember anything.'* Kathy was talking about *me*. She was complaining that she wanted more money because she had given her name and ID to the police, and she was the one taking the risk. She was supposed to deliver me somewhere."

I bite down on my tongue to keep from cursing. I want to go back, track down Kathy Sullivan, and demand some answers from that woman. But she's probably long gone. Maybe I should've stayed at the travel stop and called the police, but I was focused on getting Lark out of there.

"Then the person she was talking to said they were on their way. Like they'd decided to come get me personally. What if it was *him*? The guy who hit me with the car?"

Shit.

I think of that SUV we passed on the way out of the parking lot. The driver who got out of the car and watched us as we disappeared down the highway.

Was that him? Whoever's behind this?

"I thought he was my ex-boyfriend," Lark says. "But I can't believe anything Kathy told me, can I?"

"Some of the things she said were true. She had that school ID of yours, and they had a record of you as a student. But I doubt she's your aunt. That was probably a lie."

Tears well at the corners of Lark's eyes. I wipe them away with my thumb.

"So much for finding my family," she spits out.

I pull her against me. The unfairness and the wrongness of Kathy's lies make me sick. It's disgusting that anyone would do that to Lark, make her believe they loved her and tear it away.

That's one of the worst things a person can do to another.

"We're not giving up yet," I say. "Not even close. But for now, you're coming home with me. You have friends and a place in West Oaks. We want you there."

"You sure about that?" she whispers.

I look down at her. My fingers squeeze her chin lightly as I smile. "Nina told you that you'd always have a place to stay with us. That's how I feel too. This is more convenient, actually. I doubt anyone's changed the sheets in your room. You can move right back in."

Lark laughs, but it turns into a sob. She burrows her face against my chest again. "Thank God you were there. You saved me. Again."

"I'm glad I was there, too. But you handled that truck driver on your own. Looked painful for him, but I'll bet racking that asshole felt satisfying for *you*."

"Oh, it felt good. Trust me. But he was only bothering me because I was alone."

Jeez, there goes another stab in the middle of my chest. Because I fucking left her. "You're not alone now."

WE HOLD hands the rest of the way back, even when Lark falls asleep. Her head lolls against the seat, her breathing deep and regular. I keep glancing over at her, too many things that I can't describe jostling for space in my head and my chest.

My phone buzzes a few times. Incoming texts. Probably Nina or Matteo. I need to let them know I'm okay, and to expect Lark to be with me when I return.

When I stop for gas, I call Angela and fill her in on the developments. She says she'll contact the local authorities in Fresno and Eureka and put out a BOLO for Kathy Sullivan. That woman needs to answer for what she did to Lark.

Maybe she'll confess who she was working with. Maybe the same dirtbag who hurt Lark in West Oaks.

"Could you see about camera footage from the travel stop?" I ask. "There was a guy. Dark SUV. Came into the parking lot just as we left. I had a gut feeling about him."

"I'll talk to local police about geting the footage," Angela says.

After we hang up, I text Nina that I'm on my way home, that Lark is with me, and we're safe. I don't explain more than that. Lark seems to have taken equal billing with Nina as my top priority, and I know Nina wouldn't have it any other way.

Lark has no one else she can trust. I'm not sure *anyone* has ever needed me this much before. It's scary in a way, but it's a rush too. Holding her in my arms. Feeling that silent vow pass between us that I'll protect her. I'll be there, even when nobody else is.

And having my mouth on hers... God, that felt so right. Like I was claiming her.

Which is exactly why I can't let it happen again.

By the time we reach the house, it's dark. Lark walks inside on shaky legs. I follow behind her, my hand at her lower back. I'm carrying her bag in my other one. Jess, the night nurse, greets us. "Matteo had to head home, and Nina went to bed early. She tried to stay up, but it was a rough one. You're all right, Lark? We were surprised to hear you were already coming back."

"My so-called aunt didn't turn out to be who she claimed." Lark smiles, though I see a sheen of dampness in her green eyes. "This is better, anyway. I'm dying to keep working on that beautiful car Danny has in the garage."

"We'll do that tomorrow," I say. Plus try to figure out what the heck we're going to do next.

I offer up dinner, but Lark says she's not hungry. I walk her to her bedroom and lean against the doorframe. "We need to give a full statement to West Oaks PD about what happened. Kathy Sullivan filed a false police report claiming to be your aunt, and Angela thinks she could be guilty of attempted kidnapping too."

"You spoke to Angela?"

"Yeah, when we stopped for gas."

Lark grips the skin between her eyes. "Can I think about it tomorrow? I can't handle any more today. But...would you stay with me? Just for a little while?"

I shouldn't. But I can't bring myself to say no.

I follow her into her room and shut the door most of the way. She goes into the bathroom, taking her backpack with her, and emerges wearing a sleep T-shirt and shorts.

I toe off my shoes. Lark crawls beneath the covers, and I sit down next to her on top of the blankets, smoothing her hair back from her forehead. She blinks up at me, dark eyelashes against pale skin. Pink plush lips. I know what those lips taste like now. What it sounds like when she whimpers with need as my tongue slides in and out of her mouth.

So. Tempting.

I've always thought of myself as a good man. I took care of my guys in the Army, and when I'm on duty with WOFD, I give the people of West Oaks my all. But with Lark, it's way too tempting to be bad.

Because with her, I already know doing the wrong thing feels so damn *good*.

She's more vulnerable now than ever. I need to be that big brother I promised her I'd be. Getting intimate with her will, at best, confuse her. At worst, it'll be taking advantage.

"Lark, what happened between us earlier... It can't happen again."

Despite all my intentions, I'm slightly disappointed when she nods. "I know. Everything's a mess for me right now. You and Nina are pretty much all I have."

"We're not going anywhere. But yeah, it's complicated. I, uh, apologize for letting the moment get the better of me earlier in the car."

She smirks. "The only thing I'm sorry about is that we'll never get a repeat."

My skin heats. My eyes trace over the shape of her lips. "You liked me kissing you?"

"I felt how much *you* liked it."

Ughn. "I'm not denying it. Still can't happen."

"It's for the best," she agrees.

"Yep." Fuck me. I want to kiss her again right now. "Maybe I should go to my own room," I say.

Her grip tightens on my arm. "Stay until I'm asleep?"

Her request sets off a glow of pleasure in my chest. It spreads outward, filling my veins with warmth. I like when Lark asks for what she needs. I suspect I would say yes to pretty much anything she asked of me.

If she begs me to kiss her again? Take off her clothes and make her feel wanted? Cared for?

Shit. It's a good thing that she doesn't.

I stay there until she's drifted off, but I still don't get up. Instead, I watch her sleep. In a protective way, not a creepy one. I swear.

Back in the hospital, I promised I would help her. I didn't fully realize what that meant until now. But I know what I have to do.

I might not be able to fix Nina, but I can do this for Lark. I'm going to be the good man—the hero—she needs.

I'm going to put her broken pieces back together.

17

Lark

I roll over in bed and stare at the ceiling. The latest attempt to fix my brain was yesterday. It was hypnosis this time. The hypnotist talked me into a deep relaxation, and it felt nice. But when I came out of it, the massive black hole that is my memory remained intact.

I'm starting to wonder if anything will work.

It's now been three weeks since I ran away from Kathy Sullivan and returned to West Oaks. The first few days, I was just trying to keep my head up. Finding out that Kathy had lied to me crumpled up my heart like it was an old piece of trash. I felt low. Lower than I even let Danny see.

He went with me down to West Oaks PD, and we spoke with Angela. She said that her department had been in touch with the police in Eureka, where Kathy Sullivan filed her missing person's report about me. It seems she's on the run after realizing she was found out.

After that, Danny hired a local company called Bennett Security to run a deep-dive background check on Kathy. That report was final only a few days ago, and I nearly threw up when I read it. Kathy has never been arrested before, but her online activities tie her to multiple fraud schemes. She has a husband named Ned, but he's never even been to Alaska. He lives with her in Eureka and claims he's never heard of me.

The images that Kathy showed me of my supposed bedroom in her house? She faked them. She'd tacked up pictures of me in her daughter's room. Nearly everything that came out of that woman's mouth was a lie. I assume her story about my boyfriend "Cam" was fake too. And *I fell for it.* But that means that somebody gave her my school ID and those photos of me. Helped her make that story believable.

Kathy was hired to trick me into coming with her. Does that mean the person behind this doesn't know I'm staying with the Bradleys? Or that he isn't the same guy who tried to run me over on the street where the Bradleys live?

I have no idea. But since returning to West Oaks, I haven't gone anywhere alone. It's for my safety, but it's also getting a little…confining.

Meanwhile, Danny ordered a private background check on "Lark Richards" too, and the results of that one didn't make me feel any better. In some ways, it was worse. Because aside from that one semester at Northern California College, we can't tell that Lark Richards even exists. There are women with that name, but they're not me. My address on file with the school turned out to be an anonymous apartment with no record of me, and NorCal College didn't have my Social Security number or anything else concrete that could lead to more info about me.

My real family and friends could still be out there looking for me. But if they are, why hasn't anyone else filed a missing person's report?

Who am I?

I'm essentially back to the beginning. Struggling for answers. If it wasn't for Danny and Nina, it's scary to think about where I'd be. Aside from right here, lying in bed and staring at the ceiling, anyway.

"All right," I say. "Get moving. You're not allowed to feel sorry for yourself." The Bradleys have been wonderful to me, and I couldn't be more grateful.

But if I don't get out and do something new—something that's not therapy—I'm going to start climbing the walls.

I roll out of bed and take a shower. On my way out of the room, my foot catches on a small cardboard box and I almost trip on it. But the sight paints a huge grin on my face.

I grab the box and head into Nina's room. She's sitting up with her iPad propped in front of her. Whatever she's looking at, it's got her so absorbed she doesn't notice me at first.

"Nina?" I hold up the box. "You have an addiction."

She glances up guiltily, turning her iPad facedown.

I crack up. "Now I'm curious what you were watching. Trashy reality TV? Porn?"

She waves a hand at me. "Nothing *that* exciting. What were you accusing me of?"

"Did you buy me more clothes?"

"What makes you think it was me?"

"Hmm, let's see." I grab a pair of spare scissors from a drawer and slice open the box. Just as I expected, there's a dress inside. "Who else already bought me a bunch of girly dresses, but thought I needed one more?"

Nina's kindness has been keeping me afloat for the past weeks, whether it's buying clothes or books for me, or just letting me hang out with her. When Nina's feeling well, Danny and I take her outside in her wheelchair and sit beneath the willow tree. It's peaceful, and the branches drape so low that it feels like a secluded world all to itself. I can pretend for just a little while that I have a place here. That I'm not lost.

That the Bradleys are my family, and I'll never have to leave.

"You've been filling out," she says. "You need new clothes to show off those curves. Come on, hold it up and show me."

It's a maxi style in a shade of jewel green. Beautiful. The kind of dress I'd never buy for myself, but would wish for. And she's right about my curves. I've gained at least five pounds on the delicious food around here. See? I have plenty to be grateful for.

I smile and lean over to kiss her cheek. "Thank you, Nina. You're too good to me."

"Hush. We both know you love when I fuss over you. Try it on."

I put on the dress in Nina's bathroom and come out to show her. "What do you think?"

"I knew that green would match your eyes," Nina says. "Don't you agree, Danny?"

I turn. Danny has just walked in carrying a breakfast tray. He sets the tray on the table and looks me over. "It does match her eyes. Perfectly."

I shrug, as if his assessment doesn't make my heart race and my skin tingle.

"And she looks healthier," Nina says. "I'm envious of all that shiny hair."

"Huh, it *is* shiny. I hadn't noticed." Danny winks at me, and I discretely flip him off, as if this is just a joke between us. As if I don't want to launch myself at him and maul his face with my tongue.

Despite that hot-as-fire kiss after running for my life, we're back to being friends. But keeping things platonic was supposed to be *less* complicated. That was wishful thinking. There's an awkward distance between us now. Fraught sexual tension that we both play off as teasing. Long looks that we each pretend we don't see. Electricity when we touch that we pretend we don't feel.

Danny and I are the very definition of complicated.

"It's a pretty dress," I say, smoothing my hands over the soft knit fabric. "Thank you, Nina. I love it. But you shouldn't buy me anything else."

"We'll see." From her tone, I know Nina has no plans to stop. And really, I do love being fussed over. It makes me feel cared for, even if Nina would do the same for anyone in need.

Danny hands me a cup of coffee. "How was the hypnosis? Any progress?"

I take a sip, warming my hands on the coffee mug. "Nah, I don't think it's going to work. I'm supposed to go in for another appointment, but I think I'll skip it."

"Shouldn't you give it another shot?" Danny asks. "Nothing works the first time."

Nina frowns at him. "If she doesn't want to, she doesn't have to. If Lark is doing well, that's all that matters."

Thank you, I mouth silently at her.

During our morning conversations, Nina likes to ask me endless questions of her own. *What's your favorite holiday? What toppings do you like on a sundae?* Some of the answers I know, others I don't. Half the time, I say something ridiculous just to make her laugh.

Nina isn't so willing to answer my questions, though. I've asked her about her son Travis, the one who took off years ago. She's hinted that she'd love to see him before she loses the chance. But when I suggested Danny order a Bennett Security background check to find Travis, Nina was quick to shut me down. I guess we both have reasons to leave the past in the past.

What I need is a *future*. Somewhere to go, something to look forward to. So I'll have a place to land when Danny and Nina have gotten tired of me.

"I was thinking." I take another sip of coffee. "I should be paying rent. Which means I need a job. If either of you know someone who's hiring, then maybe—"

"No," Danny says. "Your job is getting better. That's all you should be focused on."

"But—"

"You do plenty around here," Nina cuts in. "Entertaining me, helping out in more ways than we'd ever ask. But if you want time away from the house, I have a much better idea. Danny, aren't Cliff and your old roommates having a barbecue today? And didn't they invite you and Lark?"

Now, it's Danny's turn to look annoyed. "How did you hear about that?"

She points at her iPad. "You think I don't have texting and social media? Starla will be here any minute, and I want you both to go have fun so I can live vicariously. Lark, wear the green dress." She holds up her hand when Danny tries to answer. "That will be all."

I smile fondly at her, but Danny is still glowering after we've finished our coffee.

We shuffle out into the hall. The minute we're alone, Danny pivots and faces me. "We don't have to go to the barbecue. We can stay here and work on the car instead."

"Why? I'd like to go. I could use some friends. More than just you and Nina, I mean."

"Nobody said you couldn't make friends. But you need to be careful about it. You need to be safe. That's why I turned down Cliff's invite. I thought there would be too many unfamiliar people for you."

I make an exasperated sound. "All I've managed to do for the last three weeks is stay safe!" I almost walk away, but then I turn back. "Danny, what if I never get my memory back? What am I supposed to do then?"

"That's not going to happen. Not if we don't give up. You're going to get better."

Get better. I'm not even sure anymore what that means.

Danny's been trying to fix me, and it gets exhausting, even though I know his heart is in the right place. The disappointing hypnosis session yesterday makes me feel like I'm failing at the one "job" they gave me.

"I'm sick of being cooped up here. I'm going to the barbecue. Will you give me the address, or should I get it from Nina?"

Danny purses his mouth. His dark blond hair falls across his forehead, and his fingers tug at the pendant on his necklace.

"Are you going to argue with me? We both know how that will end."

"You're worse than my grandmother."

"Sounds like a compliment."

He sighs. "I'll take you. As soon as Starla's here, we'll go." He starts to pivot away, then pauses, the muscle in his jaw pulsing. "And I agree with Nina. Wear the green dress."

18

Lark

On our way to the barbecue, I touch up the lipstick I borrowed from Starla. She and Nina wanted to go full-makeover on me, and I almost said no. But then I realized, *why not?* I decided to go for it.

That's my motto of the day—live a little. Why the heck shouldn't I?

Even if some people think I should be stuck inside the house trying to "get better."

"You're all dolled up," Danny says.

"Just trying to do what Nina requested. Go out and have an adventure so she can live vicariously. It's the least I can do to repay her generosity." I snap the lipstick cap closed.

"Lark." He sighs. He's been doing that a lot. "I can tell you're pissed at me, but—"

"Why would I be pissed at you? You've done nothing but help me." But I do sound pissed, don't I?

I'm just a woman who's fed up with the hand I've been dealt. That's not Danny's fault. But that doesn't change the fact that I need to do something different, whether he approves of it or not.

Instead of trying to get better, I'm going to try to *live my life*.

But first, I have to get one.

We pull up to a massive stucco house with a Spanish tile roof and a very distinctive paint color. "We call it the Pink House," he says.

"Gee, I wonder why?"

It's two stories, with a deck off each floor and a huge backyard. So this is where Danny lived before he moved in with Nina. It's much bigger and nicer than I would've expected, despite the bright pink stucco. But I guess that's why he has four roommates—so that they could afford a place like this.

Outdoor speakers are pumping out music, and there are about twenty people here so far, laughing and talking. Every eye turns to us as we walk into the yard.

"They're staring at me because I'm the amnesia girl, right?"

"I don't think that's why they're staring," he mutters.

He takes me over to a woman with a high ponytail and a bright smile. She's standing with Cliff, the patrol officer I met a few weeks ago at Danny's house.

The woman gives Danny a one-armed hug. "We finally get to meet your new roomie, huh?"

"He's been keeping me locked up," I joke. Danny tilts his head like he's exasperated with me. But his friend snorts a laugh.

"Lark, this is Quinn Ainsley."

Quinn gives me a hug. "Welcome! Make yourself at home."

"And you remember Cliff, right?" Danny asks me.

"Yeah. Of course."

"You're looking a lot better than when I saw you last," Cliff says.

Quinn rolls her eyes and elbows him. "You're not supposed to say things like that to a woman. You're suggesting she looked bad before."

"Not what I said!"

Quinn smiles at me. "Ignore him. I think what he means is, *great dress*."

"Thanks."

"I'll get us some drinks," Danny announces. "I'll be right back."

"Take your time," I say quietly. "I don't need you to hover."

"My mistake." He holds up his hands, backing away.

Quinn is smirking like she didn't miss a single word of that.

I chat with her and Cliff. She's a junior prosecutor with the West Oaks District Attorney's Office. "So far, I only get to try misdemeanor cases. I'm hoping they'll move me up to felonies soon." She crosses her fingers.

"So most everyone around here is in law enforcement or a firefighter?" I ask. "Should I be intimidated?"

"Hardly," Quinn says. "Around here, somebody's bound to end up making a fool of themselves by the end of the night. Some are more likely suspects than others." She points a thumb at Cliff, who is oblivious.

"What about Danny?" I ask.

Quinn laughs. "He likes to have fun too. But he's slightly more sensible about it."

Cliff sips his longneck. "Sure, if you mean hooking up with anything that moves."

She sends a glare his way. "Tact, much?"

"Am I wrong? You used to hook up with him too."

"Oh, good Lord." Quinn grabs my elbow and pulls me toward the house. "I'm sorry about that. Cliff is a sweetheart and my best friend. But he can be a clueless idiot sometimes." She chews her lip. "Danny and I did hook up a few times, but it wasn't a thing. I promise."

"It's fine." I'm trying not to choke on my tongue. "Danny and I are just friends. He's been wonderful, helping me get through all this. But it's nothing more than that." Even if my stomach is roiling at the thought of this woman in Danny's arms.

I really need to get over him.

She studies me a moment. "Come on. I could use a margarita, and I've got a secret stash of good tequila inside."

We head into the kitchen, and Quinn goes straight for the freezer. There's already a guy in here chopping chicken into cubes. He's got messy brown hair and several days' worth of shadow on his chin.

"This is Aiden Shelborne," Quinn says. "Another one of our roommates. Aiden, this is a friend of Danny's. She's staying with him at his grandmother's house."

He gives me an up-nod, barely glancing at me before returning to his cutting board.

Did I mention he's shirtless?

Aiden's got a huge tattoo spilling over his shoulder and down one arm. It looks like an ocean wave. He's a gorgeous man. It's a fact. My interest is purely scientific, but it's still true. If the goal is getting over Danny...it's good to have options.

Quinn pulls a bottle of tequila from the freezer, then grabs two glasses from a cabinet. "Aiden is one of the few non-government employees here. He's our resident antisocial loner and n'er-do-well."

Aiden runs his knife through another chicken breast. "Nicest thing you've ever said to me, Quinn."

I sit on a stool, resting my elbows on the counter. "So you're not an ex-military guy with a hero complex?"

"Ex-military, yes. I served, took my discharge, got the hell out. I don't like taking orders. Hero complex? Fuck no. I mind my own business." He turns around to wash his hands in the sink.

"Aiden's a chef. That's why we let him hang around." Quinn leans over and whispers, "Plus the eye candy."

"I heard that," Aiden says, his back still facing us.

Quinn smiles. "His little sister Madison is a cop and a close friend of Cliff's. Madison used to hang out with us. Then she went and got married and became a stepmom. She and her husband are both West Oaks PD, and it's *so cute*."

Aiden casts a bemused glance at us over his tattooed shoulder.

Quinn pours us each a shot of tequila, then adds some margarita mix and ice. "Tell us what's been going on with you." She hands me my drink, and I take a fortifying gulp.

And then I start talking.

I tell Quinn and Aiden everything, right from the beginning. Waking up in the hospital. Remembering only the last two moments from before I blacked out—the headlights and Danny's face.

Through it all, Aidan slides pieces of chicken, onion, and bell pepper onto skewers, while Quinn sips her drink. They're listening, but they're not gawking at me. Just letting me tell my story.

"Danny asked me to stay with him and Nina so I wouldn't get sent to a group home or mental institution. I'm sure a lot of people get the help they need in those kinds of places, but to me, it was pretty terrifying. I felt so alone. Danny was the only person I knew in the entire world."

Quinn shakes her head. "No, I get it. I'm sure I would feel the same thing if I'd been in your shoes."

"But Danny really went above and beyond with you, didn't he?" Aiden says.

"I can't argue there."

I take a fortifying shot of tequila before telling them what happened next. How we thought we'd found my aunt and my real identity. How it all turned out to be a lie.

Now, my new friends aren't acting so nonchalant. Quinn has gulped down the rest of her drink, and Aiden isn't even trying to make his skewers anymore. He's got his hands on the countertop and an indignant scowl on his face. "So it was all a set up to kidnap you? That's pretty fucked. Has the guy come after you again?

"Assuming it's the same person behind it all? No. It's been three weeks now, and I've been staying close to Danny and Nina's house. We haven't seen or heard anything suspicious."

Aiden nods thoughtfully. "If the guy thought you knew something and intended to keep you quiet, then finding out you've really lost your memory would take away his concern."

"But she could eventually remember," Quinn argues. "Makes sense that Danny is being protective."

These are all thoughts I've run through a hundred times in the last few weeks. "All I know is that I can't hide anymore. If I'm not going to remember everything I lost, then I want to move forward. Try to live some kind of life. You know?"

Quinn nods sympathetically.

Aiden says, "I get that Danny is worried and watching out for you. But you're exactly right. You have to be able to live. After all that you've survived, you deserve that." He announces all this matter-of-factly, then grabs his tray of kebabs. "I'm gonna head out to the grill."

He pushes open the sliding glass door and walks out.

Quinn laughs. "That's Aiden for you. Makes his opinion known, then takes off like he doesn't care either way." She tops up both our glasses. That tequila bottle is getting low.

"At least Aiden's not jumping in to try to save me every five minutes. Don't get me wrong, I'm grateful to Danny, more than I could ever say. But I can't sort out how I feel about him, either. Why did he have to kiss so well? Why can't he just be ugly and rude instead of freaking perfect and infuriatingly sexy?"

Oops. The tequila is loosening my lips even more than usual.

Quinn smiles and sighs. "What are we going to do with all these ex-military men? Can't live with 'em, can't stop noticing their sexy muscles."

I nod my head at the patio door. "Did you and Aiden ever…"

"*No*. Not even close. I have a terrible track record when it comes to men. Do you know how it is when you fall for someone completely out of reach when you're young, and you never get over it? And nobody else can ever measure up?"

I can't imagine she's talking about Danny. "Not exactly. But I can imagine."

"It happened to me."

"Who is this guy? A celebrity crush?" I hiccup, covering my mouth.

"If only. This is so much worse." She grimaces and groans. "It's embarrassing."

"Why?"

"Because he's twice my age. He would never dream of looking at me this way. And… he's Cliff's dad."

"His *dad*? Scandalous. I'm intrigued. Does Cliff know?"

"No way. And he never will. I've been trying to get over this stupid crush on Rex Easton for more than a decade. It would be easier if the man could stop being so…edible. Yet he only gets better with age."

"Okay, now I'm *really* intrigued. You have to show me a picture."

She's still grumbling, but she's also grabbing her phone and scrolling through her photos app. Our heads bend together, arms touching.

"Here he is at my law school graduation. See?"

She points to a man in his late forties or early fifties. Dark hair going silver at the temples. His beard is almost fully gray. And she's right, he's hot. Ruggedly handsome. Not smiling, but he's got that intense gaze that can stop men and women equally in their tracks.

"He's got way bigger muscles than most older guys," I say.

"He's a bodyguard for Bennett Security."

"That's the company that ran the background checks on me and the woman who claimed to be my aunt. The bodyguard life is clearly working for Mr. Easton."

"And on the side, he volunteers for a disaster-response team to use his ex-Army Special Forces skills." Quinn puts her phone away with a sigh. "I'm doomed."

"Thank you for reminding me that things could be worse. I could be in love with my best friend's dad."

"Oh, you're harsh. I like it." We both laugh. "So you see? You have nothing to fear from me where Danny is concerned."

Quinn tops up my tequila again, adding more to hers as well. She clinks our glasses together.

"I'll admit I feel…something for Danny," I say. "I can't blame him for having a past. I certainly do." I think about the old bruises that the doctor thought could be evidence of abuse. "The thing is, Danny is so determined to help me get back to my old life. But what if I don't want it? What if that's the whole point of me coming to West Oaks? If I wanted to escape, why would I ever choose to go back?"

"Then don't. Move forward. Make more friends, think about a job. I can look into how you get new identity documents. And if you ever happen to need another place to stay, we've got Danny's old room here. It's open."

"I don't want to leave Nina. But thank you. I'm glad to have a new friend."

"Me too. Could I get your number?"

"Absolutely." Danny got me a phone right after the incident with Kathy Sullivan.

Quinn programs me into her contacts, and a text appears on my phone from her.

It's me. Your awkward new friend who has questionable taste in men.

"I'm not questioning it," I say aloud. "Mr. Easton is hot."

"Then stay away, because I called dibs." She bumps her shoulder playfully into mine. "Come on. Let's go help Aiden with the grill and enjoy some of that eye candy. After all, the man's giving it away for free."

19

Danny

"You're staring," Cliff says.

"So the fuck what?"

I've had my eye on Lark for the past hour. But so has just about every other guy here. She was talking to Quinn inside the house for a while, and now they're at the grill with Aiden.

Aidan's my roommate and a friend. But is he allergic to shirts? It's not even that hot out.

He's over there grilling his skewers and displaying his usual gives-zero-fucks attitude. Not overtly flirting. But Aiden never flirts, and women still seem to flock to him. I never had an issue with that before. But at the moment, everything about my friend is annoying the shit out of me.

I take a swig of beer.

"So," Cliff says, "I can't tell what's going on with you and Lark. If she's your girl, why don't you go over there with her?"

"She's not my girl. She's a friend I'm helping out, and at the moment she's grumpy at me." Though I don't even understand the reason.

"But you want her to be your girl?"

I wipe a hand over my face. "I don't know."

For the past three weeks, I've been trying to do right by Lark. I've done whatever I could to help get her memories back, whether it's driving her to therapy sessions, ordering different kinds of food for her to try, or listening to music in the hopes that it'll strike a chord with her. Shake something loose in her mind. But it's a more difficult process than I could have imagined.

I know it's not the kind of thing where I can snap my fingers and she's better. I just wish I could do more. It eats me up to see her frustration. I feel like I'm failing her. And this longing I have for her, this craving—that's where I'm failing *myself*. Because I can't shake it even though I should.

I've replayed the kisses we shared in my dreams. Also in my bed while I'm awake, in the shower... I haven't jerked off to the thought of kissing someone this much since I was a damn teenager.

"I keep waiting for something new to come up in the search for Lark's identity," I say. "But weeks have passed, and everything's led to a dead end."

Cliff nods. "I know, I'm sorry."

Angela got the camera footage from the travel stop near Fresno, but it showed nothing useful about the mystery man in the dark SUV. Nor has anyone seen or heard from Kathy Sullivan since she took off. If Lark doesn't get her memories back, I have no idea how we'll find the guy who hurt her. I would never stress her or blame her. But she's the only one with the answers.

I'd much rather go on the offensive to keep her safe. Instead, we're on defense, waiting for her attacker to make the next move. Lark seems to think that isn't going to happen.

But I'm not so sure.

"I'm trying to do what's best for her," I say. "Put her first. She doesn't have anybody else who'll do that."

"But you want her?" Cliff asks again.

"That doesn't matter."

Cliff shakes his head. We both watch Quinn and Lark laugh at something Aiden just said, while he wears his same deadpan expression.

"For what it's worth, I'm pretty sure she feels the same about you," Cliff says. "When I mentioned that you and Quinn used to hook up, you should've seen the look on Lark's face."

"You said *what?*" My head whips toward my friend. Maybe my former friend, because I can't believe he said that.

"I didn't know it was top-secret."

"Fuck," I mutter. I don't want Lark to get the wrong idea about me and Quinn. We had a friends-with-benefits thing a while back, and it was more affectionate than much else. "What else did you tell her?"

"Uh, I may have said something about you hooking up with anything that moves?" He cringes.

"What the hell, Cliff?"

"That was my bad, I'm sorry. But you don't want to lie to the girl. If you like each other, what difference should it make?"

I shove my fingers into my hair and groan.

I've never been shy with women. I like how soft and sweet they are. I enjoy showing a woman a good time. And it's true that I don't usually do relationships. For a long time, I liked my life as it was, and I never felt the urge to change. I saved lives by day and was more than happy to hook up at night. Well, when I wasn't on shift.

But when Nina got sick, everything changed, whether I wanted it to or not.

And then I met Lark, and my world shifted again.

She's got me twisted up in a way no woman has before. I have no idea how to answer Cliff's questions because things *do* feel different with Lark.

She needs a protector. A friend. Which means I *can't* do anything about it. Even if this need for her is only getting stronger instead of going away.

I should be happy to see her over there with Quinn and Aiden. She needs more friends around her, not less.

But then Aiden pulls a skewer off the grill, cuts pieces off of it on a cutting board, and holds a chunk of chicken up between his fingers. She takes the bite *from his hand*, nodding and smiling.

I grit my teeth and growl.

"You okay over there, bud?" Cliff asks.

No, I'm not. My screws are loosening.

I find myself across the yard and next to the grill. Aiden, Quinn, and Lark all look at me. "Having fun over here?" I ask, my voice sounding testier than I meant it to.

Lark smirks at me. "We are. The chicken is amazing. You should try it."

"It's the dry rub," Aiden says.

"You going to feed it to me, roomie?" I ask him tightly.

He doesn't hesitate. He holds out a piece of chicken to me, and I swear he's laughing, though his expression hasn't changed.

I snatch the chicken from his fingers and pop it into my own mouth.

Okay, it's really freaking good.

"We were talking about you," Lark says, and a sliver of chicken goes the wrong way down my throat. I cough to dislodge it, my eyes watering.

"I didn't say anything bad," Quinn says.

Aidan shrugs. "I did." He's got a hint of a smile, the only

indication that he's kidding. At least I'm pretty sure he's kidding.

Lark grabs another piece of chicken. "Aiden said his family's catering business might be able to give me a job."

"We can always use servers," he says.

Aidan is a chef for his mom's catering company. The Shelbornes are all good people. Aiden's older brother is a drug enforcement agent, and his younger sister is a cop with West Oaks PD. Same with her husband. If I was going to trust anyone with Lark, the Shelborne family would be near the top of the list.

But there's this ragey feeling inside of me that wants to insist, *fuck no.*

"We can discuss it."

Lark glares. "Why do you think you get a say?"

"Like I said earlier. The only job you should worry about right now is getting better."

Lark's jaw sets, and she turns away from me. "Anybody else need a beer? Quinn, Aiden?"

"I could go for one," Aiden says. "Yeah. Thanks."

Lark storms off, her green dress fluttering around her legs as I watch her go.

Quinn pats me on the shoulder. "You have my sympathies."

"What?"

"You've got it bad for that girl, and you have no idea how to handle it."

Aiden doesn't add anything, but his lifted eyebrow says he agrees.

"I'm trying to keep her safe." I know, I'm a broken record. "I want to do what's best for her." If I repeat it enough, I'll get it through my head.

"Ever think of letting *her* decide that?" Quinn asks.

My jaw sets as I watch Lark on the other side of the yard.

She's pulling away from me. I feel it. Usually, if someone doesn't want to be in my life, then I don't fight it. I let them go.

But everything with Lark has been different since the moment I held her in my arms and pulled her from danger.

For the first time, I want to hold on.

I DRIVE US HOME, while Lark stares out her window.

I'd hoped that our afternoon away from the house would smooth things over between us. But if anything, Lark's even more pissed at me than when we started.

It doesn't take long before we're pulling into the driveway. I shut off the engine, but don't get out. "You really want to work as a server for the Shelbornes?"

She bristles. "What's wrong with that?"

"I wasn't suggesting there's something wrong with it. They're great people. Aiden's a good cook."

"He is. I wouldn't mind spending more time with him."

I squeeze the steering wheel, making the leather creak.

"He doesn't treat me like an invalid or a victim," she adds.

"You think I do?"

"I think you don't get what this is like for me."

"Then tell me."

"Think about it," Lark snaps. She's still looking out the side window. "Weeks keep passing, and nobody has come for me except a liar who was going to deliver me to someone even worse. What if there isn't anybody out there who loves me? Who misses me? If that's how it is, then I *don't want* my memories back."

I reach out for her. "Lark."

"Don't, Danny. Please." She pushes the door open and gets out of the car.

When we get inside, the house is quiet, which is typical for the late afternoon. Lark heads straight for Nina's room, and I follow. Nina is asleep on her bed with her iPad on her lap. Starla is dozing in the chair next to her.

Meanwhile, I'm second-guessing every fucking decision I've made in the last month. I've been trying to do my best for Lark. But the aching despair I heard in her voice when she said, *What if there isn't anybody out there who loves me?*

I just want to take that away.

"Can I talk to you?" I ask softly.

"Later." Lark picks up the iPad and hands it to me. She adjusts Nina's blankets, gently patting them over Nina's stomach.

Lark has so much kindness in her. I just can't believe that she's got no family or loved ones. I want to reassure her that we'll figure it out. We'll never stop looking. But I've already made promises to Lark that I haven't kept.

I wake up Nina's iPad, intending to shut it down. But when the screen lights up, I see Nina's email inbox, and my eye zeroes in on the message she has open.

I'm not trying to invade her privacy. But I see the words *my son Travis*, and then I find myself reading the rest.

It's about my uncle, who took off almost twenty years ago and never came back.

I don't recognize the email address that the original message came from. It's a random-sounding handle. The subject reads, *I know where your son is.*

"What the heck is this?" I say.

Lark looks up. "What's wrong?"

Starla is snoring. Nina stirs, moving her head in her sleep, so I wave Lark into the hallway. I show her the message thread.

"It's about Travis. My uncle."

"The one who Nina won't talk about?"

The original message came a few months ago, in the summer. The person claimed to be a friend of Travis's and said he was sorry for breaking ties with us, but was too proud to contact his family after so much time. *That part rings true*, I think.

But the rest of this makes no sense.

It looks like the first contact came out of the blue, and Nina wrote back right away, asking for more information. They had a few emails going back and forth, the original sender giving more info about Travis. And then the thread turned even stranger.

The anonymous sender wrote, *Don't trust anyone else who claims they know him.*

After that, the communication abruptly cut off. Nina wrote back again, reiterating that she'd already forgiven Travis and she wanted to see him. But the person never wrote again.

"This is bizarre," I say. "It sounds like the person wanted to gain Nina's trust. It's got to be a scam. They were obviously going to ask for money. But the messages stopped over a month ago, and they never followed through."

"Maybe they really did know him. It was legit."

"But then why this secrecy? Why hide their real identity? Why make Nina hope and then stop responding?" My blood is boiling with anger to think of someone taking advantage of my grandma this way.

What if it was my uncle himself? Would Travis try to be this manipulative with his own mother?

I might believe it. He stole from her before. Left me without even saying goodbye and never came back.

"She hasn't said anything about this to you?" I ask.

"No. Every time I've tried to ask about him, she shuts down. If she's had him on her mind, maybe these emails explain why." Lark grabs my arm. "Danny, if Nina wants to see Travis so badly, we have to find him."

"Find him? My uncle has been gone for almost *twenty years*. I've tried running public records searches for death certificates a few times, and nothing's come up. He's probably still alive, but he just doesn't care enough to get in touch."

"Then don't do it for Travis. Do it for your grandmother." Her green eyes plead with me. "Please."

Jeez, how am I supposed to say no when she looks at me like that?

There's so much I need to say to Lark. I need to tell her that, no matter what else we find out about her past—even if we find nothing at all—I'll still be here for her. If she wants to get a job and move forward with her life, I'll support that. I care about her.

But keeping her safe is non-negotiable for me.

Yet I also know that if I start down that path, I might say more than I should. I might make a move that I can't take back. I might pull her to me and kiss her and do all those *wrong* things that I know will make us both feel so damn good.

Lark is right. My grandmother deserves a chance to say goodbye to her son. Even if Travis doesn't deserve *her*.

"All right," I say. "For Nina." *And because you asked me.*

"Thank you, Danny."

And there it is, right there. Anything's worth doing if it makes Lark smile like that.

20

Lark

*W*e decide not to tell Nina that we're searching for Travis.

It's not an easy decision. But with all that Nina's going through, I don't want to get her hopes up only to dash them later on. I know *exactly* how much that hurts.

That night, Danny and I go out to the garage to talk it over. "I thought we could hire Bennett Security to trace the emails," I say. "If they can't find Travis directly, maybe they can find the person who sent them."

"Great idea. Bennett is the best choice. They don't do a ton of private investigation stuff, but I know the people there and trust them. Obviously I do, since I asked them to run the background checks about you. Cliff's dad is a bodyguard there. Rex Easton."

"Ah, right. I heard about Cliff's dad."

His brow wrinkles. "What's that smile for?"

I'm trying not to laugh as I remember what Quinn told me about her tragically hopeless crush. "Nothing. Go on."

Danny squints at me. "I'll talk to Rex and see what their research people can find out."

Finally, a few days later, Danny gets news from Bennett Security. "We know the IP address where the emails about Travis were sent. It's a café in Solvang, a small touristy town about an hour away from here."

"If the emails came from there, maybe Travis lives somewhere nearby," Lark says. "Someone could recognize his picture if we show it around."

"If Travis lives an hour away from West Oaks, it kinda makes it worse. He's that close and didn't bother to get in touch?"

It's like we've traded places. I'm playing the optimist, and Danny has turned into the pessimist. But maybe it's because I'm butting into *his* life now instead of the opposite.

"It's a lead. Let's just try. Can we go now?"

"Somehow, I knew you'd say that." The corner of Danny's mouth curves, and he runs the back of his finger down my cheek. Our eyes meet. Hold. My breath stutters in my chest.

Then his hand falls, and he takes a step back. Pretending that little *moment* didn't just happen, even though we're both breathing hard.

"We can go this afternoon," he says. "Starla's here, and if she needs extra help, she can call Ryan or another sub."

"Sounds good." I head for my room to get ready and try to get my lungs going again.

SOLVANG MIGHT BE the most adorable town I've ever seen. That doesn't say much because I haven't been many places that I can remember. But still, it's freaking cute. It was founded by Danish immigrants in the early twentieth century. We drive past quaint pastel buildings with exposed timbers that could've come straight from a fairy tale. There's a white windmill, a clock tower, and old-timey lettering on the signs.

"You like it?" Danny asks.

"Love it. It feels familiar, but I could've seen places like this on TV. Have you visited here before?"

"Not for a long time." His eyes trace the buildings as we look for a parking spot. "My grandparents took me here for my birthday when I was a kid. We stayed overnight, and I got Belgian waffles for breakfast. Travis came. I think it was his idea, actually. He had a thing for cute resort towns. Maybe your family took you here, too."

"Maybe."

We find a parking spot and set out to find the café. "If they sell Belgian waffles," Danny says, "I'll get you one. They're really good here."

I roll my eyes. "Is this another attempt to jog my memory through taste?"

I shouldn't have mentioned that this place seems familiar. Danny's been good the last few days about not mentioning my therapy or *getting better*, but I should've known he wouldn't give it up.

He sighs, shoving his hands into his jeans pockets. "That's not what I'm trying to do. I just thought you'd like it. Lark, I…" Danny trails off without finishing.

I'm not sure I want to know what he was going to say.

We cross the street and turn a corner. "There it is," Danny says. "Sugar & Yeast Café."

I almost miss a step when I see the storefront. It's got a bay window with blue wooden trim. A yellow and white sign with a drawing of a wooden spoon. Déjà vu overpowers me.

I know this place. I want to tell Danny, but I can't get my voice to work.

He opens the door, and as soon as I step inside, a wave of butter and cinnamon envelops me, accentuated by the rich smell of coffee. My eyes go straight to the table in the corner. There's a plant sitting on the windowsill behind it. And without even looking, I know there's a vent in the ceiling, where cold air blows on hot days. I can taste the cinnamon latte. Feel the give of a computer keyboard beneath my fingers.

While this mini atomic bomb is going off in my brain, Danny is glancing around. He leans close to me. "Let's order something, and we can show them Travis's picture and ask if they know him." He starts toward the counter, but I grab for his hand.

"Danny? I've been here before."

Then the barista looks up at us and does a double-take. "Lark! Wow, long time, no see."

21

Danny

When we walk in, it's obvious there's something going on with Lark. Her eyes are wide as she stares around the café.

Something about this place is familiar to her.

But I've resolved not to push her. So instead, I mention how cute this place is and say we should show them the picture of Travis. I don't want to put too much pressure on her. She's the one who reaches for my hand and says, "Danny, I've been here before."

Then I hear a small inhale of surprise. The barista behind the counter is staring. "Lark! Wow, long time, no see."

Lark freezes next to me. Goes completely still. I'm not even sure she's breathing.

"Hey, you all right?" I whisper. "Do you want me to get you out of here?"

Her brave expression returns. "No. I've... I've got it." She's still holding my hand as she walks up to the counter, and I follow behind her. "I'm sorry, I don't remember you. How do you know me?"

The barista laughs. Her white halter top sets off her dark

skin, and honey-colored curls are piled on top of her head. "Wait. You're serious?"

Lark nods.

"I'm Denise. But you've only been in here about a million times. What's going on with you?"

"I was in an accident. I lost my memory." Lark glances over at me like she's looking for corroboration.

I'm tempted to check Lark's pulse, but that might distract or annoy her. Instead, I stand at a protective angle near Lark's shoulder. "She was in the hospital," I say. Meanwhile, my brain is trying to sort out what the heck is happening.

Lark was at the same café where someone sent emails about my uncle. Why?

"That's insane," Denise says. "But you're okay? Was it like a head injury or something?"

"It's complicated. I just can't believe you know me. Do you know my last name?"

"Wow. Nobody has ever asked me that question before." Denise blinks for a few more seconds, then comes around to the other side of the counter and hugs her. Lark seems hesitant at first, then returns Denise's gesture.

Denise turns to the other woman working behind the coffee counter. "Hey, could we get some of those cookies that just came out of the oven?" Then she looks back at us. "I'm going to need to sit down for this conversation."

We head to the corner table. Lark is the last one to sit down. She's staring at the table like it's going to reach out and bite her.

I press my knee against hers, and she nods at me. *I'm okay.*

"I don't know your last name," Denise says. "I never even thought about that before. You used to come in all the time. Like, every day for a while. And you'd said—"

"I sat here?" Lark interrupts. "This table?"

"Yeah, exactly." Denise shakes her head in disbelief. The other barista brings over a plate stacked with chocolate chip cookies. "So, wait a minute. Is it just a coincidence that you're coming in here? Or was it like, intuition or something? Leading you back here?"

That's the big question, isn't it?

Lark seems to be lost for words.

"Maybe we should start at the beginning," I say. "The beginning for Lark, anyway. Then it might make more sense."

Lark nods for me to go ahead. Her hand rests on my thigh under the table, and I place my hand over hers. Hoping to steady her however I can.

I explain to Denise how I found Lark after she'd been hit by a car. How she's been staying with me for over a month now. I leave out Kathy Sullivan. If Lark wants to share that part of her story, I'll let her be the one to do it.

Lark squirms uncomfortably while I speak, and then she interrupts me. "But we came here for a different reason. We were hoping to find Danny's uncle. His name is Travis Bradley." Lark pulls out the picture that we printed before coming. "This is him. He would be older now. Is there any chance you recognize him?"

Denise studies the photo. "I don't. I'm sorry. I don't get how he fits into you coming back here, though."

"I don't get it either," Lark mumbles.

I try to catch her eye. *Whatever the explanation, it's going to be all right*, I want to say. *We'll figure it out.* But she won't look at me.

"Could you tell me more about, um, me?" she asks. "How do you know me exactly?"

Denise breaks off a piece of cookie, shifting in her chair. "Like I said, you would always sit at this table. You usually had a laptop with you. You did some kind of freelance work, I think? Anyway, you would come in when Cam was working, and when he went on break, he would bring you a cinnamon latte and sit down with you. We could've set our clocks by it."

A shock seems to go through Lark's body.

"*Cam?*" Lark squeaks.

"Your boyfriend."

That's the same name that Kathy Sullivan gave for Lark's abusive ex.

I feel tremors run through her everywhere we're touching.

"Sorry," Denise says. "I keep forgetting that you don't remember any of this. Cam started working here about a year ago, I guess? You guys moved down from Northern California, and Cam's the reason you were in here so much. The two of you were kind of a package deal. But then you broke up. Oh, I have a picture of him." She digs into her pocket for her phone, unlocks it, and scrolls around for a bit. Then she turns the screen to us. "He's the one on the left."

The man in the picture is in his mid-twenties. Brown hair, an easy smile. He doesn't look the way that Kathy described Lark's ex. As intimidating. That's not this guy.

Yet it still doesn't calm the nausea in my gut. I don't like how much new info is coming at Lark all at once. It's hard to follow all these different threads, and it's obviously upsetting her. It could even re-traumatize her.

If I thought Lark would forgive me, I'd be tempted to scoop her up and just get her out of here, even though I've been the one urging her to search out her past all along.

What if this Cam is the same guy who hurt her?

"Do you recognize him?" I ask Lark.

She's been examining the picture on Denise's screen for a solid minute. "No. I don't remember him. It's like I've never seen him before."

"Oh, wait," Denise says suddenly. "Cam is working today. He'll be in for his shift in half an hour. Do you want me to call him? Maybe he can come in early. I'm sure he'll want to talk to you. I mean, you guys broke up, and I figured that's why you hadn't come around in a while. He'll be able to answer a lot more questions than me."

No, I want to say. *Hell, no.*

This is all happening too damn fast.

Lark's already pale skin goes ashen. "Please don't tell him. I just... I need to think."

Denise's eyebrows draw down. "No problem. I should get back to work. But if you need anything else, let me know. These cookies are on the house." She gets up and returns to the counter, casting another glance at us over her shoulder.

When she turns around, I lean in and press my hand to Lark's neck. Her pulse is fast. Not a concern yet. But not *nothing* either.

A smile ghosts over her mouth. "I'm okay, doc."

"I can see that. You're doing great. But how do you feel?"

"Shocked. I don't know what to think or what all this means. Why would the emails to Nina have come from this café?"

"No idea."

"And Cam. He's real," she whispers. "Kathy was telling the truth."

"Or she used a bit of truth to make the lies more convincing. Maybe it was a test to see what you remembered."

"But what else is true?" Lark's voice goes hoarse. "Did he hurt me? Did he give me those bruises? Do you think he could've been the one who..."

It's the same thought I just had. "We have to consider that possibility."

But if he's done anything to you, I think, *I'll make him rue the fucking day, believe me.*

I rub her shoulders. She sighs as I work my thumbs into the knotted muscle. "Here's what we can do," I say. "We can leave and call the cops right now. Maybe they'll bring Cam in for questioning based on what's happened in West Oaks, but maybe not."

"What are the other options?"

"I'll take you someplace safe, and I come back to have a word with Cam when he gets here. I'd like to see what he has to say. If he's dumb enough to make a move, I can handle him."

Especially if he's not in the comfort and safety of his car. If he's behind the original attempt on Lark's life, then he's the kind of fucker who hurts women. Who hides behind lies and disguises.

I would *love* to face him in the light of day. And I plan to ask him what he knows about my uncle Travis, too. Cam could've sent those emails.

Lark holds my gaze for a long moment. "I'll stay here with you. I want to talk to him. Are you going to tell me no?" Her tone makes it clear she wouldn't accept that even if I did.

And I get it. As much as I want to face the guy who's terrorized her, she needs that more.

"I was going to say that I'll be right here beside you the whole time."

She exhales, her shoulder leaning into mine. "Good. I don't think I could do this otherwise."

Then I'm with you, I want to say. *However you need me, I'm yours.*

I'll stand by her. Keep her safe. But I'm fooling myself if I say it's just kindness between friends.

We've already established that we're not going to cross the line between friendship and more. But God, I want it. I want all of Lark. I want to fight for her and fucking *win* her and be able to call her mine, and that craving is getting harder and harder to resist.

∽

CAM WALKS into the café almost half an hour later. He's whistling to himself, tossing his car keys up and down on his palm. The moment he walks in the door, his eyes go straight to the corner table. As if it's a habit.

He stops mid step when he sees Lark. His eyes bulge. He flinches toward the door, like he's considering walking right back out again.

But then he turns back to face her. "Lark?" Her name is a question. His eyes move over me next, noticing how close I'm sitting to her.

Denise comes over and says something to him. She pats him on the arm sympathetically, smiling over at us before returning to the register.

Cam glances around, then walks toward our table. "What're you doing here?" he asks breathlessly. "Who is *he*?" He nods at me. I wait for Lark to answer, but she's just staring back at him.

"I haven't seen you in weeks," he says. "You didn't return any of my calls. I had no idea if you were okay."

"It's a long story," she says.

"But you decided to stop by with your new boyfriend?" There's possessiveness in his voice.

He's athletic. Someone who keeps in shape. Maybe running, lifting weights. He's not huge, but his forearms are corded with muscle. I don't sense any threat from him, at least not an overt one. Is that because I'm here? Or because he's not the kind of person who would ever lash out at anyone?

Either way, I'm not going to leave Lark alone for a minute with him. Is there a hint of jealousy behind that feeling? Damn right there is, even if there shouldn't be. I have no idea who this Cam really is. The only thing we're sure of is that he dated Lark, and for that reason alone, I'm not a fan.

"Danny's a friend. A close friend."

I lift my hand and rest it on the back of her neck. A gesture of comfort and support, yes, but I'm also claiming her. In front of Cam, in front of the whole world. This girl is mine to protect. Even if she's not mine in every way I wish she could be.

Cam looks hurt. Confused. Every bit the scorned ex. "What are you doing here?" he asks again.

I nod toward the door. "It might be better if we all talk outside." There are a few other customers here, and if Cam becomes a problem, I'd rather not have an audience.

22

Lark

The three of us file out. There's a small patio to one side of the café. The sidewalks are busy with tourists, but here it's quiet. Much quieter than the inside of my head, where alarm bells are ringing. *Why* and *who* and *what* and *how*.

None of us makes a move to sit down. Danny leans his back against the brick wall of the café building, while I stand about a foot away from him. Close enough to feel he's nearby, but still standing on my own. Since the first moment I woke in the hospital, I've leaned on him. I've relied on Danny in ways that I couldn't explain or understand. But now, it's more than that. I need Danny so much that it scares me.

And that feeling is too overwhelming right now on top of everything else.

Cam takes up a spot across from the both of us. "You going to tell me what's going on?"

"I'll try to explain. Don't ask questions, okay? Just let me get it out."

Cam seems like he's deflating as he listens. If he's the one who hit me with the car, then he's got me fooled. By the end of it, he and I are both shaking.

"You're okay? Physically?"

"Mostly."

"But you don't remember me."

"I'm sorry. I don't."

"Fuck," Cam murmurs, looking down at the concrete. "You lived with me for a year and a half. We were in love."

I hug my arms around my middle. From the corner of my eye, I see Danny lean against the brick wall as he moves his weight from one foot to the other.

"Denise said I did freelance work? I would bring my laptop here?"

Cam smiles wistfully. "Yeah, you did. You knew a little about everything, and you did whatever work you could drum up. You were a virtual assistant, did online marketing stuff and spreadsheets. Plus you and I delivered food and flowers and valeted cars sometimes. It's expensive living around here, so it can be tough. But it was good for a while. *Us*, I mean. We were good."

I wish I *did* feel something for Cam. Just so that I'd know whether his story is true. I have sympathy for him because I don't want to see anyone upset. But it's nothing more than that.

"Do you know how old I am?"

That question seems to throw him. "You said you were twenty-three. Your birthday was last month. So twenty-four."

Then Kathy didn't lie about that, either. "How did you and I meet?"

He exhales, dragging a hand over his face. "At Northern California College. We had classes together. You told me your name was Lark Richards, and I was...crazy about you, I guess. We fell for each other fast, and you moved in with me.

But you said your family wouldn't approve. We decided to run off together and move down here to Solvang."

"Why wouldn't my family approve?"

His expression darkens. "You didn't want me to meet them. You were secretive about your past. Never wanted to work at places that needed formal paperwork. After a while, you admitted Richards wasn't even your real name. You said your family was a bunch of grifters, basically. Con artists."

"*Con artists?* They stole from people?" I ask incredulously. My wide-eyed gaze meets Danny's, and he's equally shocked.

"Yeah, you grew up with that. But as you got older, you tried to be different. That's why you were taking college classes. Why you wanted to run away to Southern California. But after a few months, your family tracked you down. Your stepbrother, specifically. He found you."

A stepbrother. Fingers of ice trace down my spine. A whisper of instinctual fear.

"Does this stepbrother have a name?" Danny asks.

"Lark just called him 'Z.' He was trouble." Cam looks away from me, clearly uncomfortable. "Z was always bugging you after he tracked you down. Coming around. He was an asshole."

"What did he look like?" Danny asks.

"I don't know, average. Brown hair and eyes. Little stocky. He liked getting in my face when I tried to defend you. I threatened to call the cops on him for harassment, but you wouldn't go through with it."

My knees go weak, and I sit at one of the patio tables.

"Then, about six months ago, he came to you with a *business proposition*. That's what he called it."

"What does that mean?"

"You would never tell me the exact details. But it sounded like he'd found a mark, somebody rich, and he wanted your help setting up a con. Whatever he offered, whatever hold he had on you, it was enough for you to agree."

I cover my mouth with my hand, leaning on the table.

"You kept disappearing. Keeping so many secrets. Then one day, about two months ago, you came home covered in bruises, and I just snapped. I yelled. Told you that you had to cut ties with your stepbrother. You broke up with me, and that's the last time I saw you. If I'd known where you were, I would've come to find you and, you know, tried to make up."

Cam takes a step toward me, reaching out. Danny pushes off the brick wall to head him off, standing between us.

"Don't," I say, though I'm not sure which man I'm talking to.

The world is tilting on its axis, the color draining away. Like I'm in some messed-up movie.

How do I know what's true? What's real?

Cam's still talking, telling me more about our life together, but I've heard so many things that not much more is sinking in.

"You have friends here in Solvang," Cam says. "Everybody misses you. They've been wondering how you are. Do you want to see them?"

A swell of emotions overwhelms me. I shake my head slowly. It's not a *no*, exactly, but I can't deal with that question right now. "Maybe some other time."

"Could I get your number, at least?" he asks.

Danny takes out his phone. "I'll give you mine. If you think of anything else, you can let me know. And if Lark wants to reach you, she can." Cam seems offended that he's getting Danny's number instead of mine, but he takes the info and gives Danny his.

"Wait," I manage to say. "There's one more thing."

Cam turns back, eyes brightening with hope.

None of this is what I expected. The new facts that

Denise and Cam have shared are like small fragments swimming around without a fixed place in my head. It doesn't make sense, and this isn't why we came. The trip was supposed to be about Travis, not *me*, and I can't leave here without trying to understand how it all connects.

I dig into my pocket and pull out the photo of Danny's uncle. "This is Travis Bradley. Any chance you know him? Or you've seen him?" My voice is much steadier than I feel.

Cam shakes his head.

"What about Nina Bradley?" Danny asks. "Do you know that name? Did you ever contact her?"

Cam squints. "*No.* Those names mean nothing to me. If these are people Lark knew and never told me about, I can't help you there." The pain he's feeling is palpable. I hate that I'm the cause.

"Cam, I'm sorry I hurt you. I wish..." I shrug. I wish I could fix these things that happened in the past, things that I don't even understand. But I can't.

His frown turns bitter. "The thing is, Lark, despite *everything*, I thought I knew you. But I guess I didn't. I wonder if *anyone* does."

∾

"What are you thinking?" Danny asks.

We're on our way back to West Oaks. Danny hasn't said much since we left the café. I know he's giving me time to process, as he often does. He never pushes me. But my thoughts won't settle.

After Kathy, I'm hesitant to believe anyone's claims about me. But what motive would Cam have to lie? Cam wasn't asking me for anything, except maybe to see me again. He had no idea I would show up today.

The reason we came here at all was Danny's uncle, not

me. What does that even mean? How does it fit together? Why did the emails to Nina come from that café, a place where I spent time and where my boyfriend worked?

Who am I?

I look over at Danny and realize I didn't answer his question. "I'm thinking that I understand even less than when we started today."

He's watching me from the corner of his eye as we drive. "Want to go to the beach?"

The sudden change in topic confuses me at first. "The beach? Why?"

"Why not? We haven't gone there yet. And I find the waves soothing."

I huff a laugh, though none of this is the least bit funny. "Is that what I need? Soothing?"

His grin is lopsided. "Couldn't hurt."

Danny picks a quieter place than the more popular West Oaks beaches. We park in a lot where there's just a few other cars and walk across the sand to the water. The sun is shining, and the sky is turquoise. Someone's flying a kite down the beach, but otherwise we're alone.

Wind blows in from over the ocean, whipping my hair around my face. It's a perfect Southern California day, yet I feel like I'm in the middle of a storm.

"What if I was the one who sent those emails?" I blurt out.

Danny frowns, studying me.

"We already figured the emails were a scam to get money from Nina. I came from a family of con artists. Cam said my stepbrother wanted my help. A *business proposition*."

"No. There's no way." Danny says this with absolute conviction.

"How can you be sure?"

"Because you wouldn't do that. Not voluntarily."

"But I had choices. Cam said I chose my stepbrother over him."

Danny doesn't have an answer for that.

I go down to the water, letting the surf roll over my feet. Watching the water smooth away the footprints behind me.

I imagine how it could've happened. What the truth might be. Maybe Cam was wrong, and I *wanted* to work with Z just because I was that greedy. My stepbrother and I were con artists looking for a new victim, and we found Nina. The big house, the money courtesy of Danny's father. So I sent the emails to her from the café to gain her trust… But something went haywire. I stopped writing to Nina. Came home with bruises. And then…

Why would I go to West Oaks? Why did someone come after me and run me down? Was it to *stop* me from reaching Nina?

Am I the heroine of this story? The victim? Or the villain?

I stare into the surf and try to understand.

Danny walks up behind me. "Hey," he says. "Cam was wrong. I hope you realize that."

"Wrong about what?"

His touch ghosts over my shoulders, his fingers tangling in the long strands of my hair. "At the café, he said nobody knows you. But that's not true. It's only been a month since you appeared in my life, and there's a lot that isn't clear. I'm well aware of that. But I know everything I *need* to know about you. So does Nina. You would never hurt someone the way you're thinking. That's just not you."

I suck in a lungful of salt-infused air. "I want to believe you."

"Then do." Danny presses in behind me, reaching to cup my cheek and turn my head. I lean into his touch. I want to burrow into him, hide away where it's safe. Just disappear. I think Danny would let me.

Maybe he'd kiss me, and we'd cling to one another. Pushing away the rest of the world like we did in those brief moments in his car weeks ago. But the complications keep building up.

How can Danny know me when I don't even know myself?

My foot sinks into the sand as I retreat, putting space between us.

"You ready to go home?" he asks.

I nod. *Home*. But it's not really mine. I don't think I can call anyplace home.

We walk back to the car. I'm already feeling nauseous over everything we've learned today.

Then another shot of wrongness slams into me when I see the state of Danny's car. "What happened?" I breathe.

There are huge scratches on the driver's side door of Danny's Charger. Gouges in the candy apple red paint. I gasp, my hands flying to my mouth.

"Oh, dammit," he says, walking up behind me. "I guess some asshole doesn't like red."

"Danny. It's... I'm so sorry."

"I can get it fixed. Sucks, but it's just paint."

I clench my fist over my stomach. "It's *wrong*." And after everything today, it's just—

Wait. There's a piece of paper fluttering beneath one of the windshield wipers. With dread in my gut, I grab it and unfold it. Someone has scrawled a messy, handwritten message.

Do you still think you can run from me, Lark?

I scream. The wind catches the paper, tearing it from my hand, and Danny plucks it from the air. He turns it over and reads what it says.

"Who the fuck wrote this?"

He spins around, looking. But there's no one around. Just

the same few cars that were parked here before, with no sign of their owners. But I feel eyes on us. I know that whoever sent this is somewhere close. Watching. My skin crawls with the knowledge. I can't breathe.

Was it Z? The stepbrother Cam told me about?

Has he been following us?

"Show yourself, asshole," Danny yells. "Come out here and face me!"

Except for a mom pushing a stroller down the path, there's no one.

Danny shoves the note into his jeans pocket and wraps his arms around me. "I'm going to call Cliff. We need to file a police report about this. But we're okay. Whoever left this just wanted to scare you. He was too much of a coward to face us head-on."

How can this be okay? I want to shout.

Wherever I go, bad things follow.

Wherever I go, I drag everyone else down with me.

23

Danny

That note is fucking *twisted*.

I'm burning up inside. Boiling over with rage and frustration. How did I let the guy sneak up on us?

Has he been trailing us since we left Solvang? Or was it even before we left West Oaks?

He wanted us to know. I have to think it's because our trip to Solvang shook him up somehow. But it's shaken up Lark, too. After what Cam told her, it's too much for her. Too much for anyone.

As I call the police, I keep a hand on Lark's shoulder. I run my palm down her arm. I'm not going to let her leave my grasp, not even for a second.

Cliff isn't on duty, but they send another patrol officer, who takes our report. The cop collects the handwritten note as evidence and says they'll call if they find leads. As if I didn't know who it was, despite the lack of cameras and witnesses.

It was the guy who hunted Lark down with his car. I'm sure of that all the way down to my bones, and I'm itching to give the asshole the payback he deserves.

I would give just about anything to make this better for her. Take away the anguish I see in her eyes.

I wish I could convey to her how incredible she is. How sweet, even when she's being sarcastic. How giving, even though she's been through so much you'd think she would have nothing left to give. And the way she looked with the wind blowing her hair around her face... So beautiful it made me *ache* for her.

I almost kissed her out there by the water.

I'm starting to forget why I shouldn't.

When we get home, I park in the driveway. Lark doesn't get out, so I wait. I want to reach for her. Hold her. Make everything okay.

What do I do for her? I've asked myself that same thing so many times since Lark came into my life, but I've never gotten it exactly right, have I? Some healer I am.

"Don't tell Nina yet about the things we found out," she says. "Or meeting Cam."

"I don't plan to. I figure you'll talk to her when you're ready."

Lark nods. "Thank you, Danny," she whispers.

She's said those words to me many times, and I always get a little mushy inside. I like making her happy. Giving her the things she asks for.

But that's not enough. It's never been enough when you consider the kinds of things Lark is facing. I'm still searching for the right words when she gets out of the car and heads for the house.

What do I do? I ask myself again.

I blow out a breath, running both hands through my hair, and then tug at the cord of my necklace.

I don't see Lark when I get inside. She rushed ahead of me. But she's not getting rid of me that easily. After I check that all the locks are secure, I head to her room to look for her. Lark's door is partway open, giving me a view of inside.

She's packing clothes into the WOFD backpack I gave her.

"Whoa, what are you doing?" I ask, stepping into her room.

She stuffs a sweatshirt into the bag. "I can't stay here anymore. Not after what we found out."

I follow her into the bathroom, where she picks up her toothbrush. "No way. You're not leaving like this." If she truly wanted to go, I would let her. But like this?

I am *not* allowing this to happen.

"I can't stay under Nina's roof knowing what I might have done."

I put my hand on her arm, stopping her. "And what exactly is that? We didn't get any answers earlier. We have no idea what really went down."

"We know I probably sent those emails to Nina about Travis."

"It's possible. Or it could've been someone else. That's a big leap to make."

"How is it just *possible* when those emails were written at the café where I hung out all the time, and then I showed up here on *your* street? I was trying to get money from Nina. Tell me some other way to explain it."

I have all kinds of doubts about what's really going on here. How Lark and Travis could be connected. But I have no doubt whatsoever about her character.

From the moment I met her, Lark has shown me who she is. Whenever she runs, it's because she needs an escape. She needs help. It's not her fault she grew up in a screwed-up family. None of us can help the way we're born.

"If you're searching for an explanation," I say, "I can give you one. And it's just as plausible as yours."

She's scowling, turned away from me. I walk around her until we're face to face. "You never wanted to help your stepbrother. And when you tried to put a stop to...whatever it was he was doing, he hurt you. You needed a way out, and you knew Cam couldn't protect you. So you ran here to West Oaks. We don't know why, exactly, but we have no proof whatsoever that you wrote any emails to Nina. For all we know, you'd never heard her name before you showed up on our street."

"But I brought the danger with me."

"And I've tried to keep you safe. I'll keep trying. I'm nowhere near done." I cup my hands around her face, tilting her head so her eyes meet mine. That wild, rich green. Those eyes that make me feel alive. Like I could do *anything* so long as it was for her. "Maybe you were always supposed to end up here with us. With *me*."

"But what if I only ran away because I did something terrible?" she whispers.

"Even if you did, you're not that person now. Lark, I want *this girl*. The one right in front of me." I drag my nose over her temple, inhaling her. "I want this girl so fucking badly."

She sucks in a breath. "I want to be that girl. I want to believe she's real." Her body shivers against me. "I want to be...good."

I bite back another groan. She doesn't know what that honesty, that vulnerability, does to me. I need to kiss her. It's not a choice anymore. I need to kiss her like my heart needs to keep beating.

My lips brush her jaw. Soft presses to her skin. Her scent fills my nostrils, heady and intoxicating.

I told myself this couldn't happen because I was supposed to look out for her. But that hasn't worked either. The only way I can think of now to protect her, to care for her, is to pull her into my arms and keep her as close as I can.

"I care so much about you, Lark. Don't run away from me. I'll believe enough for the both of us."

"Show me?"

That last shred of resistance inside me vanishes. It's *gone*. And so am I.

Our mouths crash together.

She moans and grabs my hair, her other hand clutching at my shoulder. My lips part over hers, swallowing her breathless whimpers.

Her bed is behind me, so I walk us backward until I can sit against it, and Lark goes down with me. I roll us so that I'm on top of her, my mouth not breaking from hers. I suck at her lower lip until she opens up for me. My tongue sweeps inside while my hands seek out the hills and valleys of her curves. When I picked her up after she was hit by that car a month ago, she seemed to weigh nothing. Since then, she's filled out, and trust me—I've noticed. My dick has *definitely* noticed. She's got curves that I want to kiss and explore. To get down on my knees and *worship*.

It's been weeks since I last had the chance to taste this girl, and that was only for a few minutes. I want to imprint every aspect of her, the minty taste of her toothpaste and her fresh, floral smell, the silky touch of her hair. This beautiful, strong, vulnerable woman. Who refuses to be a victim, who tries so damn hard to be kind to my grandmother, to my friends, to *me*, even though I doubt many people have ever shown her the kindness that she needs.

She was even kind to Cam at the café this afternoon, even though he was far more concerned about his own feelings than her well-being. The kid claimed to love her, but how did he show it? He did too little, too late. He didn't step up when she needed him. That's what Lark needs. A man who will put her first above everything else. Especially himself.

My cock is thick between us, pushing insistently against

her through our layers of clothes. I want nothing more than to strip her down and show her exactly how much I've been craving her. But I don't know what she's ready for. I doubt she's a virgin, but this might be the first sexual experience that she remembers.

Reluctantly, I drag my mouth away from hers, separating our bodies by an inch. "This okay?"

"I'm good. I would tell you if I wasn't." She runs a trembling hand over my cheek, and I kiss her palm.

"We don't have to do anything more than what we're doing now."

"Oh, I disagree. I've been wanting to get naked with you for a while. I want to touch you. Taste you." She kisses my neck just above the collar of my tee. "Feel you." Lark reaches down to give the bulge in my jeans a little squeeze. "*All* the things."

Mmmm. I give her another slow, sensual kiss. The tip of my nose rubs against hers. "I didn't shave. I'm not scratching you?"

"I like it. I like everything about you." Tentatively, she rolls her hips against me, rocking her core over my swelling erection, and I grunt. Lark raises up to run her nose along my neck.

I take her hand in mine and press tender kisses to her knuckles. My body lowers to one side of her and I prop myself on my elbow. My other hand wanders over her, barely dipping beneath the edges of her clothes. Testing. "I thought I couldn't look out for you and have you too, but that's just not fucking working. We can figure this out. If you're willing to try with me. If you trust me, if you *want me*, then let me take care of you. Will you?"

"Yes," she whispers. "Will you make me feel good?"

"I will, baby. So good." Something she would never, ever want to forget. My dick is leaking as I think about how I'm going to spoil her. How I'll kiss and touch every part of her. Use my body to care for hers.

I'm still lying on my side. I cross my leg over her, pinning her thighs, and with my arm I gather her against me. Lark's arms fold between our chests. I'm sheltering her. A bulwark between her and the rest of the world.

"Are you nervous?"

"A little." She huffs a laugh. "What if I don't remember how to do this? What if I'm terrible at it?"

"We'll go nice and slow. I've got you." *And I'm not letting you go.*

24

Lark

*N*ice and slow. That's what Danny said.

I already want to speed up.

The way he's kissing and touching me, his weight pressing me into the mattress, the hard ridge of his cock against my hip… I've never felt more vivid, more *real*, than I do in this moment. I want all of Danny and more.

I'm trying to believe that everything he said is true. I was ready to think the worst about myself, ready to escape these debilitating doubts about who I am and what I've done. But if I trust Danny, then shouldn't I believe what he sees in me? Shouldn't I give myself a chance to have this? Feel good for once with a man who's been there for me since the moment we met?

Even when he frustrates me, I can't imagine a better, more honorable man than him. Always looking out for me. Listening to me. Staying with me whenever I've asked him, and backing off when I've asked for that too.

Maybe I'm just not strong enough to choose the right thing when Danny's here, arms around me, telling me he wants me as much as I want him.

And I *do* want him.

Desire rushes through my body like a drug. I'm delirious with it. I can't stop kissing him. Tugging him closer. Enjoying the gentle burn of his stubble as his mouth nibbles down along my jaw and my neck.

I need to feel him. See him moaning and writhing with pleasure and know that I gave that to him. But this isn't me trying to repay what he's done for me. Hell, no. I'm greedy for him. I'm eager to finally touch him, *know* him, the way I've wanted for weeks now. His tattoos and his muscles and golden skin. The wicked side of him I only get a glimpse of when he flirts.

And that thick cock. I've felt his erection twice now, and I know it's big. I want to see what he's packing. If he's cut or uncut, smooth or veined. Those dirty possibilities probably hint that I'm not as virginal as he seems to think. I'm *dying* for that cock.

"Can we get undressed?" I ask.

"You want to get me naked?"

"Obviously." I reach down between us to rub the hot length in his jeans. "Don't you want to see me too?"

"Fuck, yes," he growls, dropping open-mouthed wet kisses to my neck. "But we're taking this slow. I'm going to be careful with you."

"What if I'd rather be manhandled?"

"*Lark*," he growls, nostrils flaring. His eyes flick up to mine, all dark and stormy seas. "You said you'd trust me to take care of you. That means, right now, I'm deciding what's best for you."

The flare of heat at my center says I like that, too. The possessive, protective tone he's using, even though that same attitude annoys me at times.

Sweat prickles and goosebumps raise all over my body in anticipation.

I nod, and Danny's weight disappears as he retreats from the bed. I want to protest, but he grabs my hands so I'll sit up. He positions me at the edge of the mattress. His knee nudges mine apart, and he stands between my spread legs. I gaze up at him as he towers over me. His Adam's apple bobs in his throat as he swallows.

I'm wearing a simple knee-length cotton dress today, and it's gotten hiked up to my thighs. Danny's gaze rakes over my exposed skin.

"What are you going to do?" I ask.

"You'll see."

Bending forward, he rests his large, warm hands on my knees. His thumbs press into the flesh of my inner thighs. They drag up, up, beneath the hem of my dress, almost to my crotch. I purr and shiver, feeling my panties dampen against my skin. I lean back, propping myself against my hands on the mattress.

"Keep going." I beg.

His thumbs feather over the skin at my inner thighs. "You stay right there and be good for me, and I'll give you what you need. Nice. And. Slow. Like I said."

"But I'm not going to keep my mouth shut. That's not me."

"I love that about you. Love when you're feisty. Just don't expect to get your way."

Grinning, he grabs his T-shirt by the back collar and tugs it off, tossing it to the floor. My eyes rake over him, hungry for every inch of Danny they can get. I've seen him shirtless, and the view is just as stellar as I remembered. His chest is smooth, his pecs broad and rounded and inked with tattoos. There's an American flag on the heart-side, a compass rose on the other pec. But the true north of the compass points back to his heart.

His biceps and abs are all lean muscle with more tats, too

many for me to study them all just yet. My attention is bouncing around too much.

Then my gaze lands on the faint trail of blond hair that starts below his belly button, disappearing into the waistband of his jeans. As I trace a visual path down to his fly, Danny pops open the button and undoes the zipper.

"You still okay?"

"More than okay. Can I touch you?"

He gives me a lopsided grin. "Wait until I say."

I grumble. "You're enjoying this."

His hand pauses. "But are you?"

"Yes. *Please* keep going with your sexy striptease."

Chuckling, Danny tugs down his jeans. The bulge of his erection juts at an angle, hidden below the elastic of his gray boxer briefs. The spot of wetness at the tip of his erection makes it obvious that he's leaking.

His thumbs hook the elastic band of his briefs, and he shucks them down. His cock pops out, pointing upward. Thick and purple where the head peeks out of his foreskin. Shiny with precome. He steps out of his underwear, and his cock bobs with the movement, his balls tight and full below.

Gorgeous.

My heart is thumping, my nipples stiff against my dress. My clit throbs between my legs so hard I want to squeeze my thighs together, but he's standing between my legs, keeping them open. He's just so *beautiful*. Masculine and strong, made of swooping lines and angles and rounded muscular curves.

I lick my lips, and his cock flexes, another wet bead of precome welling at his slit. His thumb and fingers circle the base and squeeze.

Danny's standing completely naked before me while I'm fully clothed. I don't know why that's so sexy, but it is. He's showing off for me. And giving me time, even if I don't necessarily need it, because he wants to make sure I'm ready for everything we're about to do.

I can't *wait* for what we're about to do.

I sit up, my throat going dry. I'm nervous suddenly, even though I could never be afraid of Danny. I definitely want his cock and all the rest of him. All over me, in me... But I can't help thinking of his many hookups, according to Cliff at least. Who knows how much experience I have? Or if I have any clue what I'm doing?

And an even deeper fear occurs to me—what if being with Danny makes me remember a past experience that *wasn't* good, either with Cam or someone else?

"You're frowning. What are you thinking?" Danny comes closer, his fingers sliding into my hair. My nostrils fill with his musky, spicy-body-wash scent, and his dick is *right there*, but his hand is the only part of him that's touching me.

I wish he couldn't read me so easily. "Just wondering about other times I might've done this."

"Are you having second thoughts?" His free hand presses his erection to his stomach like he's trying to cover himself. "You can say no to me, Lark. At any moment. I'll listen."

"I know that. I'm not saying no. I *don't* want to stop." In fact, it's the opposite. I need Danny to give me something to hold on to, to ground me in the present. Make me feel like nothing in the past matters because this moment is so beautiful and wild and *hot* that it eclipses everything else.

Like he's my own personal sun, giving me warmth and light.

"I want to touch you," I say.

"Soon. I promise." Ever so slowly, he leans over and parts his lips over mine. My head tips back. My mouth opens and he feeds me his tongue, his palm cradling the back of my neck to support me.

But I'm sneaky. I bring my hand up along his inner thigh. He moans into my mouth. Doesn't stop me.

My fingertips tease the dark blond curls at the base of his shaft, then close around his girth. His cock flexes in my hand. All radiant, smooth skin and rigid hardness beneath.

Danny's mouth pulls away on a groan. "You really like testing me, don't you? You think going slow is easy for me when I'm around you?"

"Being *bossy* certainly seems easy for you. What now, Mr. Bossy? Or should I say, *doctor*?"

Lust fills his eyes, and another pearl of precome wells at his swollen tip.

Well, well. Somebody liked that.

"It's a very naughty doctor who's naked when his patient isn't," I point out.

Suddenly he's gripping my waist, yanking me up to standing. We trade places, Danny sitting back on the mattress where I just was, me between his knees. His cock stands tall, even redder and more engorged than before.

"When you were in the hospital and dropped your gown in front of me, I didn't look. But I wanted to. Fuck, I wanted to. Show me what I was missing?"

"Will you do it? Undress me?"

Danny's eyes close as his teeth sink into his lower lip. "You're killing me, baby. You have no idea."

But he doesn't make me ask twice. Danny hooks the spaghetti straps of my dress and tugs them over my shoulders. The dress had a built-in shelf bra, so I'm not wearing another one beneath. The moment he pulls the fabric down my torso, my breasts are exposed, nipples pointing forward and begging to be sucked.

Danny's tongue darts out, lashing over one nipple. Then the other.

"*Oh.*" It just feels so incredible. It's such a small, simple thing, but I've never felt anything so good. His hands move to my waist like he realizes I'm in danger of falling over. He looks up at me, his indigo irises drenched in naked, dark desire, as he sucks my nipple hard into his mouth.

"*Danny.*" My dress is only halfway off, the top pooled around my waist. I wrap my arms around him and straddle his lap. I'm up on my knees so he can keep sucking. "Don't stop. Please, please don't stop."

He holds me tightly by the waist, mouth latched to my breast. His tongue feathers around my nipple. His cock presses into my belly, though my clothes still separate us.

And suddenly, I can't stand that. I need to be naked so I can feel him with no barrier between us.

"Wait," I say. "Wait, wait."

Immediately, Danny pulls off, concern etched on his forehead.

At the same time, I'm shoving my dress down. At least, trying to. I get tangled up in straps and elastic and almost wind up on the floor. Pretty soon we're both laughing, but he sets me on my feet again and we get my dress off the rest of the way. I shove my panties off next. No more playing around.

"Slow," he says, all breathy and low. "Let me look at you."

I rest my hands on his shoulders, and he grasps me low on the hips. All my bruises have healed now, but I still feel them there. Like ghosts on my skin. But his eyes are devouring me like he's starving for everything he sees.

"I've never seen anything like you, Lark. So beautiful it fucking kills me."

Danny *scowls*. But it's very much an *I'm-going-to-fuck-this-woman-if-it's-the-last-thing-I-do* scowl.

I doubt anyone has ever looked at me that way, with that much primal want. The wild beating of my pulse—in my chest, between my legs—and the goosebumps rising all over my skin say this is new for me. This is special.

And it's what I want. So exactly what I want. This moment with Danny couldn't feel any more *right*.

"Come here, baby."

Now, he lets me climb into his lap. My arms go around his neck, and I guide my mouth to his, our naked bodies finally in contact. We touch and rock against one another. Give and take. No rush. His skin is hot, soft under my palms, yet corded and solid underneath. I love the feel of his needy cock right up against my belly, sandwiched between us. His precome smears on my skin.

He's got his big hands on my hips, moving me so my clit knocks against the base of his shaft as we kiss. I'm wet too, rubbing my arousal all over him. The whimpers I'm making turn to broken gasps. Danny's chest lifts as he pants. His kisses delve deeper, taking long pulls from my lips. But I can tell the rest of his energy is coiled up and controlled. Simmering just beneath the surface of him.

"Please," I whine, "need to feel you inside me."

He drags a hand over my hip and brings it between us, his fingers finding my opening. I'm so wet that he slides one digit easily inside. I bury a moan against his neck. We keep moving against one another. I'm riding his hand.

"More," I say. "I need your cock."

"Just my fingers tonight. I'm not going to go too fast with you. Besides...I don't have any condoms in here. And I'm assuming you don't either."

"Do we need one? I got every possible test and exam in the hospital. They said I have an IUD. You probably get tested during your physicals at work, right?"

"Fuck." His finger withdraws, going back to my hip. He glances at the ceiling like he's praying for strength. "I still don't think I should."

"Danny." I wiggle in his lap, nipping at his earlobe. I don't want him to treat me like I'm fragile. Or *broken*. "I trust you, but I need you to trust me, too. I can decide what I want for myself. If we're together, then we're equals. I'll listen to you, but I need you to listen to me."

He doesn't answer right away.

"*Are* we together?" I ask, leaning back to look at him. "I guess we didn't talk about that." He said he cares about me. But is this a hookup to him? A one-night thing?

His gaze softens, and he runs his fingers through my hair. "I want you more than I've ever wanted another woman. I wouldn't be doing this otherwise. I'm all in. But I can't let myself hurt you."

"You won't." I'm choosing to believe in the good he sees in me. I need him to do the same for himself. I rub my cheek against his, my breasts pushing into his chest. Every weapon I've got. "You know you want inside me, too. Please?"

"It's impossible to say no to you." In a flash, Danny grabs me and spins us. My back lands against the mattress with him above me. His chest surges like he can't get enough air. He presses his lips to my stomach, and he lingers there before looking up again with a smoldering gaze. "I'm still going to take my time, though. I'm going to get you ready for my cock, touch you and tease you until you're begging, and then make you mine."

"Get going, then."

"Impatient little thing, aren't you?" Grinning, Danny lies down next to me and turns me on my side to face him. Any last nervousness I might've felt melts away as he kisses me. I throw my leg over him as I try to get us closer.

It feels like the whole world narrows down to just us. Our shared caresses, breaths, heartbeats. The sweat co-mingling on our skin.

"Your hair is so silky," he says, running his fingers

through it. "Wish I could wrap myself up in it." Danny makes his way down my body, naming all the parts of me he finds beautiful. The admiration and praise light me up from the inside out.

"I like this freckle here. And here." He kisses one on my shoulder, then my upper chest. "And this purple tattoo. What is that flower?"

"A thistle."

When he's finally settled between my legs, he uses his fingertips to stroke my core, making me choke out a gasp.

"Okay?"

"Yes. *More*."

A finger slides inside of me, while his thumb circles my clit. His eyes move from my face to my center and back again, studying my reactions. I grab for the blanket and ball it in my fists.

The pleasure is intense. Liquid silver coating my veins.

"Look at you," he murmurs. "Your pussy is so wet for me already. You're tight. So fucking warm." He adds another finger, watching them move in and out of me. All I can do is watch *him*. The masculine cut of his jaw, blond hair over his forehead, his muscles tensing as his arm works and he holds himself up with his abs. His engorged cock is even thicker than before, the skin red. The vein on the underside of his shaft pulses, the slit leaking.

I lift my hips, needing...just *something*. Anything. More. Pleasure builds everywhere he's touching me. My clit, my pussy. His fingers stretch me, the tips curling to rub my inner walls.

"Do you ever touch yourself?" he asks.

My back arches, and I whimper. "Yes, doctor."

He growls. "Do you think about me when you do?"

"Yes," I purr. "Always."

"I jack myself and think about you." His eyes lift to my

face, though his fingers keep pumping and stroking. His irises are dark, pupils dilated. Midnight blue. "How do you think my cock will feel inside you?"

I can't take it any more. "Danny, please. *Please*."

He pulls his fingers out of me. "Are you begging for my cock? You're desperate for it?"

"*Yes*. Please give it to me." I'm babbling. That's what he's reduced me to. "I need…"

Danny moves up my body, lowers himself over me and whispers, "You are so strong, Lark. So sweet and kind and beautiful."

His words rush over me like tender caresses. Yet they lay me bare, too, exposing the worst fears I've been struggling with all day. Ever since I learned those terrible things from Cam and realized that my past could hold worse secrets than I'd imagined.

"I promised to take care of you, and that's what I'm going to do. You don't have to run any more. You made it here. Stay with me."

I sob for breath when he pushes his cock inside me. It feels…*oh*, like he's pinning me in place in the best possible way. Grounding me right here. Where I'm cared for and safe. I'm somewhere between laughing and crying and being dumbstruck with awe.

He watches my reaction with a perfect mixture of careful regard and barely restrained lust. Danny's hovering over me, supported on his elbows and knees, with my thighs spread wide beneath him. His cock is so deep, as far as he can go inside my body. The rest of him is poised. Flexed and wound tight with the effort of remaining still.

"I need to fuck you now, baby." His voice is strained. "I'm losing my mind here. Tell me you're okay."

"I'll be perfect if you don't go easy on me. Take me. Make

me yours." *Erase anyone else who might've been here before you. I only want to be yours.*

He grins wickedly. "If you really want me to, I'll make you scream my name. Then you'll have no doubt who you belong to."

I stretch my arms over my head, fanning my hair out so it's not caught beneath me. My fingers grab onto the headboard.

Then, it's *on*.

He holds himself up on one hand, grasps my hip with the other, and he thrusts his shaft hard and fast. Holding nothing back. Our bodies slap together. It's primal and it's everything I need.

Danny fucking into me is the sexiest thing I've ever seen.

He's showing me he doesn't see me as some broken, damaged girl. I'm strong enough to take what he's giving me. And I want it *all*. The beads of sweat rolling down between his pecs, landing on my stomach. The scent of him, which I'm sure I'm soaked in by now. And his rigid, girthy cock that's forcing me closer and closer to climax.

My thighs clench around him and my body tenses just before my orgasm overtakes me. Immerses me and drowns me in pleasure. I grab for the headboard, tip my head back and cry out, "*Danny!*"

His hand covers my mouth. "Shh, baby, that's a little too loud." I suck on his fingers, and he groans. His movements stutter, and I feel his cock throbbing inside me. Marking me with his hot seed. Showing where I belong.

Right here.

He lowers himself to the mattress beside me. We're both catching our breaths. "God, that was perfect," he says. "Perfect."

Time stretches as we gaze at one another.

He spends a few minutes smoothing my hair back and

running his fingertips over my arms. I'm still coming down from the high of being with him. It doesn't matter that I've lost my memories. I can say with certainty that no sex I've ever had could compare to what we just did.

"Are you happy?" he asks.

I wiggle against him, erasing every millimeter of space between us, and rest my head on his chest. "Very happy. Will you stay with me?"

"Planning on it. I need to check on Nina and Starla. Her shift will be over soon. Then I can bring you some dinner, and we can get cozy. I have a lot of snuggling on the agenda."

"I figured you'd be a snuggler."

"Even if I wasn't, I'd be a snuggler for you." He kisses my temple, which makes me fall that much more. I'm falling *hard*. Danny makes me feel calm and steady, like I can face anything if I'm with him.

But when he tugs on his clothes and leaves the room, I can't stop myself from running through the worst possibilities. What might happen if we find out more about my past, and I'm not as good as Danny believes I am. It'll tear out my heart if I let him down.

If I lose him now, that could be the thing that finally breaks me.

25

Danny

The next morning, we wake together slowly, all kisses and smiles. I don't want to go. But I have to, at least for a little while.

I run my hand along Lark's stomach. "I need to make coffee and see Nina. Stay in bed longer if you want."

"No, I'll come. I just need to shower first." A crease appears between her eyebrows. I don't like that. I want to smooth it away. I wish I could take away every single thing that might distress her. "You'll wait to tell Nina about Cam until I'm there?" she asks.

"That's your story to tell. Not mine."

It takes every ounce of willpower to get myself out of Lark's bed. We spent a lot of the night talking, and there was definitely cuddling. There were no more orgasms though. I was insistent on that, and Lark didn't push it.

I still don't know if going to bed with her was the right thing to do. Maybe a better guy would have been able to resist. I hadn't intended to let things go so far so fast, but Lark has a way of getting exactly what she wants with me. Who am I to deny her?

I've never seen her so beautiful, so *free*, as when she was in my arms last night. As if she'd let go of the usual things weighing her down. I didn't see a single sign that she wasn't all-in with everything we did.

Being inside of her... Hearing her cry out in ecstasy because of the way I'd made her feel? That's going to get addictive.

And if I don't stop thinking about it, I'm going to get hard again.

Before I can slip back under those covers, even if it's just for one more kiss, I force myself to throw my clothes on and head to my own bedroom. After cleaning up, I pad down the hallway and pass Ryan, who's just emerged from Nina's room.

"Hey," I say. "Didn't expect you to be in this early."

"New schedule. I worked it out with Nina. She thought you could use more help."

"Ah." I stick my hands in my pockets and nod. "You must have the security codes, then?"

Last night, I checked on Nina regularly, as I always do, even when her nurses are around. She was sleeping easily. I never know what the nights will bring, but Nina's was uneventful. I was careful to reset our security system after Jess left, too. The nurses have the codes, but I'm planning to be extra diligent after yesterday's scare at the beach.

Ryan nods. "I do. I'm all set. Is Lark around this morning?"

The muscle in my jaw ticks with annoyance. "In bed. I assume. Why do you ask?" *What's your business with my girl?*

"Just wondering how much coffee to make." He smiles. "I was heading to the kitchen."

Easy, tiger, I tell myself. "Oh, sure. We could all use some. Thanks."

Nina is up doing her morning crossword puzzle on her

iPad. I come in and open up the curtains, letting sunlight flood the room with its warm glow. "Good morning."

"That's quite a smile you've got there," Nina says. She sets down her iPad and studies me.

"What do you mean? I smile all the time."

"You think I don't know your different smiles? I've known you for your entire life, Danny-boy. Don't think you can hide from me. You look like the cat that caught the canary and then spent all night kissing it."

I start laughing, and that turns into an awkward cough. Shit, I should've guessed Nina would figure it out this fast. Or maybe I'm just that obvious. I've been worrying all night about Lark's safety and happiness, but mine hasn't been in question. Sunshine and freaking rainbows must be beaming out of me for all the world to see.

"Did Lark have fun on your adventure in Solvang yesterday? I'm surprised she hasn't come to tell me all about it."

Nina knows we went there, but not our exact purpose. I pull up the stool by her bed. "It was okay. Mixed." I don't want to lie, but I can't tell Lark's story, either.

"Do you remember the time we went there for your birthday?" Nina asks, a wistful look on her face.

"Sure I do." I tug my lip between my teeth. "Travis came with us. It was his idea, wasn't it?"

Her smile turns brittle. "He was a good uncle to you. When he was around."

"He was." Emphasis on *when he was around*. "Um, anyhow, Lark thought she recognized some places in Solvang, and that can be hard for her. You know?"

Nina nods. "I trust that you're taking care of her?"

"I'm trying." *Fuck, I'm trying*.

"I hope you're being *careful* with her," Nina adds, the innuendo obvious.

"I like her. A lot. I only want to do right by her. Do you not approve?"

"I approve. Lark doesn't want to admit it, but that girl needs someone. More than anything, she needs…love."

Those words do all kinds of things to my insides.

I'm thirty-three years old, and I've never been in love. I've never thrown around that four letter word before, except when it comes to Nina and some of my best friends. I don't even know if I'm capable of feeling it.

If I could be *in it* for anyone, though, I think it would be a woman like Lark.

"I've been seeing this coming for a while," Nina says. "I'm just a little surprised it took this long. The way you two look at each other is how your grandpa and I used to do, and I know raging sexual tension when I see it."

I grimace. "I don't need to hear about you and Grandpa and…*that*."

She snorts a laugh. "I care about both of you. I don't want either of you getting hurt. And Lark doesn't have a momma or daddy around to speak for her, so I'm the only one to do it. Consider yourself warned. As far as protection—"

"I'm thirty-three years old and I've had a fair share of medical training. That's not a conversation I need to have." Especially not with my grandmother.

"Maybe so, but some things just need to be said."

"We're good," I assure her.

"What's good?" Lark asks. She's just walked in.

"Nothing."

I stand up. I was going to play it cool this morning, but Lark's damp hair is combed back from her face, she's wearing the green dress she wore last week to the barbecue, and she's just too damn beautiful.

Lark smiles tentatively, and I get it now. What Nina saw between us. There's no hiding this, certainly not from Nina, who knows me better than anyone. I can't start thinking about the hot-as-fuck details of last night in front of my grandmother, because that's creepy, but I still can't control the way that my heart races at seeing her. The way my blood heats with a hunger that's only for her.

I hold out my hand, and Lark is hesitant for a moment before coming over to me. I kiss the blush on her cheek. "Hey, gorgeous."

Then Lark's eyes slide over to Nina, both women smirking. "So you know about us, huh? That didn't take long."

"Can't get anything past me. Not that it was hard to guess. Danny needs to work on his poker face. But I like the two of you together."

"Thank goodness for that," Lark says.

Nina relaxes against her pillows. "Was it your romantic trip to Solvang that brought this on? Waffles and windmills to get the blood going?"

Lark's blush deepens as she laughs. But I see the worry that her eyes betray. She's thinking of what we learned yesterday.

I promised her she could decide when to tell Nina the truth. Now, Lark is looking at me for reassurance. She wants to double-check that I'm okay with this. Not because she needs my permission, but because she wants to know we're on the same page. We're in this together.

I nod.

"Something's up," Nina says, glancing between us. "Out with it."

"Don't be mad," Lark says to Nina.

"That's a terrible way to start a conversation," my grandmother replies.

"You're right. Let me start over. So last week, Danny and I saw some emails on your iPad. About Travis."

Fault lines appear around Nina's mouth. White-hot fury

glows in her eyes. She knows exactly which emails we're talking about.

"It was my fault," I say. "I read them and showed Lark." If she's going to be mad at someone, I'd much rather it's me.

"Of course you looked. Because you can't mind your own damn business when it comes to me, can you, Daniel Bradley? This is one time that I wish you'd stayed *out of it*."

26

Lark

*N*ina turns her scowl on me. "And *you*, Lark. I can believe my grandson getting nosy, but you?"

"I thought I was helping. We both did."

"I'm sure. But my email inbox has got nothing to do with either of you." Nina crosses her arms like that's the end of the discussion, and she sets her jaw.

She's a stubborn lady, but I've never seen her this furious and defiant.

No, that's not it, I realize. Nina's gone pale, and her clenched jaw hides a tremor. She's *afraid.* That's something I understand too well. I hate seeing Nina this way.

I walk over to Danny and rest my hand on his lower back. "Could you grab us some breakfast? And give me and Nina a couple minutes to talk?"

"If you think you can defuse this," he murmurs, "I'm happy to do whatever you say." Danny kisses my temple and leaves the room.

"Snooping in my email wasn't enough? You're both conspiring against me now?"

I return to Nina's bedside. I take her hand, and she grasps

mine lightly. She's got such inner strength, this lady, even when her illness makes things harder on her.

"Why didn't you tell Danny about the emails?"

Her jaw is set. She doesn't respond.

"You've done so much for me," I say. "I wanted to do something to help you. But I should've told you right away, and I'm sorry about that."

Nina sighs. "Lucky for you, I've never been very good at staying mad." Her gaze drags toward the family photos on the walls, though Travis isn't in any of them. "I didn't tell Danny because he would've insisted I have nothing to do with Travis or anyone associated with him."

"Are you so sure about that?" I ask quietly.

Danny knows I might have a connection to Travis, but he swears it doesn't matter. I'm doing my best to believe him. Why would he be upset with Nina for wanting to see her son? If anything, she's far more blameless than me.

"Get me a fresh glass of water?" Nina asks. "It'll take me a while to get this story out, and you know how my throat gets dry."

After I get her a glass and she takes a few sips, she starts talking.

"I got the first message a few months ago. If you've read them, you already know what they say. *Your son misses you.*" She closes her eyes and flinches, as if she's bracing against a sharp pain. "I was skeptical of course. I didn't want to get my hopes up, and I could smell a scam a mile away. I'm not some little old lady who's ready to send her money overseas in exchange for empty promises. But whoever is behind it, I guess they knew that Travis was my weakness. The one thing that would grab my attention. And then, they stopped writing at all. Pulled the rug out from under me. Like a cruel joke."

Every word makes me flinch inside. I'm praying I didn't

write those messages. Please say I couldn't be that cruel. "Maybe there's an explanation behind it. Maybe they did know Travis and wanted to help reunite your family, but for some reason got cold feet. Or...something else stood in the way."

"More likely, the author of the emails talked to Travis and couldn't convince him to come and see me. Danny would say that Travis never came home because he simply doesn't want to. I thought I'd accepted a while ago that my son was gone, but getting those messages? They broke me open again, Lark. Right down the middle." Nina's jaw trembles, her face shutting down the way she always does around this subject.

"You still miss him, don't you?"

A tear slips down her cheek, and I gently wipe it away. "Of course I do. Every single day."

When I came here and the Bradleys took me in, I was looking for my real family. I thought my biggest problem was that I couldn't remember them. But Nina has every one of her memories, and she's *still* lost someone who belongs in her life. I hate that.

She's afraid of the truth about Travis. And I'm freaking *terrified* of the truth about myself. What if one leads to the other? If I really have some tie to Travis Bradley, is it worth the risk of finding out? I don't know how to make that kind of calculation. But it's easier to be brave to help someone else, rather than just yourself.

If there's even a *chance* I could help Nina find him...

"Could I see a picture of Travis?" I ask.

"What good would that do?"

"I'm curious. He's someone you love, and that matters to me."

She side-eyes me. "You're plotting something. But, fine. I'm still a proud momma, even when it hurts. Hand me my iPad?" Reluctantly, she opens a window on her device. "A lot of my old photos of him weren't digital, but I scanned them a few years ago. I keep them in a special folder."

I flip through a slideshow of images. Nina's husband and their two sons on road trips. Travis's high school graduation. There are dozens of him with a baby I assume is Danny. Danny's cute. Big eyes, wisps of pale blond hair. Chunky legs.

"Travis had always been a wanderer, much like me, but he rarely held down a steady job. He would travel around to teach at ski resorts in the winters, surfing in the summers. That was fine by me. It was the life he wanted. But Chris, his older brother, took it as a personal insult that Travis wasn't driven by money. Then when Danny was a kid, he got so close to Travis, and that bothered Chris as well. Danny wanted to be just like his uncle."

She flips through more photos of Danny and Travis. As he grows, Danny looks so much like his uncle, it's uncanny. All the Bradley men are blond and blue-eyed, but Travis has the same tilt to his head as Danny when he smiles. The same gentleness to his eyes.

There's something here in these photos, chiming in the empty spaces of my heart. Something *big*. Hidden and shifting in the shadows inside me.

Do you still think you can run from me, Lark?

I shake away that memory. The dry scratch of the note in my hands, and the wind blowing my hair into my face.

"Why did he leave?" I ask.

"I've gone back and forth on that over the years. It was a small thing that blew up into something big. When my husband died suddenly, Travis didn't make it back in time for his dad's funeral. And when he *did* show up, he asked for money, which made his older brother furious. Travis took off in a huff. Then it turned out that my husband's nice pair of cuff links had gone missing, something he'd worn at our wedding and left to Chris in his will. Chris accused Travis of stealing them. It got ugly fast. I always tried to stay neutral between my boys, but I was already hurt from Travis missing the funeral."

She blinks, and another tear escapes.

"We all said shitty things. To make it worse, Danny heard a lot of the argument. He saw Travis storm off without even a goodbye. I figured, if Travis wanted to go, let him go. I didn't think we'd never hear from him again. It took me years to realize what a mistake I'd made. I wish I'd reached out right away to say I loved him and that nothing else mattered. Especially not a pair of cuff links. But I didn't get the chance."

We keep scrolling through the pictures of Travis, and the feeling of recognition only intensifies. Those deep blue eyes. Not just the color, but that way Danny and his uncle both have of looking out at the world. Like they're really seeing.

Seeing *me*.

It's like the moment that I walked into Sugar & Yeast in Solvang, and I just *knew*.

I've met this man. Not just Danny, but his uncle.

What do I do with that knowledge?

"Sometimes I go months without looking at these," Nina says. "And other times, I can't stop. Hurts either way."

"Then it's better to look, don't you think?"

She huffs a laugh. "I guess it is. Now you see how those emails gave me hope. I wanted to tell my son how much he meant to me. When they stopped, I felt all the hurt all over again."

"I'm so sorry."

"You shouldn't be sorry, Lark. You had nothing to do with it."

But... What if I did?

I can't speak. All my fears are squeezing my windpipe. Finally, I get my voice to work. "After Danny and I saw the emails last week, he asked Bennett Security to look into it.

They found the IP address where the emails were sent. It was a café in Solvang."

"And that's why you went there yesterday? You and my grandson are sneakier than I gave you credit for. I had no idea. But I see why you didn't tell me. You didn't want to get my hopes up."

"We went to the café to show around a picture of Travis, just in case someone recognized him. It was a long shot."

"And?"

I almost tell her all of it. But then I just…can't. Not yet. Because then I'll have to tell her about that awful note left on Danny's car at the beach after we returned from Solvang. The implied threat, and my deeper fear. That if I keep digging for answers about my past, it won't just lead to Travis. It'll lead to someone far worse.

"They didn't. Recognize him, I mean. I have no idea if we can pick up the trail and find Travis. But if there's a way, do you want us to keep looking for him?"

I hold my breath while I wait for her answer.

Then she says, "It hurts either way. So it's better to look. Isn't it?"

"Then we'll keep searching." *No matter what we find.*

27

Danny

I step into the backyard. "Lark? You out here?"

It's mid-morning, and I haven't seen her since I left her and Nina to talk. I found Ryan brewing the coffee in the kitchen and hung out with him instead. I can't figure the guy out. He's in the medical field, so we should have a few things to make small talk about. At the very least. But dragging more than a few words out of him was impossible.

Finally, I gave up and tried buffing the scratches out of my Charger's red paint. But I was too distracted thinking about Lark. Missing her, replaying our night in my head... And wondering what she and Nina were talking about. Once I couldn't wait any longer, I went to look for her. I stopped by Nina's room, and then Lark's.

And that's how I've ended up out here. The backdoor camera recorded Lark coming outside, and we've established that I'm not above a little spying if it keeps her safe.

"Lark?" I ask again.

"I'm here," she calls out softly.

It's a perfect fall day today. This is Southern California, so everything's in bloom, but the temps stay nice and mild.

Yellow sunlight bathes the yard. There are brightly colored blooms and green foliage everywhere I can see. But I don't see my girl.

Then I reach the far corner of the yard and catch a darker shade of green beneath the willow tree. It's her dress.

I head over, brushing the branches out of the way. She's sitting on a picnic blanket at the base of the trunk, staring off into space in deep thought.

"Hey. I wondered where you'd gone."

"Just needed to think."

I take a seat beside her on the blanket and lean in for a slow kiss. Her skin is warm, and I feel the frown on her mouth and the tightness in her arms when I touch her. "What is it?"

She chews her lip. "I told Nina that we went to Solvang looking for Travis, but not that the barista recognized me. Or about Cam. Or the note on your car."

I exhale, toeing off my shoes. I don't want to get the blanket dirty. "Yeah. Nina didn't say anything, so I guessed as much." I trace my thumb over the crease between her eyebrows, wishing I could take her stress away.

"I don't want to lie or hide things from her. Once we know what really happened with Travis, I'll tell her everything."

"So you want to keep looking into it?"

"Yes," she says firmly. "I do. I want to find Travis for Nina."

I have my own mixed feelings about my uncle. And a lot of ambivalence about whether it's worth finding him. We can't forget that there are people out there who want to hurt Lark, people who may be trying to find a way to reach her even now.

But whatever we discover, nothing could change the way I feel about her.

This is the kind of woman she is—determined to help Nina, even if she might put herself in greater danger in the process. I'll stand by Lark's decision, but I'll continue making it my mission to keep her safe. She'll be right at my side.

"You're okay with that?" she asks.

"I am. If it's what you want. As long as we do it together." I lift her hand and kiss her knuckles. This brave, incredible woman. And she's mine.

"I'm not taking you away from Nina?" she asks. "Between yesterday and today, I feel like I'm getting all your attention."

"There's enough of me to go around."

Lark rolls her eyes and smiles.

I'm still determined to take care of Nina and Lark both, even if it means relying on the hired nurses a bit more than before. It just happens that I have two people who mean everything to me instead of just one. I've seen the way Matteo juggles all his responsibilities. I might've considered it crazy before, but now I'm getting it. This is that *big* feeling he's described to me. Like you could be a one-man army for the people you care about. Your family.

That girl needs someone, Nina said. *More than anything, she needs...love.*

"C'mere," I say, opening my arms. "Let's get comfy."

We stretch out on the blanket. Lark pillows her head against my chest, while I draw shapes with my fingertips on her back. I love this, getting to touch her and be affectionate. If I had my way, I'd have my hands on Lark as much as possible.

"You really like this willow tree, don't you?" I ask. "You sit out here a lot."

"I do. I think this is my favorite spot in West Oaks. Even more favorite than the garage with your beautiful cars."

"Damn, that's saying something." I lean over to kiss her

forehead. "You can enjoy being happy. You deserve that. As for the rest, we don't have to figure it out right now."

She smiles up at me coyly. "There's something else I'd rather do right now."

"I hope it's kiss me."

Lark fists my T-shirt and pulls me down until our lips meet.

Last night, Lark admitted to being nervous about having sex. And the truth was, I was nervous too. I was afraid of hurting her, of going too fast and doing something she would regret. I felt like I was taking her virginity, and that's a big responsibility. A responsibility I welcomed, but I took it seriously. I wanted everything perfect for her.

I think I did a decent job, judging by how loud she got. So fucking sexy. I love it when a woman shows me what she likes.

But as I kiss her now, things feel more settled between us. This is exactly where we should be. In each other's arms. Looking back over the last month, I'd say this was inevitable. There was a gravity between us that we couldn't escape. We only tortured ourselves by trying.

Now that we're together, I want to give her every kind of pleasure. To fill her mind and her heart with only the best experiences. And the fact that we're under the willow tree, Lark's favorite place? I'm getting all kinds of dirty ideas. I've never claimed to be a perfect angel, but this woman does something downright wicked to me. Makes me want to be good to her by being *oh so bad*.

I shift us so Lark is on her back and I'm above her. She wraps her legs around my waist, the green fabric of her dress bunching up a bit. I run my hands over her body, using a firm touch as I squeeze her curves. I started off gentle with her last night, but I noticed that she liked things rougher.

I want to keep trying things. Finding out what else makes her lose control.

I slide my hand downward, lifting up the hem of the fabric enough to reach underneath. My hand wanders over her panties and bare smooth skin for a while as we make out. Then I separate from her, sitting back on my heels, and grab hold of the elastic waistband of her panties. I tug until I've pulled the scrap of cotton all the way over her legs and off. The panties tuck into the back pocket of my jeans.

She looks up at me with a shocked smile. "Are you doing what I think you're doing?"

I put my finger to my lips. "Unless you want me to stop, then you should stay quiet," I murmur. "We don't want anyone coming outside to investigate what we're up to."

She sucks in a breath, but she doesn't tell me no. Instead, Lark watches me with wide eyes to see what I'll do next.

I lift up her dress, slowly, slowly, until I've exposed her body below her hips. There's dark, trimmed hair at the cleft between her legs. I bend forward and spread her open with my fingers. So pink and pretty.

"*Danny,*" she whispers.

I hear her arousal in the waver of her voice. I can smell it on her too, see the evidence on her lower lips. Glistening. I drag my tongue over her folds. Lapping up her wetness and adding my own.

She moans, and her hand digs into my hair. "Someone's going to…see…"

"Then I'd better make you come as quick as possible."

Nina's got a tall privacy wall around the yard, and the neighbors' houses aren't close. And inside the garden, the willow tree's branches are mostly blocking us from view, but not completely. If Ryan decides to take a stroll to this corner of the garden, or hell, the guy who checks the water meter, it won't take them too long to figure out what's up.

It's not likely. But the thought is still exciting. My cock strains against my fly, fully hard and raring to join the fun.

I flick my tongue over her clit, concentrating my efforts there. I bring two fingers to her opening and push inside to rub her G spot at the same time. I really do need to make this quick because this angle isn't great for my neck, but she tastes way too good to stop. Her small whimpers are driving me wild.

In less than a minute, she arches her back and her legs shake. "Danny. Oh, *oh, God*." Her hand fists in my hair, tugging hard at the strands.

I don't stop licking and fingering her until she sits up, looking down at me with heavy eyelids, plush lips hanging open.

I smile up at her. "Did you like that?"

Lark's eyes are glazed. Pleasure-drunk. "I want you to mark me."

I don't understand what she means at first. "Mark you?"

"With your mouth. I want you to mark me with something I asked for. Something…good."

Oh. She's thinking of the bruises she had before. The ones that probably came from Z, her stepbrother.

The seriousness in her eyes and her voice tells me this means a lot to her, more than she can probably convey. "I'd love to do that." I'm still kneeling between her legs. I move to kiss the soft, pale skin of her inner thigh. My lips press to the unblemished skin again, feather-light.

Then I open my mouth and suck on her. Small pulses of arousal jolt through my erect cock.

"Yes. Please. Like that." Lark's breaths quicken, growing louder. She runs her fingers through my hair again. Both encouragement and permission to keep going. Lifting my eyes and holding her gaze, I sink my teeth into her thigh in the same place I was just sucking.

Another bolt of lust thumps in my balls.

She whimpers, but nods.

I look for any sign that it's hurting her or that she doesn't like it, but all she does is tug at the strands of my hair while more of those small whimpers and moans fall from her lips, urging me on.

Then I sit up. "That what you wanted?"

Lark pushes herself upright and launches at me.

We're both on our knees, a storm of wild kisses, caressing hands. Lark fumbles with the button and zipper of my jeans with halting, desperate movements. "Let me." I get my fly open, then push my jeans and boxers down. My swollen cock pops out, pointing upward and achingly hard.

"Fuck me?" Lark begs. She turns and tugs her dress up over her ass. Baring herself to me. I can't hold back an animalistic groan that comes from the bottom of my chest.

This is, hands-down, the most erotic display I have ever laid my eyes on.

Lark's on her hands and knees. Her gorgeous, smooth skin is laid out, her pink center glistening. I can just make out the hickey that I left on her inner thigh.

I grab her by the hips and sink my cock into her in one swift, unrelenting movement. She closes her mouth, cutting off a gasp.

"Lark. You're fucking ruining me." I have to stop and just breathe before I lose it altogether.

She's so snug around me. So hot and wet and *mine*. She's unleashing a feral part of me I didn't even know existed. I grunt as my breaths drag in and out of my chest, my teeth clenched and bared.

My hips pull back, then snap forward. We both stifle our cries. Again. Again. So many times a pleasure-fueled haze settles over my brain. This is the hottest, dirtiest sex I've ever had. Most of our clothes are still on, and we're outside, the cool breeze running over our heated skin as our bodies slide and rut together.

Somehow, I drag myself out of that haze of blinding lust and lean over her. I kiss her bare shoulder where the strap of her dress has fallen down. Then I pull out of her. She looks back over her shoulder, frowning. "Danny?"

"Come here. I want to see your face."

Lark turns around. I sit back on my heels and tug my jeans down even further. My dick is hard and slick and ready, jutting upward from my crotch. She straddles me and lowers herself down. My shaft slides into her again, the skirt of her dress pooling around us. Then she's sitting in my lap in the most intimate of embraces, and I wrap my arms tight around her.

"Right where you belong," I murmur.

She holds my face as we gaze into each other's eyes. Exchange unhurried, messy kisses.

I move her up and down on my cock as we rock our hips together. Our movements are small and gentle, nothing like the wild thrusting of a few minutes ago. I fucked her hard last night too, and it was incredible, but this is exactly what we need. This beautiful moment, sharing pleasure and showing her tenderness.

I'm so gone for this girl. I just want her to have everything. To give her everything.

Pleasure coils at the base of my spine and in my balls. "I'm close," I say. "Do you think you can get there again?"

"Yes. When you come in me."

Ughn. That's all the encouragement I need. I cinch my arms around her waist, bucking my hips upward. My cock pulses, erupting deep inside of her as starbursts go off behind my eyes, and Lark presses her face to my neck, shivering and riding me through her second orgasm.

For as long as I can, I hold her there as a breeze ruffles the willow branches. My legs are getting tingly from being on the hard ground, but I don't want to move from this spot.

I want to freeze the present moment with Lark, as if nothing else exists but us. As if there's no danger or heartache waiting beyond our door.

28

Lark

For the next week, I feel like I'm living someone else's life. Someone else's blissful, buoyant, over-sexed life.

Some things stay exactly the same. Like spending time doing crosswords and online shopping with Nina, and holding her hand when she doesn't feel well. Or working on the '71 Charger with Danny. But then, Danny will walk into the room or glance over at me with *that look* in his eyes, and suddenly we're sneaking away and tearing off each other's clothes. In his room, my room, the hall bathroom. On top of the washing machine in the laundry room. And underneath the willow tree again, because that was insanely hot.

One afternoon, Danny takes me from behind while I'm bent over the red Charger's hood. The garage smells like cars and sex afterward, and I wish I could bottle it up and give it to Danny to wear as cologne. But that would probably make me even more insatiable for him than I already am.

I figure Nina realizes what we're up to with all the smirks she's giving us. But I'm thankful she doesn't comment on it directly. I'm bold about plenty of things, but whenever I think about Danny and me, my face burns red like a girl about to be kissed for the first time. He makes me...*glow*.

At night, we slow things down and savor each other. One of my favorite things is kissing down Danny's smooth pecs and stomach to his happy trail. Then I keep going, kissing and nuzzling the base of his cock. I love watching him get hard for me. Then I take his crown into my mouth and nurse the tip while he gets closer and closer to losing control. Finally, I take him all the way into my mouth and hollow my cheeks and suck, my tongue licking up and down the vein underneath, until he comes in thick, hot spurts, panting and groaning.

And I love it when he sucks hickeys onto my skin. My thighs, my hips, under my breasts. Leaving his mark. Not where anyone else can see them, but just for us. No matter what, *I know*. I can't describe how good it feels to belong to someone and know that he belongs to me.

I still know so little about my past life, but is it possible I've ever been this happy? This at peace and content with each day as it passes? This is our little world, and it's enough for me. Being with Nina, seeing friends like Quinn or Matteo and Angela when they stop by.

And Danny. He's everything.

As far as the great big *everything else* that I'm supposed to figure out—finding Travis, my past, my future—we haven't found any more clues yet, so I'm putting it off. Danny thinks I don't notice the way he watches the cameras and patrols the house and grounds like a bodyguard. But I do. There's been no sign of whoever left that note on Danny's car, and we haven't tracked down any leads on Travis. But it still feels like danger is waiting right outside the door. Looking for a way in.

Do you still think you can run from me?

Whenever I recall those words, a thread of horror winds

its way down my spine. Nina's illness is a different kind of threat, and it's ever-present. Something's going to happen. I know this perfect interlude has to end.

But that just makes me want to enjoy it for as long as it will last.

One morning, I wake up next to Danny in his bed. His arm is draped over me, and I'm snuggled up against him, my back to his chest. We're both naked. I used to sleep in T-shirts, but there's not much point with Danny. We always end up skin to skin, though Danny keeps a pair of sweats handy in case Nina needs anything in the night.

Danny kisses my neck. "Morning, beautiful."

As usual, my hair is a crazy mess. I smooth it down and try to get it under control. "It is, isn't it?"

"I remember when you used to be full of eye rolls and sarcasm."

"If you miss my cynicism, I can work on that. More smirking and rolling of eyes. Noted."

He chuckles, burying his nose in my tangled hair. "I like all the versions of you. But if this is how you are when you're happy, then I want this Lark every day."

I turn over, and we kiss, our bodies intertwining, skin against skin. But before things can escalate, Danny pulls back reluctantly. "Cliff and my roommates are having a get-together at the Pink House today. You up for going?"

"Like a date?"

"Sure. You want to go on a date with me?"

I shrug. "If Aiden's cooking, I'm there."

Danny purses his lips and tries to look annoyed, but he's hiding a smile. "I'll tell Cliff we're in." He grabs his phone and unlocks the screen.

Then he frowns. A real one.

"What is it?"

He wipes a hand over his mouth. "Rex Easton wrote me. Cliff's dad, from Bennett Security. They have news."

My pulse speeds up. "Did they find Travis?"

"No, not yet. But a possible lead."

After our trip to Solvang, Danny updated Bennett Security about the possible connection between Travis and me. The company has been helping us search for more clues, since we've got almost nothing to go on.

"What did they find?" I ask.

"Rex wanted to share it with us in person. He'll be at the Pink House today if you're up for that."

"Of course I am. We have to."

Danny turns to study me. "There's always a choice. We could just say *fuck it* and do something else instead. Go on a real date." He sets his phone aside and rolls on top of me. "I want to take you out. Show the whole world you're mine."

I like the thought that he wants to show everyone we're together. That he's proud to be with me. It makes my chest feel light, like my heart is ready to float away. Even though, way down underneath, I'm scared to death about what Rex Easton will tell us.

And I'm scared about people following us. Leaving threatening notes...or worse.

"If we go to the Pink House, you can show Aiden Shelborne I'm yours while we're there. Since you're *so* jealous of him."

Danny growls. "The man was feeding you from his fingers!"

"He was just fishing for compliments about his food."

Danny makes a grumbling sound in his throat. "Complement his food all you want. But if anybody's going to be feeding you, it's me."

His cock is thickening against my thigh. I press my leg to his erection. "You could feed me something else right now," I say. "Then we go talk to Rex this afternoon. And save our date for later."

"Sounds like a plan." He lowers his weight onto me, capturing my mouth with his.

DANNY DRIVES us to the Pink House, and we head straight to the backyard. Aiden is over by the grill, wearing a shirt this time, while fragrant smoke billows around him. Quinn dashes over as soon as she spots us.

"So you decided to give this guy a shot," she says to me. "How nice for him." She gives me a hug and Danny a playful punch on the arm. Quinn knows all about me and Danny already, so she's just giving him shit in front of their other roommates.

"It's a trial run," I say.

Danny puts his arm around my shoulders and kisses my temple. "She makes me look good though, doesn't she?"

I meet his eyes, and we smile at each other until Quinn snorts. "The two of you could turn anybody into a hopeless romantic. Keep your distance in case that's contagious." I give Quinn a knowing smile, and she adds, "Don't even say it."

What? I mouth silently.

"Wait until we're alone. If your man can spare you for five minutes?"

"Five minutes. I'm setting a timer." Danny gives me another kiss, then lets me go. I still have a warm glow all over my body as I walk over to the beer cooler with Quinn. The way Danny claims me in front of all his friends, no hesitation… I don't think I'll ever get enough of that.

We grab a couple of pale ales and pop the tabs. "You two

look obnoxiously happy," Quinn says. "I've never seen Danny like this. So lovey-dovey and over the moon for someone."

"You think so?"

"Face it, you're made for each other." She nudges me with her elbow. "Expect everyone who's not in love to complain about you guys all day long."

I panic a little at those words. *In love.* Is that how we seem? I've suspected that my heart might be headed in that direction, but it's way too soon. Nope, not gonna think about that.

I'm not going to start thinking about how I'd break into a million pieces if this all goes away.

I take a sip of my beer. "I heard a certain older, distinguished bodyguard would be here today."

Quinn shrugs, schooling her expression. "Rex tries to come by a few times a month for father-son moments with Cliff."

"Are he and Cliff close?"

"Sort of. There's a complicated history there, but isn't that true for everyone?" She drops her voice. "The only thing that's clear is that Rex barely notices me. You haven't said anything to Danny about my ridiculous crush, have you?"

"Of course not. What kind of girl do you think I am? These lips are locked tight."

I'm amazed at how easily I've fallen into a close friendship with Quinn, despite her past with Danny. But I'm not jealous. If anything, I want to ask her more about him. But there are several subjects I haven't touched with Quinn. We don't talk about her history with Danny, and I haven't shared what I learned in Solvang about my *own* history. I've just wanted to have a friendship that wasn't tainted by the darker sides of my past.

"Danny's waving like he needs you for something,"

Quinn says. "And he's standing with Rex. What's that about?"

I glance over. Danny and Rex are waiting by the back door to the house.

Anxiety floods my stomach and rises in my throat. Crap, it must be time. I insisted that we speak to Rex about the investigation, yet I'm not eager for it to actually happen.

"Bennett Security has been investigating some things. Rex has news. They must be ready for me."

Quinn gives me another quick hug. "Good luck, then. Hope you like what you hear."

That isn't likely, I think.

But Nina wants to see Travis again while she still has the chance. No matter how much the truth scares me, I have to remember why I'm doing this.

∼

"It's good to meet you, Lark." Rex Easton takes both of my hands in his, focusing on me with a dark gray gaze.

Rex is just as tall and handsome as he looked in the photo Quinn showed me, though his hair and beard are threaded with more silver. He's got the deep, sexy tones of a voiceover actor, combined with the same kind of calming presence that Danny possesses. But while Danny is all easygoing charm, Rex is more contained. I imagine he's the type of guy who's difficult to read, which is perfect for a bodyguard.

And he's got that enigmatic, older-man mystique. No wonder Quinn can't get over him.

We head to the living room at the front of the house, where it's quiet. Danny and I sit on the couch by the window, while Rex sinks into the chair across from us. "You're familiar with the company I work for? Bennett Security?"

My knees are bouncing. I can't keep still. "Just what

Danny's told me." And Quinn, but I leave her out of it. "You're usually a bodyguard?"

"I am. Investigations aren't my typical gig. But most of the guys on our team are ex-military, and a lot of us are ex-special ops. We're creative problem solvers. Because I know Danny personally through my son, I've been acting as point on the search for your missing identity, as well as the search for Danny's uncle, Travis Bradley."

"You found something new about Travis?" Danny asks.

"We have. And just this morning, an update came in about Lark, as well."

My stomach lurches. Danny squeezes my hand.

You've got this, I tell myself. *You can handle it.* For Nina.

"Okay," I say, sitting up straighter. "Tell us about Travis first."

Rex sits forward and clasps his hands between his knees. "As you both know, it's been hard to pick up Travis's trail because he disappeared almost twenty years ago, before a lot of records were fully digital. We did all the obvious searches, criminal records, credit check. Nothing came up. But we didn't give up after that. Our research team managed to find a DUI charge in Las Vegas from about eight years ago, filed under the name 'Travis Bradlee,' with two e's at the end instead of e-y."

Rex pulls up a photo on his phone and shows Danny the screen. "The Vegas police provided a copy of the mug shot from his booking. Is this your uncle?"

Danny nods. "Yeah. That's Travis." I already knew how much Danny and his uncle look alike, especially their eyes. But Travis's are bloodshot in this photo, and his arm is in a sling.

"What happened to him here?" I ask.

"He was in a car accident," Rex says, "injured pretty badly, the only vehicle involved. His blood alcohol was over the limit, and it was severe enough to make it a felony, given all the circumstances and the property damage. He got bail, but he skipped town and didn't appear for the trial."

Danny tugs at his necklace. "I never heard of Travis having a problem drinking, but the skipping town part? That fits."

"After finding this lead, we expanded our search to include the misspelling of Travis's last name. One of our researchers got a hit on a local newspaper from near Solvang."

"*Solvang?*" I blurt out.

"That's right. The article was about a support group for people with chronic injuries." Rex flips to another image on his phone screen. "They hosted a fundraising event in a park, and this article was posted on the newspaper's website about six months ago."

In the photo, a few dozen people mill around in a park, holding signs that say *Better Care for Chronic Pain*. With the bright sunlight, the faces aren't super clear, but it looks like Travis is standing to one side of the group. I spot his name in the caption, misspelled like Rex said. Travis Bradlee with two e's.

Then Danny mutters, "What the hell?"

"I'm guessing you see the same thing we noticed?" Rex asks.

I glance from one man to the other. "What? What are you talking about?"

Danny points at Rex's phone. "There. Lark, it's *you*."

On the edge of the photo stands a girl with long black hair. A girl who looks exactly like me. At the same picnic that Travis attended.

Danny rests his hand on the back of my neck. "It's your hair," he murmurs. "I would notice it anywhere."

"But...my name isn't in this caption."

"Danny gave us a reference photo of you. One of our researchers has a sharp eye and made the connection. We called the clinic that runs the chronic pain support group. They refused to give out any info about Travis Bradley. Medical privacy laws. But they did have a record of a Lark Richards in their list of volunteers. You'd been volunteering at the nonprofit clinic. Helping organize the support group meetings, making food deliveries to people with mobility issues. That kind of thing."

I'm still staring at myself in the photo, begging for something to click in my brain so this all makes sense.

"Did you find anything else to suggest Lark knew my uncle?" Danny asks.

"Not yet. We're still looking into it. But we did learn something else." Rex pauses, and sympathy fills his dark eyes. "Lark, you left their volunteer list a couple of months ago. Apparently, there was an incident."

"Incident?" I ask.

"Accusations that you'd stolen from a patient you'd been delivering food to."

"*What?*" I choke out.

"They wouldn't give us any more information than that. And they chose not to press charges, so the real story is probably different. Misunderstandings happen."

Shudders run through me. "It doesn't sound like a misunderstanding. They think I'm a thief."

"We can't jump to conclusions," Danny says. "Don't assume you did something wrong." He's still gripping the back of my neck, but the rest of me keeps shaking. I'm going to be sick.

I swallow down what I'm feeling, all the shame and dismay, before speaking again.

"Will you tell us right away if you find out anything more?" I ask Rex.

"Of course. I'll let you both know." He gets up, shakes both our hands, and excuses himself.

"We knew it might be bad news," Danny murmurs.

"*Bad news?*" I've been trying to hold back my disgust, but now it's all spilling out. "Danny, I got kicked out of volunteering because I stole from people who *couldn't leave their homes*. What kind of person does that? What kind of person *am I?*"

"You were accused of something. That's all. Doesn't mean it's true."

"But—"

"*No.*"

He barks the word, as if he's laying down the law. I scoff. "You don't even know what I was about to say."

"I didn't need to. You were doubting yourself, going to those same dark places again. You said you wanted to keep searching for Travis, and I went along with it, but I've changed my mind. It's *hurting you*. And I'm not okay with it."

"My past is tied up with your uncle, and—"

"And my uncle has been in Southern California for at least the past six months, if not longer. He *left*. He could've come back to us. But he chose not to. You know who did come to West Oaks? *You*." He raises a finger to my lips when I try to open them. "You've done more for Nina in the past weeks than my uncle has in years. We all have shit in our pasts. What matters is *now*."

Danny holds my face in his hands and nudges our foreheads together. Pinning me right there. In the present. Like the two of us are all that matters.

"Maybe you don't remember your life from before six weeks ago, but you know who you are now. *I* know who you are. Nothing that Rex told us changed how I feel about you. And you know what? I'm done looking for Travis. I don't give a *shit* about finding him."

He's speaking so intensely, so passionately, that I feel the vibrations in his hands where he's touching me.

"But what about Nina?"

"If finding Travis means hurting you, there's no question about what she'll want to do. I don't care about the past. Not if it will take you away from me." Danny pulls me to him, my head against his chest, and I listen to his heartbeat. "I just want to hold on to you."

Guilt is eating me alive. I was supposed to do this for Nina. But it's one thing to choose the hard path when it's abstract. Another when the terrible facts are laid out in front of me.

"I want to hold on to you, too," I say.

"Then we will. I'll tell Rex we're not interested in knowing more. We're *done*."

29

Danny

*L*ark insists she doesn't want to leave the Pink House yet, so I go through the motions of catching up with my friends. But I've got her in the corner of my eye.

I swing by the grill to say hi to Aiden, clapping him on the back. "Food smells great."

"Thanks. You look happy." He's scowling, but I don't take it personally.

"I am." Hard to believe, but it's true.

This past week with Lark, my reluctance to keep searching for my uncle has only grown. I'd told Lark I would help her with it. We'd do it together. And I tried to follow through. But then we get the first bit of news from Rex, and it upsets Lark this much? No. I'm not playing along anymore.

I'm at peace with my decision about Travis. If I have to choose between finding my uncle and protecting Lark, there's no contest. I'm going to discuss it with Nina because this is her decision too, but I'm confident in what she'll say.

When I first met Lark, I was so determined to heal her. Put her pieces back together. But she's not broken. Took me a minute, but I finally got that through my head. She doesn't need her old memories if they're just going to drag her down.

If I could, I'd scrub my brain of the bad shit, too. Who wouldn't?

The news about my uncle's DUI, his being in Southern California without saying a word to us... It reminded me of the time when I was ten that Uncle Travis promised to take me to Knott's Berry Farm. I waited all day excited about rollercoasters and ice cream, and he never showed. Later I found out he'd argued with my father that day. My dad thought Travis was a bad influence and forbade Travis from spending time with me. I was so pissed at my father. But did Uncle Travis try to let me know? He didn't. He let me down.

When I was a teenager and Travis took off for good, I used to wish he'd come back. But as I got older, I accepted the fact that my uncle wasn't going to return. You can't make people love you, and it's far better to move on than to be the idiot who sticks around longing for something that will never be. I can't ever forget that lesson.

I'm finished with Travis, and as far as I'm concerned, Nina is too.

Aiden and I both look over at Lark, who's talking with our other roommates. "Why shouldn't I be happy?" I ask. "I got the girl, and I'm taking her out tonight."

"Something tells me you had that girl from minute one. You'd be stupid not to see that she's crazy about you."

Slices of skirt steak are waiting on a cutting board for tacos. I grab a piece and pop it into Aiden's mouth. He smirks at me as he chews. "You know, you're a good guy deep down, Aiden."

"Take that back."

"Nope, it's true. Someday, you'll find the right person who turns you into a softie and you'll be smiling like an idiot, too."

He shakes his head. "I'm immune."

Just you wait, I think, and clap him again affectionately on the back.

Not long after, Lark and I head home. I park in the driveway, tapping my hands on the steering wheel. "Go in and pack an overnight bag. And wear a pretty dress."

She arches an eyebrow. "Oh, really? You have big plans?"

"I do." I lean over and kiss her nose. "We're leaving in an hour, just as soon as I get Nina settled. I'm taking you on a date."

I'm going to give Lark all the happiness she deserves. Even if I have to remake the world, slay every dragon, even rewrite history to make it happen. I feel it with a desperate determination that goes all the way to the marrow of my bones.

I won't let the past hurt us. I refuse.

WE PULL up to a valet stand. "A hotel?" Lark cranes her neck as she stares up at the white building. "This is our date?"

"I thought we could use a night away. They have this courtyard full of exotic flowers. And botanical themes to all the rooms. I've never stayed here, but I read about it online. If you're not feeling it, though…"

She turns to me, eyes wide with wonder. "You picked this for me?"

"Of course I did." I slide my fingers into her hair, my hand resting at the back of her neck. "Just for you."

"Danny, I…*love* it."

"Wait until you actually see it."

The valet takes my keys while a bellhop gets our bags

from the trunk, and we head inside to check in. "This is too expensive," she whispers to me.

"Don't worry about it. I wanted to do this for you."

I've booked us an ocean-view suite. This place is on one of the fanciest stretches of Ocean Lane, and it's not my usual scene. But I have a little nest egg saved up from my military days, and if I can't dip into it for an occasion like this, then what's it for?

When I told Nina the idea, she was one hundred percent on board. Ryan's going to come in this afternoon, and between him, Starla and Jess, Nina is covered.

This night is just ours. I want to spoil my girl.

The bellhop takes our bags to the room, and Lark and I head straight for the courtyard. It's gorgeous, an open space several floors high, with huge trees growing in the center and long, flowering vines trailing over trellises and railings. Lark and I hold hands as we make a slow circuit, and she examines every unique bloom. But I can't take my gaze off of her. She's wearing a simple, knee-length black dress in a silky fabric, and her hair is pinned halfway up, the rest trailing down her exposed back.

She fits right in here. Her green eyes are as bright as the lush foliage surrounding us, and her smile might as well be the sun. This woman is turning me into a romantic. I'll probably start writing poems next, and Matteo will have to suffer through hearing my various drafts, because he's the most romantic asshole that I know.

Maybe I'll torture Aiden with them a little, too.

While she's studying a plant with spikes all over its stem, I wrap my arms around her waist and kiss her earlobe.

I've never had anyone who means what Lark does to me. Every other relationship I've had has been light and easy. But I don't want that with Lark. With her, I'm all-in for the complications, so long as we're focused on the present and our future. I've decided nothing else exists.

"Danny," she says quietly, "I should tell you something. When you were talking with Nina and Starla earlier, I called Cam."

"Oh, yeah?" I say, extremely nonchalant. I gave Lark her ex-boyfriend's number a few days ago, and I knew she had programmed it into her phone.

But Cam is one of those *past things* I'd much rather bury.

I reach around her to link our fingers, rubbing the back of her hand with my thumb.

"I wanted to ask him about what Rex told us," she says. "My volunteer work for that clinic where Travis was a patient. Cam said he didn't know anything about it. Another secret I was keeping from him, I guess. It's not that important, but I wanted you to know I spoke to him." She turns her head to look up at me. "I don't have secrets from you."

I lift my hand to cup her cheek. "I know, baby. It's okay."

"I don't want to be the person I was before."

My shoulders tense at the fresh reminder of the Bennett Security report. I refuse to believe that Lark would steal from some helpless person. And if she kept secrets from Cam, she had reasons. *None of it matters.*

"I don't want to be the same guy I was before, either. You make me better." I lean forward to capture her lips. We kiss for a little while in the courtyard, surrounded by sweet-smelling flowers and trees heavy with fruit.

For dinner, I've got a reservation at the hotel's beachside restaurant here. Our table is outside on the patio overlooking the water. We're there just in time for sunset, which I *totally* planned. Turns out I'm a natural at this romance thing. We sit next to each other at the tiny table, arms and thighs pressed together, as we sip champagne and order too many courses. I want to memorize Lark's expressions as she tastes each dish, her moans and gasps of surprise.

We order red wine with our entrees and another round of bubbly with dessert. Lark's cheeks bloom with pink, and as the sky darkens, fairy lights illuminate on the patio, reflecting in her eyes.

"I've been thinking about what you said last week. That you want to get a job?" We're sipping the last of our champagne. A jazz trio is playing over in the bar, and the soft strains of music drift over us.

"And you said no."

"I said we'd discuss it."

"Even though it's my life and my decision?" She tilts her head sardonically.

"What I'm *trying* to say is, if you really want to work for the Shelbornes' catering company, we can figure out a way to make it happen. My top priority is that you're safe. But Aiden would be around, obviously. He'd look out for you."

"You're okay with Aiden looking out for me? Assuming I can't do it myself?"

"We made our peace."

Lark smothers a laugh and leans over for a quick kiss. "Quinn said she could set me up with a lawyer to figure out my documents and legal status."

"There's a way to make it work. I have no doubt about that. But I also think you should consider going back to school. You should take the time to figure out what you really want to do." Twenty-four years old might not be too young compared to thirty-three, but it's still young. I want her to have every option.

She bites her lip and looks out at the ocean. "Maybe. I might like to do something related to plants. Like studying how they fit into their environments. That would be amazing.

But how could I afford it? I have no savings that I know of. *Nothing.*"

"We can figure that part out, too. I'll help you." I'm still determined not to take my father's handouts, and the salary of a firefighter isn't much to speak of. But if it's for Lark's benefit, then I would consider asking my dad for a loan.

I'd do just about anything for her.

"Danny, I can't—"

"Nope. I can be just as stubborn as my grandmother when I want to be."

She leans her shoulder into mine, our foreheads touching. "How did I get lucky enough to find you?"

"Funny, that's what I've been asking myself since we met."

"I want to deserve you," she whispers.

"You do. I promise you do."

When we get upstairs to the suite, I leave the lights off. I throw back the curtains and open up the balcony doors overlooking the hotel patio and the water. The warm glow of the restaurant's fairy lights gives us enough to see by, and lights from boats play across the waves, weaving with the moonlight. A cool breeze blows in, just this side of chilly. We huddle together on the balcony to admire the view. Below, glasses clink and utensils clatter in the restaurant, and the jazz trio sends up its rhythmic melodies.

Lark stands at the balcony railing, and my arms circle her waist from behind.

"I feel like Cinderella," she says. "Like this is all going to disappear because it's too perfect."

"I can't afford to move you in here. But if it's champagne and ocean views you need, I can work on that."

Lark turns around in my arms and looks up at me. "No, my needs are a lot simpler than that." She touches my face and pulls me down into a kiss.

We start out slow, gentle, our lips meeting and tongues brushing. I hold her face and trace her cheekbones with my thumbs. I'm trying to make every moment of tonight last, but our kisses turn heated almost immediately, the usual simmer between us already stoked by the sparkling wine and the nighttime ambience.

My hands rest on her hips, and I back us both up until we're through the door and just inside the room.

"Want me to close the balcony door?" I ask, kissing her neck. "Or leave it open?"

"Open."

I smile against her skin. "I knew you'd say that. You naughty girl, you." I slide the straps of her dress over her shoulders, kissing her breasts as soon as they're exposed. When the fabric pools at her feet, I find she's got nothing on underneath. "Mmmm." The humming sound I make mixes with the ambient noise and laughter drifting up from outside. "You're gorgeous."

"I want you naked, too."

I strip out of my clothes as quickly as possible. My button-down, my black jeans, my boxers—everything ends up in a pile on the floor. My cock bobs, long and heavy and ready to go.

"Somebody's excited." Lark drags her fingertip along my shaft, then grazes my slit, and my cock spasms.

"*Ughn*," I groan. Feels so fucking good. "It's not my fault. You're the one who does this to me." I fist the base of my swollen dick. "You like the fact that we can hear people downstairs with the door open. The possibility someone will see us."

"Maybe," she says. "It clearly turns you on too."

"Can you blame me for wanting to show you off?"

It's dark in this room, and given where we're standing on the fourth floor and the angle of the balcony and beach below, someone would need to have a high-powered scope on a ship at sea to spot us. But it's hot to think about it. Being with Lark in the open air does get my blood going. She seems freer and happier when we're outdoors.

Her arms circle me at the waist. I reach down to grab her ass, lifting her slightly so she has to go onto her tiptoes. I bend to kiss her neck. "You're stunning all the time, but especially naked, with your hair falling down your back. Your smooth, soft skin bared for me to kiss." Then I go to my knees at her feet. "And your pretty little pussy on display for me to tease."

I bring my hand up between her closed legs to tease her folds. Lark gasps, hands resting on my shoulders. I kiss her stomach. Her thighs. I suck a hickey into her skin just the way she likes, this one at her hip bone. While I worship her, Lark runs her fingers through my hair. When I glance up, she's looking down at me with reverence. Such innocent, sweet awe.

And *damn*, that makes me want to do such bad, dirty things to her. Because I know how much she loves it.

I stand up and lift her into my arms, carrying her to the desk, which is off to one side of the balcony door. My fist wraps around her hair and I tilt her head back as I kiss her, my tongue petting hers inside her mouth. She's got her hands braced behind her on the desk, back arched in a way that lifts her breasts.

Down on the beach, someone laughs and shouts. Glasses clink and the jazz musicians play in the restaurant.

"Don't scream too loud when I fuck you," I whisper in her ear, "or everyone downstairs will hear it. Probably everyone on the whole beach."

"No promises."

My hands go to her knees, pulling her legs open. I tilt her pelvis so she's at the right angle to take me, and then I work my dick into her with deliberate slowness. At first, just tiny pulses of my tip at her opening that make her gasp and whimper.

Lark's thighs clench at my hips, trying to draw me closer. "Please," she whines, "need you all the way in me."

I grab the edges of the desk and thrust hard, driving my pulsating shaft all the way inside. Lark cries out, arching her spine.

"Shhh. Everyone will hear how much you love my cock. That's supposed to be our secret."

Lark grins at me wickedly, clearly enjoying this game of ours. "You're just that good."

I laugh because being with Lark is more fun than I ever remember having. Making her smile, making her happy. Seeing our bodies meet in the mixture of darkness and moonlight—it's sexy and so incredibly beautiful.

I bend over to suck her pointed nipples while my dick pumps in and out of her slick channel. She moans.

"Shameless," I say. "What'll we do with you?"

"Fuck me harder?"

"Need you on the bed for that." I pull out and lift her into my arms again. We cross to the bed, where I drop her on the mattress, then roll her onto her stomach, dragging her hips up so I can kneel behind her. "You want my dick, baby?"

"Yes. Please! Give it to me."

My cock shoves back inside of her. Right where I belong.

"Danny!" She babbles as I thrust my swollen, aching shaft into her again and again. I've got one hand pressed to her lower back, the other gripping her thigh. The sounds of our heavy breaths and moans and bodies meeting combine with the ambient noise from below. And there *is* a real possibility someone outside could hear us. Especially if there's another hotel guest with their balcony open. But I can't bring myself to care.

Whatever my girl asks for, that's what I'll deliver.

When I feel the telltale clench in my balls, the tingle at the base of my spine, I pull out of her again. She complains, but I lie down on the mattress on my back. I enjoy every way of fucking Lark, but my favorite way to come is while I'm looking into her eyes.

I tap the tops of my thighs. "Right here. I want to watch you ride me."

Lark swings her leg over me, and I hold my cock upright so she can impale herself onto me. Her dark hair curtains around us. Brushes my arms and chest. The downstairs restaurant, the beach, the rest of the world—it all falls away in this little world that's just ours. Her hand rests on my pec just over my heart, and I press my palm to the same spot on her body.

Our hearts beat. Fast. Wild. But I'd swear they're in perfect time.

I can tell from the pitch of her cries, the clench of her legs, that she's close. I lift my upper body, propping against my elbows, just as she comes undone. Our mouths meet, her cries muffled against my own. My orgasm rips through me, turning my vision white despite the darkness. My balls empty. Filling her with my aching need. My incurable desire for this girl. Filling her with my love.

I love her.

Shit. I really do.

It takes me a moment to come back to this universe. For the world to resume. Dinner service continues downstairs, and it sounds like the jazz trio is wrapping up their set.

Lark is curled over me, her face tucked into my neck.

I'm in love with her.

I'm not sure if I'm ready to say it yet, or if she's ready to hear it. Except for Nina, I haven't said those three words to *anyone* since I was a child. But this feeling is bigger and deeper and, if I'm honest, fucking scarier than anything I've known.

I only met her a little over a month ago. During that time, she's been dealing with the kind of mental stress that most people can't even imagine. I've witnessed it, but that's not the same as experiencing it in my own head. Not just losing her memories, a massive piece of herself, but also facing a sick predator who's tried to hurt her and terrify her.

Lark needs someone to put her first. She needs love.

She keeps worrying that she doesn't deserve to be part of my family. But I'm just praying that my love can be enough for *her*.

30

Lark

*D*anny and I are both quiet, and the ambient noise from outside fills the silence. He draws circles on my back.

We've had a lot of good sex since we got together, but tonight is really something else. And it wasn't just the physical part. It was everything. This hotel, the courtyard full of plants, the dinner. The way we tease each other and manage to laugh while we're turning each other all the way on.

I've had a lot of bests with Danny, but this night takes the cake.

"Are you tired?" he asks.

I prop my chin on his chest. "Not even a little." It's not that late yet. But even if it was, I don't want to go to sleep. I want to enjoy this perfect night for as long as possible.

"Want to take a shower?"

"In the giant, luxurious bathroom fit for a princess? How is that even a question?"

Danny heats up the water, and we step under the spray. We wash each other with expensive body wash, kissing and caressing in between, and then we just hold one another. I love how affectionate Danny is.

"Nina said you've traveled a lot. What's your favorite place in the world you've visited?"

"Hiking Mount Kilimanjaro. That was incredible. Or anyplace where I can see the Milky Way at night."

I snuggle my head against his chest as the warm water sluices over us both. "I want to see the stars."

"We'll go camping. We've got some Dark Sky Parks here in Cali. Or we could hit Canyonlands and some other spots in Utah. All the red rocks and painted canyons. It's like another planet."

"You'll take me there?"

"Absolutely." He kisses my forehead. "I'll take you everywhere. New York and Paris and Berlin and Tokyo, when we've saved up enough to afford it. We'll pick places I haven't been, too. So we can experience them for the first time together." He holds my face and looks at me like I'm something he treasures. Someone who's worth all this effort.

I want so badly to see myself the way he does. I want to travel to all those places he's mentioned and more.

But when I venture out and dig into my past, that's when danger has threatened. Maybe my stepbrother—or whoever hurt me, whoever's continued to harass and follow me—will give up and leave me alone if I stay here. With Danny and Nina in West Oaks.

Maybe I was supposed to find Danny, not just so that he could help me through this, but so that I could help him with Nina too. So that I could *love* him. He's the best man that I've ever met, and if he cares about me, then I'll do whatever I can every single day to earn that.

"Where should we go first?" he asks.

"I just want a life here in West Oaks. A home. Being who I am now."

Danny smiles. "Good, because I think you're amazing. I wouldn't change a thing."

I shrug. "You're okay, too."

"Wow, careful with those over-the-top compliments. I'll get a bigger head than Matteo's."

"You're amazing," I whisper to him. "And I wouldn't change a single thing."

I want the future he talked about. *I want a life with you.* It's on the tip of my tongue. I don't say it yet, but I feel it all the way to the core of my being. The clearest, simplest truth that I know.

If he loved me… Could I ever be that lucky?

Danny is worth everything, and that includes letting go of my doubts. Letting go of my fears about myself.

～

WE FALL into bed and sleep. In the morning, the bright sky wakes us. We make love bathed in diffused sunlight, Danny moving on top of me. He pins my hands over my head, his cock hard and thrusting as he covers my neck and breasts with love bites and kisses. We're all golden skin and white sheets and contented sighs. A perfect contrast to the moody darkness of the night before. I'm with Danny, so of course it feels exactly right.

We're supposed to have this. Nights and mornings and all the hours in between.

We come staring into each other's eyes. Danny's are endless blue, just like the sky. Then it's open-mouthed kisses and cuddles and sweet whispered words. Quinn was right. We're so adorable, I can hardly stand us. But I can't stop smiling either.

After another shower in the luxurious bathroom, we dress and walk down the beach to a small bakery. We stroll along the water and drink our coffees, holding hands. "Have you checked in with Nina?" I ask.

Danny's fingers slide under my hair to the back of my neck. Seems to be one of his favorite places to touch me. "Yeah, Matteo is there. Nina's up, and Ryan just got on shift. But Matteo's going to stay until we're home."

"That's nice of him."

"We're going to owe him and Angela a million hours of babysitting once their kiddo arrives. You up for that?"

That thought makes me smile. "I doubt I know anything about babies, but it would be fun to learn." *With you. Everything with you.*

On our way back to the hotel, we stop at a fancy florist's shop on Ocean Lane. I slow down and linger, admiring the bunches of long-stemmed flowers that the florist has on display out front.

"Want to take some home?" Danny asks.

I smile. "I'll make a bouquet for Nina."

"She'd love it. I'll go inside to pay."

I hum a melody as I pick and choose from the array of flowers. Some pink roses, because they're classic like Nina. Pink dahlias. A few eucalyptus branches.

But I stop moving when goosebumps prickle all over my skin. My happy feelings wither and decay.

It's that instinct I get sometimes. That awful feeling that someone is watching me. I try to breathe through it as I scan the faces of people on the street. Most of them aren't paying me any attention, just going about their mornings.

Then I see him a block away. A man with a dark windbreaker, his hat pulled low, his eyes in shadow. His body is turned partly away from my direction. But I'd swear he's watching me. I can *feel* his eyes.

Every instinct inside me is screaming. My throat closes

up. My lungs stop working, and the flowers droop in my hand.

I know him I know him I know

Danny walks outside, and the bell on the shop door jingles. "Paid up. Are you—Lark? What's wrong?"

"Danny, I saw—" I start to turn back and point. But the man is gone. "He was just…" The words won't come out.

"What did you see?" Before I can reply, his phone rings. Danny pulls it from his pocket. Looks at the screen. A crease appears between his brows. "It's Matteo."

I'm still trembling. I stare down the block at the corner where the man in the cap was standing.

Who was he? Was he really watching me?

Is this how I'll always feel, terrified I'm being followed, looking over my shoulder and wondering, *will this be the day that it all catches up to me?*

The perfect bubble of our night together vanished so quickly. Like it had never been real.

Danny shifts his weight as he answers the phone. Matteo starts talking, and the color leaches from Danny's face.

"Is she…?" Danny's Adam's apple quakes in his throat. "Okay. Okay. I'm on my way." Danny lowers the phone, his face stricken.

A dahlia drops to the sidewalk. "Nina?" I ask.

"We need to go."

～

I GRAB our bags from the room while Danny gets the car. We race home, pushing the Charger's engine. Danny has barely said anything, but I feel the tension and anxiety pouring off of him in waves.

"Matteo said Nina isn't breathing well," he says haltingly. "It's possible she's overdosed on morphine."

"Did Matteo call an ambulance?" I ask.

"No, Lark," Danny says tightly. "She's in hospice. That means no treatment or resuscitation. That's not how I want things to be, but it's Nina's choice."

My stomach twists. I can't imagine having to make these kinds of decisions for my life, or for someone I love.

I reach over and touch Danny's arm, but he's gripping the steering wheel with both hands. I can't tell if he notices my touch or not. I want to say something to reassure him, but what?

If he loses Nina now, when he was with *me*, I don't know if I'll be able to forgive myself. I know that's ridiculous because it's not my fault. Nina's illness is terminal. We all know that. But it's too soon for her to be gone. Way too soon.

Danny punches the gas at the next green light. It feels like hours by the time we turn onto Danny and Nina's Street, though it couldn't have been more than fifteen minutes.

The moment we're out of the car, Danny races for the door. I'm right behind him. When we get into the house, voices are coming from Nina's room. Danny runs straight there, but my steps slow in the hallway outside Nina's door.

I can't bring myself to go in there. If she doesn't make it...

Matteo comes out into the hall. "Lark, you should go in," he murmurs. His olive skin has gone pale. "Nina might not have long."

Oh, God. I clasp my hands over my mouth. "Isn't there anything they can do?"

"Ryan and Danny are doing what they can to make her comfortable. She's still breathing, but it's touch and go."

"But what *happened*? How could she have overdosed?"

"I don't know." Matteo's phone makes a noise, and he

glances at it. "That's Angela. I need to call her back. Do you need anything?"

I shake my head. What I need is for Nina to be all right. "No, go ahead." Matteo steps into the living room. I keep vigil in the hallway because I just can't go in there and see Nina lying unconscious in her bed. I can't bear it.

How could everything seem so wonderful this morning and fall apart so fast? It really was a Cinderella moment. A fantasy.

And you always fall for it.

"She's going to be okay," I mutter, pacing. "She has to be."

I didn't even get the bouquet for her. I left the roses and dahlias behind. And that makes me think of flowers at a funeral, on a grave, and I just can't let my mind spiral. I *can't*.

My chest is too tight. I can't breathe in here, can't handle the fear that Danny will walk out of Nina's room with a heartbroken look on his face.

Get away from here. That's what my instincts are telling me. I have a tendency to run away from things. I know that. But right now, the impulse is too strong to ignore.

Just for a minute. So that I can breathe.

I open the front door and step outside, gulping down fresh air. My feet take me out into the yard. Normally, the fresh smell of greenery steadies me. Since the moment I arrived here, I've loved all the trees and plants that surround Nina's house. This place has felt like a refuge. Even knowing about Nina's illness, I still convinced myself that nothing could touch us here.

But that's always been a lie.

The front yard has never looked so dark before, filled with so many pockets of shadow between the trees and the hedges.

My eyes are drawn down the street. I can't see the skid

marks on the concrete. Hedges block the stretch of road where that car ran into me. But my heart races, picturing the scene.

Then I get that eerie feeling. Eyes, studying me. As if someone's watching me, closing in. But is it *real*? Or just fear playing tricks on me? Like seeing that man on Ocean Lane this morning when I was at the flower shop…

My phone rings, the sudden shrill sound jolting my entire body.

Jeez, I am *way* too wound up.

It could be Danny calling me from inside the house with news. No matter what's happened, I need to be there for him. I scramble to take out my device. My screen says, *Cam*. Maybe I should let the call go to voicemail. But I find myself swiping the screen to answer.

"Hello?"

"Hey. How are you?"

My eyes are still darting around, searching the shadows of the yard. For what, I don't know. "Did you need something?"

"You sound upset."

I grit my teeth. "There's a lot going on. If this isn't important, then it's really not a good time to—"

"Lark, wait. I've been thinking a lot since you called yesterday. There's something I didn't tell you before."

"Yes?"

"I still have a box of things of yours, stuff you left behind. A sweatshirt and a shell necklace I bought for you. I'd like you to have them." I don't respond, and he rushes to go on. "And there's a planner too. Like a calendar? Where you kept track of your schedule. Since you're trying to figure out how to get your memories back, I thought this could help."

I briefly close my eyes in frustration. Cam should've told me about this stuff before. But Danny and I already decided not to look into my past anymore. "I don't want my memories. I just want to move on."

"But the journal mentions the name 'Travis.' He's the person you were looking for, right? That picture you showed me?"

My shoulders hunch forward. I almost say yes. But Danny and I have been through this. We made our decision.

"We're not looking for Travis anymore," I say.

"Could I bring these things to you? Could I come see you?"

"*No.* That's not a good idea."

"Lark, I—"

I end the call without saying goodbye, my heart thundering in my chest.

When will this be over? Truly over?

Danny and I both thought it was enough to choose to be happy. But that's not really true. We can't make Nina healthy again.

I can tell Bennett Security to stop investigating, close off my mind and my heart to who I used to be. But I can't stop my past from finding me, can I?

Can I?

A twig snaps behind me. I go to whirl around, but a rough hand covers my mouth, another clasping my throat so tightly I can't scream.

Cold. Ice cold.

"Hello, little sister," a low voice hisses in my ear. "Still think you can run?"

31

Lark

*E*very cell in my body is frozen in place. I can't move. Can't breathe. White fills my vision.

Headlights, aiming straight for me.

And I'm caught in their snare.

"Do you know who I am?" He's speaking quietly, a hoarse whisper. Almost as if he's trying to disguise his voice. Or maybe he's just trying to avoid being overheard. We're right outside Danny and Nina's house. Minutes from help. Two muscled, overprotective firefighters are nearby, but they might as well be a world away.

I'm paralyzed. Trapped in a nightmare.

"I'm going to loosen the hand over your mouth, but if you scream, I'll make you very sorry." His grip on my throat tightens for a moment. A warning. Though I doubt I could get my vocal cords to work enough to curse him, much less cry out.

The fingers over my mouth shift enough that I can speak.

"You're Z," I manage to croak.

My stepbrother.

"That's what you used to call me to your little boyfriend. The old one, not the new guy. I'll give Bradley credit. He's good at keeping you close. Better than I was."

My arms and legs shake with indignation. "Don't talk about Danny."

"I'll say whatever I want. I know a lot more than you imagine, baby sister. I know you were just on the phone with Cam. You really don't remember anything from before, do you? Because if you did, you wouldn't give Cam another moment of your time. You wouldn't trust him for a second."

My bravery surges. "You're the one I don't trust. Show me your face, you piece of—" I choke on the words, fighting to breathe as he squeezes my windpipe again.

"There was a time you wouldn't have dared speak to me that way." He loosens his grip, and I gasp in a lungful of air. Z leans close enough that his exhales tickle the back of my ear. "You thought you could run from me, double-cross me, and I meant to punish you for that. But you're like a cockroach, Lark. You don't go down on the first try, do you?"

I blink rapidly, praying someone will come out of the house. Walk down the street. Anything. But we're in the shadows of Nina's front yard, completely alone. "You were driving the car."

"Of course I was. I found out you were planning to come to West Oaks. I caught up to you, like I always do when you run. I *always* catch you. And Danny Bradley might've helped you get away for a while, but I've known where you were every second that you've been in West Oaks. I've been close. Watching. Since before you went to Solvang, even before you got back from the hospital."

No. I squeeze my eyes closed.

But I felt him, didn't I? Felt him watching. Right on this street.

"At first," he says, "I thought you might be faking the

amnesia thing. I wasn't sure if you were setting a trap for me, so I stayed away. We needed Kathy Sullivan to check on your story."

"You're the one who hired her."

He doesn't respond to that. Probably because it's obvious. "I was surprised as anyone to find out your mind really was a blank. Kathy was supposed to deliver you to me, but once again, Bradley played your savior."

I remember Kathy's phone conversation. She must've been talking to *him*. And then, the dark SUV that Danny told me about. The driver who stared as we fled the parking lot. "You were there at the travel stop."

"I've been *everywhere*, Lark," he hisses. "You thought you could start a new life with a new family, but I've been here. I've been *close*. Biding my time for an opportunity like today."

My skin crawls where he's touching me. I'd turn myself inside-out if I could to make it stop. "Did you do this? Did you hurt Nina?"

"Maybe I did, maybe I didn't."

"I swear, if you did anything to her, I'll—"

He grabs my throat hard enough to leave bruises. "You'll *what*? Scream for your boyfriend? He's busy. I can do whatever I want to you. Deep down, you know that's true. You're brave enough to run, but not to fight me."

No. No, no, no.

I want to deny it.

But when he tried to run me down in the car, I froze. And even now, I can barely move. My legs are stuck in place, as if vines and roots have sprung up from the ground and tangled around me, holding me fast.

"Why won't you just let me go?" I force out. "Just leave me alone and forget about me. I don't know who you are or what you look like. I'll tell the police to stop looking for you."

"If they knew why you really came to West Oaks, they

would've arrested you before you got here. You want to know why I won't let you go? You want to know the *real* Lark?" He drags me a few steps back. Deeper into the shadows between the trees and the hedges. "You grew up the same way as me. Scraping to get by. Lying, cheating and stealing. We got good at it. But I was fair to you. Always. I took care of you, and you betrayed me."

"Cam said you were controlling. You weren't taking care of me. You were *hurting* me."

"Bullshit. Cam didn't know anything except the lies you told him. He was a mark, like all the rest. You used him." I try to shake my head, but he's still holding onto my throat. "You volunteered at that clinic so you could scout for sad, lonely people who needed a friend. Like Travis Bradley."

"*No,*" I whisper. Tears sting my eyes.

"You're the one who realized Travis had a loaded family he hadn't seen in decades. Nina Bradley was a perfect mark. Rich old lady, sick, eager to reunite with her son. You sent the emails to her. You were supposed to get her to send money to an account I set up, and then we'd vanish. That was the plan. Simple. We'd done it plenty of times before."

Acid burns in my stomach. I'm going to throw up.

"But then, you decided you wanted more. You wanted to cut me out of the deal. You came straight to West Oaks to meet Nina in person, get enough money from her that you could run away and disappear forever."

"That's not true." It can't be.

"You *knew* I'd come after you, just like I did. But then you forgot your own plans. You were pretending to be a good, sweet, innocent girl, and when you lost your memory, you became your own cover story. But that's not you, Lark. You're just as devious and cruel and vindictive as I am." He pulls me against him, close enough his lips graze my ear. "You're mine, and you always will be."

"No!" I struggle against his hold. For the briefest moment, his fingers slip from my neck, but then he's got me cinched up against him, my back to his chest.

"Still refuse to believe me? Fine, you can keep up with your charade. But it's going to cost you. Two hundred thousand dollars to buy your freedom."

"Two hundred *thousand*? Are you insane?"

"You're underestimating how rich the Bradley family is. If you pay up, you can stay in West Oaks and play house with your firefighter and his dying grandma."

"I won't."

"Then I'll hurt you again when you least expect it. But I'll take out your firefighter too, like I tried to do the night I first chased you here to West Oaks. I'll run him down and leave him nothing but a smear on the—"

I don't know where the courage comes from, but suddenly it's there, surging up inside of me. Pure rage. Danny has protected me, cared for me, and damn it, I will do anything to protect *him*. I won't let anyone hurt Danny or Nina.

I slam my head backward into Z's face.

Z screams. For several seconds, time moves in slow motion. I turn toward him. I have to see him. I have to *know*. But his hands are covering his face, and blood is gushing from his nose. He's stumbling backward into the hedges.

So I decide to get the heck out of there.

I run for the front of the house, screaming at the top of my lungs.

I dash up the porch steps. The front door flies open, and both Danny and Matteo race out of the house.

I collide with Danny's open arms. "Lark, what—"

"It's my brother! He's here!" I point at the hedge where Z just disappeared through the gap, fleeing to the next-door neighbor's property.

"Matteo, stay with her," Danny shouts.

Then he takes off. My arms are still outstretched, reaching out for him, but he's gone.

32

Danny

I push through the hedge, ignoring the scratches the rough branches leave on my skin, and tear across the next property. The neighbor's yard is dappled in sun and shadow.

There. I see a man's back as he flees. Dark clothes, dark brown hair. A sturdy build. He doesn't pause or hesitate. The man shoves his way through another set of hedges.

I race after him. Branches snag on my clothes. I come out on a street that runs perpendicular to mine. My head swivels as I search up and down for the guy who's running.

But he's gone. Fucking vanished into thin air.

I tug my phone out and call the police. "I'm Danny Bradley, West Oaks FD. A man attacked my girlfriend. He tried to kill her before. He's fleeing on foot as we speak." I give the dispatcher the cross streets and my address, plus my best attempt at a description of Z.

If West Oaks PD moves fast, they'll be able to set up a perimeter and catch some sign of him. If he's got a car parked in the vicinity, hopefully they'll spot him.

After I hang up, I bellow a curse, slamming the side of my fist into the nearest tree trunk.

I can't believe Z was here. Right here in Nina's neighborhood. Outside her home. And I had no clue. I don't know what exactly he did to Lark, if she just saw him and ran or if it was worse. But rabid, virulent fury is pouring through my veins like a toxin.

I almost lost Nina today.

And then, Lark.

I'd ask how this day could get any worse, but that dumbass question answers itself. If I had lost them, it would've been *my fault*.

The two people I love most in this world, and I didn't protect them.

I smack my fist into the tree trunk again. Blood wells from cuts across my knuckles. I allow myself five seconds of feeling the tsunami of shit that almost came down on me today. *Fuck*.

Then I stop, panting as I catch my breath.

I head back to the house. My teeth grit as I jog, taking the sidewalk this time.

Lark is on the porch with Matteo, hugging her elbows. She stands when she sees me. "Anything?"

"He's gone. West Oaks PD is on their way." I mount the steps, and Lark walks into my open arms. I run my hands over her, searching for anything that might be wrong. "You're okay? Did he hurt you?"

Then I spot the smudges on her neck. The beginnings of finger-shaped bruises on her fair skin. And I nearly snap. Red paints my vision.

If I find him, I'm going to kill him.

"I'm okay," Lark says. "What about Nina? Please tell me she's all right."

My rage settles when I see the fear in Lark's eyes. I pull

her close and slot her as tightly as I can against me. "She's getting there. It was bad. But she's pulling through."

Nina was in terrible pain last night. While I was gone with Lark, my grandmother was in *pain*, and Jess was trying to help. She gave Nina a hefty dose of morphine. Ryan gave Nina more meds this morning, and it turned out to be too much. Not enough to paralyze her lungs and stop her breathing entirely, thank God. But too much.

The morphine is wearing off now, and we're not going to give her any more for a while. I'll make sure she doesn't get that high a dose again. But I've known all along that this kind of thing can happen. Pain management isn't an easy calculus. I have no reason to think Jess or Ryan did anything wrong. But everything went to hell this morning all at once, and I wasn't ready for it. Not even close.

And somehow, Lark's stepbrother managed to strike at the very moment we were most vulnerable. Like he'd been waiting for it.

"Are you sure you're not hurt?"

Lark nods. But I see a flicker in her eyes. There's more she's not telling me. Maybe she can't say it in front of Matteo, who's standing off to the side, watching us with a fierce frown.

I kiss Lark's forehead. "Why don't you go inside, and I'll be there in a second?"

"Okay. I'll check on Nina."

"Sure. She's not awake, but Ryan's with her."

Lark goes inside. I hold my breath until the door closes again. Then I turn to my friend.

"I tried to get Lark to wait inside when you ran off," Matteo says, "but it was all I could do to keep her here on the porch."

"Thanks, man. You've done a lot for me today."

He reaches out to squeeze my shoulder. "I'd do it all

again. Just ask. I feel like shit for not realizing Lark had left the house before. I was answering a call from Angela."

If blame is going around, it'll fall squarely on my shoulders. Not my best friend's. "We're all doing our best." Even if that's nowhere near enough. "Is Angela all right?"

"Yeah, some Braxton-Hicks contractions. They're no big deal, but it's not pleasant."

"Do you need to get home?"

"Nah, she's at work for now. You know Angela. Not much can drag her away from her cases. I'll stay here a few more hours. Make sure everything's kosher."

We both go inside. "Could you let me know when West Oaks PD arrives?" I ask. I'll have to check our cameras as well to see if they caught anything.

"Sure thing."

"Thank you."

I make a quick detour to the bathroom to wash the blood from my scraped knuckles and slap a bandage over them. I find Lark hovering in Nina's doorway. Nina's still unconscious, and Ryan is monitoring her vitals closely. He handled the crisis well, actually. He was already giving Nina oxygen when I stormed in earlier. I don't know him as well as Jess or Starla, but I'm glad I can count on him. Too bad I can't clone myself so I can be everywhere I need to be at once.

"Hey," I whisper to Lark. "Can we talk?"

She leads the way to her bedroom. It's dark in here, but Lark doesn't bother to turn the light on. Her bed is made, but there are a few items of clothing out. Must've been from packing for our night out.

Lark tugs the curtain closed, blocking off the view of the backyard that she loves so much and pulling us further into shadow.

She sinks onto the edge of the mattress, and I sit beside her, turning to face her. "I'm sorry," I say. "This is on me."

Last night, I let down my guard, focusing on how much I wanted Lark instead of the danger that's constantly surrounding us. As if I could banish Z and every other threat just by wishing it. I should've known better. I *do* know better. I fucked up.

But my words manage to make things worse. Because Lark's face crumples. "No, *I'm* sorry."

"Why?"

"Because of what I did. He…he told me."

Her stepbrother. I take Lark's hands in mine. "What did that fucker say to you?"

She speaks in a monotone. "It was exactly what I was afraid of. I'd met Travis through my volunteer work, and I found out about Nina having money. I'm the one who sent the emails to Nina. Z and I worked together on planning it out. I decided to double-cross Z and come to West Oaks directly, but it was always about conning her. Getting her money."

"Lark. The guy tried to kill you. Kidnap you. Who knows what else. You can't believe him."

Her eyes harden. "But it makes sense with what Cam told me. Today, Cam said he found my planner, and I'd mentioned Travis in it. I—"

"Wait, what journal? You spoke to Cam today? When?"

"It was right after we got home. I went outside. Cam called. Said he'd found some calendar of mine that had Travis's name. Cam wanted to bring it to me. I was distracted. And the moment I hung up, that's when my brother grabbed me."

Another wave of rage roars through me, so intense my vision fades at the edges.

So it wasn't just her stepbrother involved in this. Cam called her. Was his timing coincidental? Or did he actually have something to do with Z's attack on Lark today?

Was it all bad luck? Or was Cam's phone call part of some choreographed dance? I don't know what the hell to believe anymore.

"Did you recognize anything about him? Anything that could form the basis of a description for the cops?"

"I didn't see his face. His voice was...hoarse. Quiet."

"Was it familiar?"

Her eyes are glazed, staring and unfocused. "I can't tell anymore. What's familiar, what's not. What instincts are real. Z admitted he's the one who tried to kill me. He said he's been close. Watching me. *Us*. Z said I can buy my freedom for two hundred thousand dollars, but if I don't pay, he'll come after me. He had his hand around my throat, and the whole time I couldn't move. I couldn't do anything. I was too scared."

"But you did get away. Matteo and I came running because we heard you screaming."

She blinks her long lashes. "He said he would hurt you, and I couldn't stand it. That's when I finally fought back."

I tuck her hair over her ears, looking into her beautiful, soulful, sorrowful eyes. Those eyes prove to me that she's not what her brother says. "Exactly. When it counted, you did what you had to."

"Did I, though?" Her voice is a whispered plea. "Every time we learn something new, it's worse."

There's a soft knock at the door. "Danny?" Matteo says. "The officers are here. They're ready to take your statements."

"Are you up for talking to them?" I ask her.

"They can come in." That glazed look is back. As if she doesn't care either way.

"Do you want me to stay?"

She shrugs, her gaze cast downward. "You don't have to. Go be with Nina."

"But Lark—"

"Don't you *dare* say this doesn't change anything, Danny. Please. I know when a man is humoring me." She wraps her arms around herself and walks to the other side of the room. Away from me.

And that new distance rips me right down the middle.

"Are we okay?" I ask. "You and me?"

"How can we be?" she whispers.

There's another knock. I go to the door and open it. Cliff is right outside with Matteo and another patrol officer, a woman. "Did you catch him?" I ask Cliff.

"We're working on it. I need whatever info you can give us."

I nod, then clear my throat as I step out into the hall. "Can Lark and I give our statement together? Or…"

Cliff frowns. "It really needs to be separate. That's policy."

Shit, that's what I figured.

If Lark had asked me to stay with her, I would've found a way. But she didn't. And unlike when she asked me to leave at the travel stop, I think she meant it this time. She needs space from me. What Z said to her snapped something inside of her that was already wounded. And it's ripping out my guts to witness it.

How do I help her? What do I do?

I've asked myself that question so many times. I've never felt more unsure of the right answer.

"Okay, let's get it done," I say.

The female officer goes into Lark's room, while Cliff stays with me. "Tell me what happened?" he asks me.

I go through the events from this morning from my perspective. I give the best description of Z that I can, which isn't much. I don't share what Lark told me, leaving that up to her. Whatever she wants to tell the police, that's her story and her choice.

But as I speak, my thoughts are spinning out like tires over wet concrete.

From that first glimpse I had of Lark, bathed in the fierce glow of headlights, I was pulled into a situation I didn't fully understand. I've been reacting. Trying to do what she asked of me, give her what she needs. I've tried to make her feel safe. Told her that the past didn't have to matter.

How fucking *wrong* I was.

Z came here to our home and hurt the girl I love. That is never happening again. I have to make sure of it.

But I can't just keep reacting.

I have to make a move. Lark managed to fight for herself this afternoon, and I'm going to fight for her, too.

I have to find some *answers*.

When I'm finished with Cliff, I leave him there in the hall as he makes notes on his phone. The other officer is still with Lark.

I go to the living room, where Matteo is standing. But he's not alone. Quinn and Aiden are here. Both of them step toward me when they see me, concern and empathy all over their faces. Even Aiden's.

"What're you doing here?" I ask.

"Cliff told us something was up," Quinn says. "We came straight here, and Matteo was just filling us in. We want to help."

Aiden nods at a cooler that's sitting on the couch. "And I brought stuff to cook. Figured somebody might need to eat."

Every muscle in my body is wound as tight as a spring, but I loosen up just a notch. My friends are here. Wow. I have never been so relieved to see them. "That would be incredible. And really good timing."

"Where's Lark?" Quinn asks. "Giving her statement?"

"Yeah, in her room. She's…" I clear my throat. "She's not okay."

"Then I'd better go see her." Quinn gives me a quick, one-armed hug as she passes on her way to Lark. I blow out a breath. *Thank you.* Lark needs her friend right now.

Then I turn to Aiden and Matteo. Two guys who, when it comes down to it, I trust nearly as much as I trust myself. Both trained ex-military. Both more than able to watch over Lark and Nina while I'm gone and bring down hell on anyone who gets in their way.

"There's something I need to do," I say. "An errand I need to run. Can you both stay a few hours?"

They tip their heads affirmatively. "But do you need backup on this errand of yours?" Aiden asks.

"No. I'd rather you stay here. I think it'll be faster if I handle this alone."

"Be careful," Matteo says, frowning.

I grab my keys, making no promises.

33

Danny

This drive into Solvang is nothing like the one I took with Lark.

That day, I remember how hopeful Lark seemed as we arrived in town. She thought she was doing something to help my grandmother. We had no idea that Lark's own history was tied up here.

Was Z following us then? Lark said he's been close enough to watch us. That was the day some asshole keyed my car and left that note for Lark. I assumed it was her stepbrother, and I'm sure I was right.

If he's been close this whole time, then where the hell has he been hiding? Lark doesn't know what he looks like, so he could've been in plain sight.

I thought I was satisfied with my life before her, but I had no idea what happiness really felt like. It's wholeness when you know the sting of being alone. Pledging your heart to someone, fully aware of the risks. There's no true happiness without feeling the possibility of loss. I didn't let myself take those risks before because I didn't want to get hurt.

What I feel for Lark, the *love* I feel, is worth it.

But losing her is not an option.

I park and head toward Sugar & Yeast Café. The answers are here somewhere, the clues to Lark's past, and I'll do whatever it takes to find them. Even if it means tearing apart every inch of this town.

Even if it means tracking down my uncle, someone I had no desire to ever see again.

But there's one person who definitely knows more than he's been saying. If I have to tear *him* apart to learn what he's hiding, that's what I'll do.

I barge into the café. Denise is behind the register again, and her eyes widen when she sees me. My fists are clenched as I storm over to the counter.

"Where's Cam?"

I'm usually an easygoing guy, but I've got a scowl that can get some shit done. I honed it back when I was Doc to a bunch of wily soldiers. They could've told you that when I'm on a warpath, you might want to clear the way.

Denise steps aside, and there he is. The target of my ire. Lark's ex-boyfriend who just *happened* to call her offering up new info just before Z attacked her.

"Danny?" Cam says, glancing around. "What's up? Is Lark here too?"

"No, she's not." I vault the counter and collide with Cam, backing him up until he hits the opposite wall. Stacks of paper coffee cups topple over. Cam yelps, and there are shouts of indignation and surprise from others in the café. I bar my arm across his neck. Cam looks ready to piss himself. "She's back in West Oaks, terrified because her stepbrother attacked her today."

"*What?*"

"He had his fucking hands around her throat. Right after you called her up like you were trying to distract her. Were you working together? Do you know where her brother is? If you do and you don't start talking, I swear to you—"

"I'm calling the cops," Denise yells behind me.

Cam holds up his hands. "No. It's fine. It's all...fine. Danny and I are going to talk out back. If you'll let go of me long enough for that?" he asks me.

Slowly, I step back from him. But then I grab his bicep and drag him toward the café's back door, hauling him out. Cam stumbles, catching himself against the brick wall of the next building over.

"Is Lark all right?" he asks. "Did Z hurt her?"

"Not yet. She got away in time. But you'd better tell me what you've been holding back. *Everything*. Right now."

"Okay. Okay." He wipes at the sweat beading on his forehead. "I have a box of things that belong to Lark in my trunk. It's parked right around the corner. That's why I called her earlier. I'll just give it to you. I had no idea about her brother being there."

"And why didn't you tell Lark about her stuff before? Because you wanted to have something else to hold over her?"

He flinches, looking down at the concrete. "It's stuff she left behind on purpose, mostly. Things I gave to her and she didn't want anymore when she left me. Okay? And yeah, maybe I was trying to find a way to see her again, or I was trying to hold on to some small piece of her. Do you really have no idea how that feels?"

My fists clench and unclench.

With any other woman before Lark, I wouldn't have known what he meant. But Cam said before that he loved her. So I guess we do have something in common.

"I want everything that belongs to her," I say.

"Fine. It's yours."

Cam takes me around the block to a parking lot. I'm

watching for any sign that he's trying to trick me or pull a fast one, but he just pops his trunk, grabs a cardboard box from inside, and lifts it up.

"This is everything."

I take the box. A sweatshirt is folded on the top. "All right. But what else does Lark need to know? I want every confession you've been holding back. About her identity, her stepbrother. I don't care how small." It's clear there's something else. I can read the guilt all over his face.

He's chewing his lower lip ragged. After another moment, he says, "Z came by once when Lark wasn't home. This was maybe three months ago. Z said Lark was sneaking around and planning something dangerous. He said he wanted to protect her. She'd already told me enough about him that I was wary, but...he offered me money to find out where she'd been going. She'd been keeping secrets from him, too."

"And you took the payoff?"

"It wasn't about the money! I was worried about her. I started trying to figure out what she was up to, and Lark caught me following her. She was so angry. She stormed off. It was that night she came home with bruises, and we argued and broke up."

"Do you think she went to confront Z about it? That's where the bruises came from?"

"Maybe. I don't know. But that's the last that I saw her until you guys walked into the café."

"Do you have her stepbrother's address? Phone number? Anything we could possibly use to find him or identify him?"

"If I had anything on him, I would give it to you if it meant helping Lark. But I don't."

I glare at him until I'm convinced he's telling the truth. "I don't want you contacting Lark anymore. If she decides to call you, that's her choice. But you're done."

"Would you at least tell her I'm sorry?"

"No."

"Come *on*, man. You got her. You don't have to be a jerk about it, too."

I tuck the box under my arm. "Fine. I'll tell her you're sorry. Because she deserves to hear it, not to make you feel better."

He slinks back to the café.

I CARRY the box to my car and set it in a rear bucket seat to sort through. I'm not trying to hide. If Z followed me here, I would love for him to show his face. That would mean he's not in West Oaks with Lark.

I set aside the sweatshirt, as well as some other clothing and pieces of jewelry. There's a single sneaker, probably forgotten by accident.

And then, the planner Cam mentioned to Lark on the phone. It's for this calendar year. Did she leave it behind by accident? Did Cam purposefully keep it in his effort to spy on her? Impossible to say.

I flip through it carefully, noting Lark's expressive hand-writing. She wrote down her appointments and tasks, including several mentions of *the clinic*. That's where she volunteered, the same place where Travis was a patient.

And there it is—Travis's name and a phone number. She's underlined it twice.

Right away, I take out my phone and dial the number. But it's out of service.

Is it possible that what Z told her is true? She really meant to con Nina out of money with those emails about Travis? What did my uncle really have to do with the scheme?

The thing is, I wish I didn't need to know. Not if it could

hurt Lark. And maybe there's an inkling of fear inside me, too. A worry that I'll eventually learn something that makes me doubt her. *What if...*

But if my uncle is our only lead to finding Lark's evil step-brother, then I'll have to follow it.

I study every page of the planner, hoping for something useful to pop out at me. Nothing does. Then I start at the beginning and try again. There has to be something.

Finally, I notice an address. It's written sideways on a random page, easy to miss. Easy to disregard, because Lark wrote down lots of things in her planner. But when I plug the address into Google Maps, I find that it's for a vineyard that's about twenty minutes from here, where the land is hilly and rural. The street view shows a quiet road with rolling hills in the distance, the kind of place Lark would adore.

And then I spot a weeping willow tree a little down the road from the vineyard entrance. Like the tree in Nina's backyard.

A hunch slots into position in my brain.

I toss the cardboard box into my trunk and jump into the driver's seat.

～

LESS THAN HALF AN HOUR LATER, I pull the Charger onto the side of a rural road. Fields of wine grapes grow on hills into the distance. About a hundred yards ahead, I spot a stone and wrought-iron sign, which marks the entrance to a winery. But there's a low-lying area to my right, with a small creek, where a weeping willow grows on the bank.

Over near the willow, the only sign of life is an old camper, which is parked just off the road.

The moment I step out of my car, warm air and sweet-smelling plants greet me. A gentle breeze ruffles the hanging branches of the willow. This place says *Lark* all over it, so much that it makes me ache for her.

I wish she were here with me right now. Even if she's got no real connection to this place, she'd love it. She'd want to move right in. I'd lay down a blanket for her, and we'd just relax together for hours until it was dark, until the stars came out.

I want to take her camping, like I told her last night at the hotel. Out in the middle of nowhere, just us, making love in the open air. I want to see her smiling and laughing without any trace of sorrow knotting her brow. No more fear. No more running.

Don't run from me, Lark. Don't run from us.

A metal door slams, pulling me out of my fantasy. Someone just climbed down from the camper. He comes around the side toward me, work boots crunching in the roadside gravel.

"Hello? Can I help you?"

At the sound of his voice, my breath stops.

His hair has grown long enough to dust his shoulders. He's got a thick beard, and his skin's a burnished copper from years in the sun. But when he gets a good look at me, his blue eyes go wide. Same eyes I see in the mirror.

"*Danny?*" my uncle sputters. "What on earth are you doing here?"

"I could ask you the same question."

"How did you find me?"

Unbelievable. First time I've seen Travis in almost twenty years, and that's all he has to say?

I'm surprised he even recognizes me. Last time he saw me, I was fourteen. A kid. And that reminder is a cold slap in my face. He left, and he didn't want anything to do with me. He *still* doesn't want me here. That's clear from his stiff back, the way he's keeping his distance.

This isn't some heartfelt reunion. I have a purpose here, and it's not to tell Uncle Travis how I missed him all these years.

"I'm here about Lark."

His eyes narrow. But I don't think it's because her name is unfamiliar.

I take out my phone and pull up the first picture I can find of her. It's a selfie I took of us at the restaurant last night. My mind boggles to think it was less than a day ago. The two of us are smiling with the ocean in the background.

That night, she was *mine*.

I turn around my phone and show him the picture, ignoring the vicious tugs at my heartstrings. "Do you know her?" I ask gruffly. "Yes or no."

Travis looks at the photo without taking the phone. "Of course I do."

"How?"

"How do *you* know her?"

"You first."

"About a month and a half ago, she was staying here. With me."

That statement hits me like a kick in the stomach. Rearranging my insides, threatening to make me vomit. "Were you...were you and Lark..." I can't even say it.

His eyes widen. "Lark is like a daughter to me. She's practically a kid."

"She's twenty-four, but...yeah." I wipe away the sheen of sweat on my skin. Jeez. Freaked me out for a moment there.

"Lark and I are friends. Or maybe *were*. We don't always agree on things, and she got angry with me and took off. It's a thing she does."

"I've learned that about her."

"So it seems. Though I don't understand *how*. Clearly a whole lot's happened I don't know about." He shoves the hair back from his forehead. "She looked well in the picture. She's all right?"

"Mostly." I jam my phone into my pocket. "About six weeks ago, she came to me and Nina." Tried, at least, before that asshole got to her first. But she ended up with us, thankfully. No one is ever going to convince me that Lark isn't better off with us, or that we're not better off with her. "Someone followed her. Hurt her. We think it was her stepbrother. She called him Z. And he's still threatening her."

My uncle shakes his head, cursing under his breath. "I had no idea where she'd gone. She wouldn't answer her phone or email. I didn't think she would go to West Oaks, though."

"If you had known she was in West Oaks, would you have come to us to find her?"

Travis glances away, and that's all the answer I need.

No, he wouldn't have come. Because he didn't want to see us.

"Nina is sick, not that you would care. You don't want to come to West Oaks, and I don't want you there either. Fine. The only reason I'm here is for Lark. Just so we're clear."

"Then what do you need?"

"I need to know the fucking *truth*."

34

Lark

I'm so caught up in my thoughts that I don't hear at first when Quinn comes into my room. She taps me on the shoulder. "Lark?"

I jump up from my seat by the window. "Oh my gosh, what are you doing here?"

"Cliff sounded the alarm. Aiden and I got here as soon as we could." Quinn wraps me in a huge hug, and that makes me realize how badly I needed it.

"Do you want to tell me what happened?"

"I do. I really, really do."

I just finished up with Cliff and the other patrol officer. I'm starting to become an expert on giving police statements. It's not anything I would ever want to learn. But that wasn't the same as telling Quinn.

There are too many thoughts in my brain and I need to get them out. I desperately need my friend.

"Hold that thought," she says, going over to my window. She pulls back the curtain, and warm sunlight floods the room. "There. That's better. Now, tell me all about it."

She sits on the bed beside me and keeps her arm around me as I speak.

"He actually *came here*? That's brazen."

"Yep. Steps away from this house and from the public street. But even though he was right there, I didn't see his face. He's like this bogeyman hiding in the shadows. With all he's done, I still haven't even figured out his *name*."

Cliff told me he'd accessed Nina's security system, and the cameras didn't show anything useful. As if Z somehow knew exactly where they were pointing and how to avoid them. Which only adds to the superhuman mystique he's taken on in my head.

"He'll mess up at some point," Quinn says. "Everyone does, and that's when we'll get him."

"Spoken like a prosecutor." Then I tell her the rest of what he said.

That I'm a horrible person who lies, steals, and cheats.

But Quinn's reaction surprises me. "So, what if it's true?"

I turn my head to look at her, words evading me for a second. *So what?* Isn't that obvious? "If it's true, how can Danny ever forgive me? How could anyone see past the things I've done?"

At some point, Danny is going to decide he can't stand it, can't stand *me*, anymore. He might claim he doesn't care. But the resentment is going to grow, eating away whatever we try to build.

That's my greatest fear. That I'll ask Danny to stay, and he will, but he'll end up hating me for it.

Quinn sits back a little and fixes me with her fiercest expression. If I was a criminal defendant in her courtroom, I'd be quaking.

"Lark, if that guy Z is your brother, then it's no wonder you have a hard time trusting yourself. He's probably undermined you for years of your life. Told you that you weren't good enough. That's what abusers do. But you got away from him when you came to West Oaks. Sure, Danny helped you along the way. Nina too. But *you* escaped him again when Kathy Sullivan pretended to be your aunt."

"Sort of." I didn't get far. But...I did realize just in time that Kathy was up to something.

"And *you* got away from him today. You're already fighting back, and you're already *winning*. Every battle with him, you've won."

"I didn't think of it that way."

"You should. You seem pretty tough to me. But it's not my opinion that counts. *You* are the one person who gets to decide who you are. Nobody else. Not me, not your creepy-ass brother, not even Danny. The question is, who do you want to be now? Let's say all the worst things you fear about your past are true. Can't you still move forward? Let yourself be happy?"

I shift my gaze to the window, with its view of the garden outside. "What if I'm too cynical for that?"

"Hey, you do you. That's the whole point, isn't it?" She bumps my shoulder. "Be whoever you are today. Right now. If Danny wants to be with that gal, he should be so lucky."

Danny. The best thing that's ever happened to me.

What if I find out the truth, and it's just as bad as I fear? Is there a way forward for Danny and me? I know he would say yes. That's what he's been saying to me since our trip to Solvang. I think I'll always be cynical, but I want to have faith in him. In *us*. And in myself, too.

He's always been willing to stay with me. I'm the one who's been running. I need to tell him that *I* want to stay. I want to be with him, facing whatever comes at us together. I *am* strong enough for that. I have to try.

"I think I'm in love with him." I stand up. "I'm going to tell him."

"Good for you, girl. Go get your man."

"I will, but it's your turn next. If I can find a way to be happy with *my* messed-up history, then you should be able to ask out a certain sexy older bodyguard."

"Ugh, we're not talking about me." She grabs my arm, and we go out into the hall. Near the living room, we nearly collide with Cliff, who's striding through the entryway with purpose, as if he just came through the front door.

"Is Danny still here?" Cliff asks.

"He should be," I say.

Matteo walks in from the living room, a line appearing between his eyebrows. "Danny took off about half an hour ago."

I cross my arms. "He *what*?"

Aiden strolls in next. I didn't even realize he was here. "Yep, Danny left on some kind of mission. Made it sound life-or-death important. But he insisted that Matteo and I stay here."

I swear, if Danny ran off to do something stupid because he thinks it will help me, I will never forgive that man.

Quickly, I send off a text to his phone, asking where he is. Then I turn my attention back to Cliff. "Why did you need Danny?"

"We found the guy who attacked you today. He's in custody."

Quinn hisses as she inhales, grabbing my arm. I can't even make myself breathe.

"A neighbor spotted someone sneaking into a house that's for sale, and the perp had blood streaming down his face," Cliff explains. "We picked up the suspect nice and easy. He was polite enough to have an ID on him. The guy is named Zander Richards."

Zander. That name echoes in my brain. Z for Zander.

And Richards. That was a last name I used in the past,

but according to Cam, it was fake. Figures that Zander would be using the same one.

"I doubt Richards is his real name," I say.

"Entirely possible. We'll find out. Looks like he's been squatting in that house he was sneaking back into. It's two streets over from here."

Quinn squeezes my arm.

Jeez, no wonder my stepbrother said he was close. The thought makes painful goosebumps sheet my skin. "You arrested him?" I ask.

"We're in the process of arresting him for trespassing. Plus he's our top suspect for assaulting you, but we'll need you to ID him."

"I didn't get a good look at his face."

"Eh, even so. The damage to his nose suggests we got the right guy." Cliff grins. "Nice job with that head-butt, by the way."

Matteo holds up his hand for a high-five, and Aiden gives me a fist bump.

"When does Lark need to make the ID?" Quinn asks, still holding tight to my arm.

"I'm going to head back to the station. The detectives assigned to this case are questioning Zander, and I'll let you know what I find out."

I had my issues with cops before, but I'm glad Cliff is a friend. Thank goodness he's around to tell me what's going on. Same with Quinn. As a prosecutor, she understands all the ins-and-outs of investigations.

I thank Cliff, and he takes off. Matteo locks the front door behind him.

Quinn rubs my arms. "They caught the guy. How do you feel?"

"I'm relieved. But it's weird. He was like the bogeyman

before, no face and no name except an initial. Now he seems human. I thought it would take more to catch him."

"It often feels that way when we grab a perp we've been hunting," Quinn says. "They're just flesh and blood, and they make mistakes."

"Made a big one messing with you," Matteo adds.

I smile at him. "What about Nina? How's she doing? Does she need anything?" I haven't even had a chance to go see her. It's been too chaotic.

"Still resting. The other nurse showed up, Starla, so Ryan could head home for a while. But both of them said they can work extra today to help out."

I exhale. "Good." If Danny would just get back here, everything would be back on track.

Quinn slings an arm around my shoulder. "I'm afraid you have no choice, Lark. You have nothing better to do than relax and have fun with your friends. Oh, the humanity."

I laugh, returning her hug. "Relaxing with friends sounds perfect."

"I say we head to the kitchen." Matteo nods in that direction. "Something smells promising. I'm intrigued."

"That's all me," Aiden says. "I need to get back in there. Nobody in the kitchen until I'm finished."

Matteo cocks his head. "I've heard these rumors that you can cook. I have doubts. Good cooking runs in families, but I know your brother, and Jake doesn't strike me as the kind of soldier we'd want on KP duty."

Aiden purses his lips and says nothing.

"Oh, Aiden can cook," Quinn assures Matteo.

"So can I, as everyone at Station Two will attest." Matteo claps his hands and rubs them together, his crooked grin turning devious. "Perhaps a little friendly competition is in order."

"No." Aiden folds his arms over his chest. "This isn't a reality show."

"Oh, this is happening." Quinn hooks her arm through mine. "Lark and I will judge."

"No arguments here," I say.

We start toward the kitchen, and Matteo steers a reluctant Aiden to come with us.

But on the way, I check my phone again. No word.

Danny, where are you?

QUINN and I commentate from the sidelines while Matteo and Aiden cook more food than I even knew we had in the house. Matteo is all smack-talk and boisterous laughter, while Aiden is gruff and reticent. But it's just an act. He keeps snorting to cover his laughs.

Matteo whips up homemade pasta, while Aiden does some kind of savory cream-puff things filled with cheese and an array of other small bites. It's ridiculously good, and since I skipped lunch, I'm ravenous. Afterward my stomach is stuffed and I'm smiling so much that my cheeks hurt, despite all the terrible things that happened today.

In between, I go check on Nina and bring Starla samples of the food. Nina's exhausted, looking more frail than I've ever seen her. But when she wakes, I sit with her and hold her hand, just grateful she's got more time with us. Matteo and Aiden take a break from cooking as well to say their hellos, and Quinn gives Nina a rundown of all the gossip from the West Oaks DA's Office. Nina isn't feeling well enough to talk much, but she smiles and chuckles along with us.

I need to update her on the rest of what happened earlier, how Z was here on her property. I have no intention of keeping anything a secret from her. But that can wait. For now, it's enough just to be with her.

Quinn is right. I *am* tough, and I want to fight for the friends I've made here. This family. I doubt I've ever been a part of anything like this, and I have to find a way to hold on to it. The only thing that's missing is Danny. I keep checking my phone, but he hasn't written back.

I need Danny here. His absence is an ache that just gets worse with every minute we're apart.

And *finally*, he texts me.

Danny: Got held up. Heading home.
Me: Hurry back. Did you hear from Cliff?
Danny: Yeah, he told me they caught the asshole. Thank God.
Me: I miss you.
Danny: Miss you, too. So much.
Me: We're okay?
Danny: We will be.

I'm on pins and needles until I finally hear the door open. The rest of us are back in the kitchen to give Nina some quiet. I can't eat another bite, but somehow Matteo and Aiden are still at it.

"Danny!" Matteo says. "Get your ass in here. You need to break a tie!"

Aiden makes a face. "Bradley is the deciding vote? Can't we get someone with a decent palette?"

Quinn rolls her eyes at them both.

Danny's still in the foyer, but I hear his footsteps approaching. I walk toward the front to head him off, too eager to wait another moment. "Hey, took you long e—"

The words die on my tongue when I see Danny isn't alone.

I recognize the man with him from the photos Nina

showed me. Travis Bradley's eyes rove over the kitchen and then land on me, widening in recognition. "Lark. My God. It's really you." He races toward me, and before I know what's happening, he's swept me into his arms.

Danny stands slightly behind his uncle, his face carefully impassive, revealing only a slight frown.

"How…" I stammer. "What…"

Travis lets me go, and I realize Matteo, Aiden and Quinn are crowded behind me, staring at us. Danny's eyes are as dark as stormclouds.

"You found him?" I ask. *How? When?*

"The three of us can talk alone," Danny says. "My uncle has a lot to tell you."

"But what about Nina?" I ask.

"He's not here for her," Danny growls, and Travis seems to bite down on whatever reply he might've made. Danny looks over at his friends. "Sorry to interrupt, everyone. Matteo, could you take my uncle to the living room? We'll be right there."

Quinn obviously has questions. Aiden's watching with a thick brow slightly raised.

Danny takes my hand and leads me past the kitchen to the hallway at the back of the house, where there's access to the garage and utility rooms. After a moment's deliberation, he pushes into the laundry room and closes the door behind us.

Starla must've put a load in earlier, because the dryer is running. The minute we're alone, Danny pulls me to him. "Fuck, that feels good. Holding you."

It does. I melt into him, breathing in the scent of him, masculine with hints of leather and spice. "Where were you? You left without telling me."

"I'm sorry, but I had to do it. You were so upset after what Z said to you."

"Zander Richards." I want to use an actual name for him, even if it might be fake. I need to prove I'm not afraid. That he doesn't control me.

"Zander, yeah. That prick. The police are dealing with him, so we don't have to. I left to talk to Cam. He gave me that journal he mentioned to you, and I found Travis's address inside." Danny cradles my face. "Lark, I don't know yet what Travis is going to tell you. I explained that you'd lost your memory and filled in some of what's happened to you. I wanted to wait to hear the rest when we're together. But whatever he says, I need you to know—"

"That it doesn't matter. It's okay. I get it now. I talked everything over with Quinn, and even if I did things I hate in the past, that's not who I am now."

A sweet smile slowly rises on his face. "That's all true. But that's not what I was going to say. I need you to know that I love you."

I gawk at him, staring into his ocean-and-sky eyes. "I'm... going to need you to repeat that."

Danny presses our foreheads together. Nuzzles my nose with his. "I. Love. You." Between each word, he drops a kiss onto my cheeks. And then he reaches my mouth, whispering the words against my lips. "I love you."

"I love you, too." I brush a few strands of hair from his forehead. "I do need to know the truth. I won't hide from it anymore. But no matter what, I'm going to stay here with you as long as I can."

"Make that forever, and we're agreed."

We're both smiling as we kiss. Slow meetings of lips, tongues dancing, teeth nibbling. He lifts me up and sets me on the dryer, which is warm and rumbling beneath me.

I'm so ready to get lost in him. The man I love. But there's still a lot we need to talk about.

"Why did you say Travis isn't here for Nina?" I ask. "Doesn't he want to see her?"

Danny takes a long, deep breath. "He didn't say that outright. But he chose to stay a stranger from us. He doesn't deserve her forgiveness."

"But Nina deserves the chance to offer it. I know it's not really my place because she's your grandmother—"

"No, Lark, it is your place. I value your opinion. I love you."

Something bright and beautiful lights up inside me every time he says that. Like a flower blooming. "And I love you. But if you can forgive me for what I did, whatever that might be, maybe you can give your uncle the benefit of the doubt too."

Danny's lips press to my forehead. "You're amazing, you know that? You fill up spaces in my heart I didn't even know were empty."

"Is that a yes?"

His smile flickers at the corners of his mouth. "When it comes to you, it's always a yes from me."

Our mouths draw together. His fingers thread into my hair, and mine into his. Need builds, stoked by the heat of our kisses and the friction of our bodies together and the vibrations of the dryer. I always need more of Danny.

This isn't the time, though.

"Travis is waiting for us in the living room," I say.

Danny tilts my head and sucks gently at the pulsepoint on my neck. "But I need what's mine. And I need to give you what's yours."

Chills of desire rush through me. It's not easy to say no to him, especially because Danny rarely asks for much. "Everyone will know exactly what we're doing in here."

"You think I care?"

"No, I think the opposite. You'll like it. Because you're a

very bad boy." I slide my hands up the firm, etched curves of his biceps. "But we're saving that for later. We'll have all the time in the world."

He drops his forehead onto my shoulder, grumbling. "There's one more thing. Cam admitted he spied on you for your brother, and you found out. That's why you broke up with him. He said he was sorry. Not sure what that's worth, but I told him I'd pass it on. Even though I didn't want to."

I'm not sure what it's worth, either. But it means something to me that Danny shared it.

The muscle in Danny's jaw pops. "I told Cam not to contact you. But if you want to get in touch with him, you should."

"I probably won't. But thank you. I love you, Danny," I murmur.

"I love you, too."

We go to the living room, hand in hand.

35

Danny

"It's really something to see you two together." Travis's gaze keeps bouncing from Lark to me. "You and my nephew. It's doing a number on me."

We're sitting on the sofa across from him, hands clasped. Travis seems unsure of himself, and he's trying to ease the tension. *Sorry, Uncle Travis. It's not flipping working.*

On the drive to West Oaks, Travis tried a few times to ask me questions, especially about Nina, but I just couldn't. I was so furious with my uncle that I could hardly see straight. My vision was feathering, and I worried I'd crash the car. So we traveled in silence that was thick enough to slice through.

But of course, seeing and talking to Lark calmed me down. She's the perfect drug, making me euphoric and settling me at the same time. Loving her makes everything else more bearable. I guess she's doing the same thing for me that I did for her in the hospital. Giving me an anchor in the middle of a storm.

"You look healthy, Lark," Travis says. "Better than the last time I saw you."

"Danny's been taking care of me. Nina too."

"That's good. Really good." His eyes are shining. Lark is returning Travis's intent stare, and I wonder what she's thinking.

In the hospital, she seemed mesmerized by my eyes. She seemed to know my eyes before anything else. Is that because of Travis? She was remembering *him*? *She was like a daughter to me*, my uncle said, and it wouldn't surprise me if he sucked as a father. Just like my own.

But my eyes comforted her. That means she must have trusted him.

I told Lark I'd give him the benefit of the doubt, and I'm going to try. She's got a kind, giving heart, and Lark has wanted to reunite Nina with her long-lost son since the moment she first heard Travis's name.

But if Travis was a father figure to her, then why didn't he protect her when she needed him? Why did she end up in West Oaks alone with a car bearing down on her?

"I used to wish the two of you could meet. Danny, I used to wonder how you were and—"

Anger flares in my stomach. "Don't make this about me," I snap. "Just start at the beginning. How did you meet Lark?"

"If you want the beginning for *her*, I should start before that." Travis licks his lips, aiming a hesitant gaze at the carpet. "Lark, this is all stuff you told me. But if you lost your memory about everything, then I'll try to give you back as much as possible."

"Did I say anything about my parents?" she asks. "Someone told me they were hippies in a commune, but I don't know if that's true."

"From what you told me, they were young when they had you, but they were just suburbanites in Northern California." He clears his throat and rubs a hand over his gray-stippled beard. "You said your dad left early on, and your mom's family had disowned her when she got pregnant. You were ten when she passed away, and you ended up in foster care. Those years weren't easy for you. But eventually you got settled. You had a foster brother. Zander."

"Z?"

"You called him that sometimes, yeah. The people you and Zander lived with weren't as bad as the others. You felt like a family. But they had their own schemes, and it sounds like having foster kids was one of them. It was like Oliver Twist. You and Zander had to go out, picking pockets or conning people for money. You and your brother worked as a team. Your family would find an opportunity, a mark, and the two of you would go in to sell a story."

Lark clutches my fingers like she's holding on for dear life. "That's close to what Cam told me. My ex-boyfriend. He said Z was my stepbrother, and I grew up in a family of con artists."

"Doesn't surprise me that you muddied the details. You weren't quick to trust, and it took a long time for you to trust me. But I'm getting ahead of myself. Even though your foster family cheated people for money, you weren't like them. You never wanted to take more than you needed to get by. You just wanted a fair shake. A chance to earn something real for yourself. By the time you were eighteen, you had a real job at a plant nursery in Northern California."

"Was it in Eureka?" I ask, remembering the story Kathy Sullivan told Lark weeks ago. So many pieces of it have ended up being true, even if not directly.

Travis nods at me. "It was near there, yeah." Then he turns back to Lark. "Your job at the nursery lasted a few years, and then you got a really lucky break. You'd befriended a woman who owned a bunch of fancy restaurants and needed flower arrangements for them. She hired you to work for her, and you were able to take college classes on the side too. You started dating Cam. He seemed like a nice enough guy, from what you told me of him. You had a life you were proud of. But Zander had done the opposite. He'd gotten better at faking credentials, documents, tricking people. He talked his way into your boss's home and stole from her, just out of spite to you. Got you fired and almost arrested. That was the last straw for you. You cut ties with him and the rest of your foster family, picked up with Cam, and left without telling Zander where you were going."

"And I came to Solvang."

"You did, about a year back. But I didn't meet you until about six, seven months ago. In the spring." Travis smiles, though tears shine in his eyes again. "You were volunteering for the clinic where I went for help with my migraines. I had a car accident a while back. My head hasn't been the same since. Chronic pain."

I can't keep the sneer off my face. "We know about the DUI. How you took off afterward to avoid responsibility. Typical for you."

A flash of red works up my uncle's neck. He scratches his head. "Guess I don't have to explain that part. There's a shit ton of other stuff I need to explain to you though, Danny. If you'll let me."

"Not now," I say through gritted teeth.

This time, when Lark squeezes my fingers, I know she's trying to give comfort instead of take it. I smile at her reassuringly, even though my insides are churning.

My uncle and I both go silent. Lark is the one who speaks next.

"Cam, my ex, said I agreed to help Zander with something. I would disappear, and I wouldn't tell Cam where I was going. I kept secrets."

"Probably because you didn't fully trust Cam. Like I said. After your history, who could blame you?"

"But Cam said I was helping Zander con people."

"No. No way. You wouldn't lift a finger for Zander after what he'd cost you in NorCal. You were volunteering because you wanted to help people who had nobody else."

Lark exhales a small breath. I touch her cheek briefly, and she looks up at me.

You see? I try to say with my eyes. *That's who you are.*

"You were different from the other volunteers," Travis says. "A lot of people are all sunshine and false cheer, but not you. You were sarcastic, and I liked that. I looked forward to seeing you at the support group. And you sometimes came by my place with groceries and stuff when I was having an episode and couldn't get out the door. I work for a wine-maker, doing odd jobs around the vineyard, whatever they need, and she lets me park my camper on her property. I count myself lucky. But it's not a steady salary. No health insurance or sick leave."

So that explains why he was able to live on that beautiful stretch of road in Santa Barbara wine country. Not cheap real estate by any means.

"You and I struck up a friendship," Travis says to Lark, a glow of fondness in his eyes. "An unlikely one, I'll give you that. But it helped that I lived in such a beautiful place." He chuckles. "Half the time, I think you were visiting just to sit under the willow and admire the view. I didn't mind."

"There's a weeping willow here, too," she says.

I glance over at Lark, whose cheeks are pink. I wonder if she's remembering how we made love there. Lark adores that tree. Travis's camper and the land must have been a refuge for her. Another small piece of the puzzle slots into place.

"There was a willow at the house where Chris and I grew up," Travis adds, nodding. "That's why I picked that spot to park my camper. My mom always loved those trees. They're not common in California, so it reminded me of home."

Lark gives him a small smile.

He laughs wistfully. "We had fun together, though. Watched dumb TV shows. Worked on the car I've been trying since forever to fix up. Danny, you remember that Charger my dad used to have? How your grandpa tinkered with that thing?"

"I remember," I say stiffly. Did Travis not recognize the '68 Charger we rode in earlier? Maybe he was as distracted as I was on the drive here, his mind in a hundred different times and places.

"I have a Mustang I bought on the cheap way back, and Lark, you helped me with it sometimes. We loved talking cars." Travis goes on with his story. "I opened up to you, told you more and more about myself. Including the DUI, by the way. Things about my family. Regrets. You encouraged me to get in touch with my mom again, even though I was too much of a coward to do it."

"Did you talk about emailing Nina?" I ask.

Lines crease around Travis's eyes. "No. Not that I remember."

Lark changes the subject. "There's a lot more I don't understand. I got fired from my volunteer spot with the clinic. They said I stole from someone."

Travis's expression darkens. "That was Zander. You see, it hadn't taken him long to track you down, and he was still trying to keep his hooks in you. It stressed you out. I think that's a big reason you liked visiting me, just to get away from that. Finally, Zander decided to punish you. He caused some kind of controversy at the clinic, and once again you got blamed. You weren't an official volunteer anymore, but still came to see me. That's when you really opened up. You told me everything about Zander, how you ran away from him and your family. Were still running. You told me your real last name was Swanson."

Lark Swanson. I tuck her hair behind her ear. Simple name, but it fits her.

"I didn't trust anyone, but I trusted *you*." Lark doesn't sound skeptical. More like she's struggling to understand.

He laughs gently. "We're alike, and I think you saw that in me, too. Weird as it seems. Some people just fit. We were both running from our mistakes, our pasts, even though our situations were completely different. When we were together, neither of us felt so alone."

I don't know what to think of this bond between Lark and my uncle. If he was her friend when she needed one that badly, why couldn't he have done the same for me, his own nephew? Yet it's hard to keep up the anger when he helped Lark. Both then, by being her friend when she needed one, and now, by telling her the truth she needs to hear.

Lark shifts around on the couch cushion. "What happened next?"

"Well, you got fired from volunteering at the clinic about two months ago. Not long after, you showed up at my door with all your belongings. Bruises on you and hellfire in your eyes. You were furious, damn near *dejected*, and you wouldn't tell me what was really going on. But you kept mentioning my family. My mom. You insisted again that I get in touch and try to mend things." His gaze meets mine before darting away. "But I just...couldn't do it."

"The emails," Lark mutters.

"Second time you guys have mentioned emails. What's that about?"

"Someone sent emails about you to Nina. It was probably me. But the emails started months ago. Not weeks."

Travis sighs. "You must've been trying to help us reconnect since I didn't have the courage to do it on my own. I bet you tracked down her email address online. You're good with computers. Good at just about anything you set your mind to."

"But I did that without telling you? And then I came all the way here to West Oaks to Nina's house? Why?"

He shrugs. "All I knew is that you disappeared. I thought you might've gone back to Cam. Or worst case, to Zander. I tried calling your phone but never got any response. I was freaking the heck out, honestly. Worrying over you."

But he didn't go to the police because he'd run from that DUI in Vegas a decade ago, and he was afraid of getting caught. He doesn't need to explain it for us to connect the dots.

And there's that fucking anger again, burning the underside of my skin.

"Plenty of reason to worry," I spit out. "Zander followed her here and tried to kill her. He was trying to stop Lark from getting to us." Though I still can't understand that part. Was it just Zander being cruel? Trying to get revenge on her for leaving him?

No, I realize. Zander was concerned about whether she had her memories. He told Lark that was why he hired Kathy Sullivan—not just to lure Lark away from us, but to find out what she remembered.

There was something Lark knew that he wanted to keep secret. Something worth killing her over.

"I'm sorry," Travis says. "I really am."

I can't tell if he's talking to Lark or to me.

Sighing, I turn to the woman I love and slide my fingers into the hair at the back of her neck. "At least we know that just about everything Zander told you was bullshit. You weren't trying to trick Nina or steal from her."

"But we still don't know exactly why I came to West Oaks."

"You were trying to help."

She opens her mouth, brows drawn down in thought. Finally, she nods. I kiss her temple.

My girl. My beautiful, sweet girl. I told her that nothing Travis said would change how I felt about her, and it hasn't. All he's done is confirm how good a person she is. And it doesn't surprise me. I know the woman I love. That's what I've been saying this whole time.

"Thanks for telling me all of this." She looks over at Travis. "From the moment I met Danny, when he saved my life, I felt like I knew him. I trusted him without knowing why. It was because of you. I think some part of me remembered you."

Travis's face crumples, and he tries to cover it. "Shit. Maybe I did something right, then? I hope."

"You must have." Lark smiles at me. "I fell in love with Danny because of the man he is, all on his own. But that first feeling that I was safe with him came from a good place. Sounds like you two have a lot in common."

She stands up and gives Travis a hug, which he gratefully returns. They're both wiping their eyes. Then she gives me another kiss. "Talk to him," she whispers, before heading down the hallway.

Her footsteps echo, and then fade.

Guess I can't delay this anymore.

I get up and stand in front of my uncle, digging my hands into my jeans pockets. His mouth flattens into a tight line.

"Almost twenty years," I say. "Twenty *fucking years*."

"I have no excuse. But I can try to explain. If you'll let me."

I shrug and walk over to the living room window. It's getting dark. Fuck, it's been a long fucking day. And I know I'm wearing thin when every other word in my brain is an f-bomb.

"How long have you known about that DUI?" Travis ask softly.

"A few days. Private investigator." I don't feel like explaining Bennett Security and what they do.

"That must be how you found my address."

I turn around, crossing my arms over my chest. "Actually, it was Lark. Indirectly. She had your address written down, though she didn't realize it. I don't see the need to discuss logistics with you, though. If you have something you think I want to hear, then say it."

He sniffs, nodding. "You probably know about what happened before I left. Your grandpa's funeral. The cufflinks."

"The cufflinks you stole? Yeah, I remember. I was a four-teen-year-old kid, but I was old enough to overhear what everyone else was saying and figure out what I needed to. How you stole from my dad and Nina, and when they got upset, you took off and never came back. Never said a *word* to me. Like I didn't mean shit."

Travis wipes a hand over his face. Then he sticks a hand into his pocket. Pulls out his wallet.

From inside the fold of leather, he produces two gold cufflinks.

"I did take them. But it wasn't to sell them like your dad accused me of. It was stupid and sentimental. I did a lot of stupid, impulsive things back then. I wish I could take them back."

"So you've been carrying that shit around all these years? For what? You could've come back, and you didn't. You live an hour away from here. You mentioned the migraines and chronic pain, and I'm sure that's rough. But you haven't been out of commission every minute for the past twenty years."

His fist wraps around the shiny gold trinkets. "I tried to come back. A year after I left. I wanted to apologize. Explain myself and make things right. But Chris told me I wasn't wanted in your life."

"My dad said that?"

"He told me you and Nina were both better off without me. That I was a bad influence on you, and he didn't want me around you anymore. He'd said it before, but that time, the truth sank in. I'd missed my own father's funeral. I felt like a waste of space."

I'm ready with another biting comeback until I actually process what he just told me. I can imagine my father saying that. He said the same about Travis to me plenty of times.

"You didn't talk to Nina or me? Didn't let us decide?"

He hangs his head. "I figured Chris was right. That you were better off without me in your life."

I'm still pissed, and I still want to argue. But if I take a step back, if I try to separate myself from the pain of rejection, I can see how he might've believed my father.

It's the same thing Lark was doing. Believing the worst about herself because of the cruel words of someone else. And while my dad is kind of an asshole, he's not the evil villain here either. He and his brother just let pettiness and fear make their decisions for them.

I exhale and tug at my necklace. I haven't thought about it in years, but Travis gave me this necklace for my thirteenth birthday. I've been wearing it all this time, like he's apparently been carrying those cufflinks. Tiny pieces of jewelry. But both of us have been hauling around an invisible, back-breaking weight.

"Do you want to see Nina?"

"Of course I do," he rushes to say. "More than anything. And I want the chance to get to know you, too. To know the man you've become. Seeing you with Lark, how you treat her, I'm just so damn proud of you."

I nod begrudgingly. "She deserves it. She's an amazing woman."

"She is. It's not fair that she's had to deal with so much. But if you two end up together, if you make each other happy the way I know you can, then it'll be worth it. Who the hell knows, maybe it's meant to be."

That's something else my uncle and I can agree on.

"Let's go see if Nina is awake," I say. "She's had a hard day, but I know she'll want to see you."

36

Lark

When I walk into the kitchen, Aiden, Mateo, and Quinn are chatting quietly with their heads together. The two men look up, and Quinn dashes over to me. She's got her arms open, and I sink immediately into her embrace. I could get used to all these hugs.

"How'd it go?" she asks.

"Pretty well, actually. No, *really* well."

I'm so relieved that the whole story tumbles out of me. I couldn't hold it back if I tried.

I've heard so many versions of my history. From Kathy Sullivan, from Cam. A twisted interpretation from Zander. Each one had shades of the truth. But I'm sure that what Travis just told me was accurate, at least as far as he knows. It felt like a key sliding into a lock. Not opening up my real memories, because it seems nothing is ever going to do that. But it still felt right. Travis's story explained so much.

Of course I responded to Danny the way I did. I saw his eyes, heard the kindness in his voice, and I knew to trust him. I was already primed to consider Danny a friend, someone I knew instinctually would help me.

None of that explains why I love him. That's everything to do with the man he is. But if I hadn't already felt that bond with his uncle, then I never would've taken the chance of getting close to him. Letting him into my heart.

Aiden crosses his arms, leaning against the kitchen counter. "So it worked out. Cool."

Quinn snorts, and Matteo shakes his head. "Nah, that won't cut it. We're going to need a group hug for this one." They wrap me up in their arms, Aiden finally joining after Quinn bugs him.

"Is Danny still in with his uncle?" Quinn asks when we break apart.

"Yeah, I'm hoping they can work things out. We'll see."

I slide onto a barstool, feeling exhaustion creep up. I'm shocked to realize that the windows are dark, and it's nearly dinnertime. This has been a long, trying day, but it's ending in a great place.

Quinn and Aiden are finishing up the last few dishes. Matteo pulls up the stool next to me. "I was just in to see how Nina's doing. She's resting, and Ryan just got back on shift. Starla's still here too. You guys are lucky to have so much help."

"Definitely. I think that's because of Danny's father." I know Danny doesn't have an easy relationship with his dad, but at least he's providing for Nina.

Matteo rubs a hand over his beard. "Ryan was asking about you, though. Sounded like he was anxious to talk to you."

"To *me*? Why?"

"Don't know. It was odd, if I'm being honest. Has he been a nurse for Nina for very long?"

"A few weeks, I think. He got added to the schedule after I arrived." My cheeks warm. "I thought it was because Danny was so busy with me that he didn't have as much time for Nina."

"Could be. I got a vibe that he might have a thing for you. Or at least, more interest than I would be comfortable with, in Danny's place."

"I...don't think so." But then I remember Ryan giving me some assessing looks, asking me about myself before. I'm sure it's nothing but friendly curiosity.

"Maybe I'm wrong," Matteo says. "Angela always claims I'm overprotective." He grins. "Speaking of my lovely lady and mother of my child, I need to get home to her. You guys good here? I don't want to interrupt Danny's heart-to-heart with his uncle."

"We're good, yes. Thank you so much for everything."

I give Matteo another hug. Aiden and Quinn offer to stay the night if we need, but I tell them to head home. I'm sure Travis will be staying here tonight, and if all goes well, there might be some emotional family time ahead with Nina.

After last goodbyes and seeing our friends out, I head toward the living room. Danny and Travis are just emerging. Both are smiling, which I take as a positive sign.

How'd it go? I try to ask Danny with my eyes.

"I'm going to take Travis to see Nina." Danny reaches for my hand and tangles our fingers together. "Thanks for telling me what I needed to hear. I love you, babe."

"Love you, too." We sneak a kiss, and I see Travis grinning at us over Danny's shoulder.

I walk with them to Nina's room. She's awake, and Starla's reading to her. Danny goes inside, while Travis and I hang back.

"Hey, how you feeling?" Danny asks his grandmother. "Someone's here to see you."

Travis tenses up beside me. "What if she doesn't want to see me?" he whispers. He reaches for my hand and squeezes.

"She will," I murmur back. "It's going to be great."

Then Danny is waving Travis inside. I hear a hoarse gasp, probably from Nina, and a sob from Travis. Nina's son makes a beeline for her bed and sweeps her into an embrace, both of them crying. Danny's wiping his eyes too.

Starla steps out into the hallway with me. "Now, that's a sight."

"It is." A beautiful one. I just want to stand here and admire it.

"Do you have family, Lark?"

I glance over to find Starla scrutinizing me.

"I have a family." I nod at Nina's room. "Here." I used to get upset at Danny for trying to *fix things*. He wanted to make things the way they were before, and often, that isn't possible. But this family can make something *new*. Forge new bonds and find the kind of happiness and peace of mind that we all need.

Starla follows my gaze and smiles.

"Have you seen Ryan?" I ask. "Matteo said he was looking for me."

"Oh? He was just here. I'm not sure where he went. What did he need?"

"I was going to ask him."

Her smile turns stiff. "I don't want to speak badly of a co-worker." She takes my wrist and walks me further down the corridor. "But I was *very* concerned to hear about the incident earlier. The morphine? Ryan gave Nina too much. Jess always leaves clear notes behind about the doses she gives at night, and I suspect Ryan was being careless."

I frown, uncomfortable that she's sharing this with me. "Shouldn't you talk to Danny about it? Or the hospice service?"

"I will. But sometimes, Ryan seems distracted from his

duties, and now he's been looking for you? If he's bothering you…"

"He hasn't been. No." I don't want to get the guy in trouble at his work unless there's a real reason. The morphine could be an issue, but I have no way to judge. I'm not a nurse.

"Then perhaps I'm just old-fashioned." Starla lifts the strap of her bag onto her shoulder. "I heard about what else happened. The police? You're all right?"

"Oh, yeah. The police caught the guy." I'm not sure how much Starla knows about my past, and I'm way too tired to get into it.

Her face flushes. "Did they say what the man wanted? Why he went after you?"

"Just that they know his name, and…he's my foster brother. That's what Travis told me."

Her brows draw together. "You and Travis already knew each other. I've been trying to keep track, but it's confusing. Sorry, I just overhear a lot."

"No, it's fine. It's a long story, though. Maybe I can explain it all to you another day? I'm pretty tired."

"Of course you are. So am I. I have another patient to see, so I'll have to be on my way. But please, have Danny give me a call if Nina needs me." We walk together to the front door. She sets her bag down, rummaging around to organize something. "I'll just let myself out. Get some rest. You deserve it."

"Night, Starla."

I head into the kitchen, thinking I'll warm up some leftovers for Danny and Travis, and hear footsteps behind me. I assume it's Starla again, that she forgot something.

But it's Ryan.

He's dressed in black scrubs. His spiky hair looks especially unruly tonight. The scent of cooking in the room combines with the bitter medicinal scent that's lingering around him.

"Hey, Lark. There you are. Can we talk for a minute? Alone?" His voice sounds oddly bright, but his hands are fidgeting.

"Is it important?"

"I think it is. Yeah."

I sigh. "Okay." I gesture around us. "We're alone here already."

"I mean…" Ryan looks toward the front door, which isn't visible from here, but we can both hear Starla humming quietly as she gets herself organized to head out to her car.

Whatever Ryan wants to say, he doesn't want Starla to overhear. Maybe because she was talking bad about him? I don't know what kind of workplace drama this is. I'm *far* too tired for it. But the sooner I listen, the sooner we'll be done and I can get back to Danny.

"This way," I say.

I walk down the hall toward the garage with Ryan padding quietly behind me. When I glance back, he's scrubbing his hands nervously against the sides of his pants.

I open the door to the garage and switch on the main over-head light. We're in Danny's workspace, with the hood of the '71 Charger propped up to reveal the engine block. The two other stalls of the garage are still in shadow. Nina's minivan, and then her storage area, with its stacked furniture and boxes.

I spin around to face Ryan. "Well, here we are. What's up?"

He's still in the open doorway. Ryan steps toward me, shutting the door behind him. Then he rests his back up against it. I have a momentary flare of anxiety. I guess when he said *alone*, he really meant it. He's blocking the door back to the house.

But there's the exit on the far side of the garage, and obviously, the overhead doors. Plenty of ways out of here. Not that I need one. The guy just want to talk, and both Danny and Travis aren't far away.

Still, I back up until I'm resting my hip against the workbench. I cross my arms and tap my foot. Waiting.

"It's about Starla," Ryan says.

"Okay…"

He grimaces. "This could be something, or nothing at all. But I heard your friends talking about how the police caught somebody who assaulted you earlier, and it sounded like he was the same guy who hit you with a car. Guy named Zander?"

I hug my arms tighter around myself. Guess Starla isn't the only nurse around here who overhears things. "Right. What about it?"

"So, this is weird. But a couple days ago, Starla's phone kept ringing. She was just wrapping up her shift, and I was coming in. And she took out her phone and I saw the name *Zander* on the screen. Zander with a Z."

Cold runs through me, freezing my arms and legs with a sense of unreality. "It's not an unusual name."

"Isn't it, though?" He holds up his hands. "You're right. It could be a total coincidence. I'm not meaning to upset you. Really. But the thing is, other stuff has been weirding me out about Starla too. I've seen her on Nina's iPad. When Nina was asleep."

"They like to watch shows together on Netflix."

"Yeah, but when I walked into the room, Starla closed whatever she was looking at. Like she didn't want me to see. And other times, she's been sloppy with Nina's care when Danny's not around."

Practically the same thing Starla said about him.

"I don't understand what you're accusing her of. I guess you don't like her. That doesn't mean something is wrong."

Ryan shrugs, looking down. "But the Zander thing. I felt like I needed to tell you."

Beads of sweat roll down my sides. "It's strange. Definitely. But I'm sure it's a coincidence. The other stuff, you should talk to Danny about it. I didn't hire Starla. It's not my place."

"I'm sorry. Wasn't trying to upset you, *Lark*."

I look up sharply at the edge in his tone.

Ryan's pupils are dilated, his gaze going dark. And now I really don't want to be out here anymore. "I'd like to go back inside. *Now*."

Glowering, Ryan slowly steps aside. But he doesn't get out of the way. Instead, he twists the knob himself, frowning at me as he turns toward the door.

But when he opens it, Starla is standing there on the other side.

"Gossiping about me, Ryan?"

She's got both hands behind her back.

He sputters. "Were you spying on me? You see, Lark? This is why the lady weirds me out." Starla comes forward, forcing Ryan to stumble backward so that she doesn't run into him.

With a sudden violent movement, her hand comes out from behind her back. She's holding a syringe. It all happens so fast that I can barely react.

Starla stabs Ryan in the neck with it.

"What the *fuck*?" He trips backward, hands flying to the needle, yanking it away. I'm sucking in a breath to scream. And then Starla's other hand comes out from behind her back. I cannot believe what I'm seeing.

She's aiming a gun at me.

"Make a noise, Lark, and I swear it'll be your last."

37

Lark

*S*tarla is pointing a gun at me. In the corner of my vision, I see Ryan slumped and losing consciousness on the ground.

"What is going on?" I stammer. "What're you *doing*?"

Her eyes flick down to Ryan as he struggles to breathe. "Some people don't know when to keep their mouths shut. You've often had that problem."

I keep staring at her, as if she'll morph into someone else and this will make sense. But she's still the same nurse with round cheeks and prim lipstick that I've known all these weeks.

But she had the name Zander programmed into her phone. *Zander*. He was calling her.

"D-Do you know Zander Richards?"

Starla glances at the gun in her hand, but her expression barely changes. "I knew this was coming," she mutters, "but I thought I'd have a little more time to sort it out."

Ryan flops onto his back. He's making awful noises as he tries to get air into his lungs. She must've given him an overdose of something.

"He's suffocating. Help him!" I cry.

I move toward him, and Starla raises the gun at me. "Now you see what'll happen to you if you don't do as I say. I thought I made that lesson clear to you a long time ago, but a mother's work is never done."

"*Mother*?"

Using the gun, she gestures for me to go toward Danny's workbench. "Sit down," she commands. I back up until I'm against the bench. "Not there. The floor. Put your hands behind your back." She uses one hand to dig into her bag again, coming up with a plastic zip tie.

An image suddenly fills my mind. Handcuffs snapping onto my wrists, fixing me to a kitchen table. *That's what you get for talking back to me, Lark.*

"*Lark*," Starla snaps, pulling me out of that strange moment. But her voice is the same one I just heard in my mind. What the heck?

Sweat soaks my armpits. I slide to the ground and clasp my hands at my lower back, doing what she asked.

"Try anything, and I'll kill everyone in this house." She bends quickly behind me, using the zip tie to secure my wrists together. "Legs out."

Starla uses another two zip ties, looped together, on my ankles. Then she stows the gun in her pocket and walks briskly to the other side of the garage. She starts digging around over there.

Starla knows Zander. She must've been helping him. She's involved somehow. She was using Nina's iPad…She may have *killed Ryan* and just tied me up.

Why? What the heck does all this mean?

Starla pulls a shoebox out of a hiding place in Nina's storage area. "What is that?" I ask.

She lifts the lid. "Always with the damn questions. You

never change." Starla pulls stacks of cash out of the box. Small items that clink like jewelry.

Another surreal image assails me. I'm slinking through a crowd with a dark-haired teenage boy. I bump into a passerby, apologizing as my hand slips into the woman's purse to grab her wallet. The dark-haired boy takes a wallet from the jacket of the man next to her.

I gasp as that image vanishes.

Zander. That was him. I'm sure of it.

That was something that really happened. I *remembered it.*

"Who are you?" I ask.

"You already know that, Lark. All the answers are in your head." She finishes emptying the box, stowing the contents in her messenger bag. Then she crosses to my side of the garage again, grabs my chin, and tilts my head. "I taught you everything, and then you were ungrateful enough to forget it."

"You're not my mother. You're *not.*"

Another image. A memory. I'm yelling those same words. *You're not my mother.* Zander is holding my arms, keeping me from lunging at her. The woman with Starla's face, though that's not the name she used before. Zander shoves me into a closet and slams the door. I scream and bang on the wood.

I blink, and the garage is back. But it still feels like I'm in the middle of a nightmare.

Starla's thumb caresses my chin. "Not technically your mother," she says. "But I'm the closest thing you or Zander will ever have. We're family. That's why it breaks my heart that you're so ungrateful."

"This isn't happening," I whimper.

A cruel, closed-lip smile spreads her mouth wide. This is the real Starla. Not a kind, old-fashioned nurse, but a predator.

And the wall inside my mind—already cracking—gives

way. The barrier collapses in wave after wave of memories. I'm drowning in them.

I remember *everything*.

Foster care. New faces. It wasn't that different from when my mom was alive, sadly, because she had to work so hard to take care of us. Her family had kicked her out, so she relied on neighbors and friends. After she was gone, even those familiar presences scattered.

Some of the foster families were kind. Others not so much. But one thing was the same. They never lasted.

Until Mother.

She had a nurturing quality to her, firm yet fair. Starla went by a different name back then, but to me and Zander, she was always Mother. We were a little family, her and my new foster brother and her boyfriend, who was a cop.

When I showed up, Zander had already been with her for a while. Mother took me under her wing. Teaching me, keeping me safe and warm and fed. More than I could say for some of my prior "families." But only if I followed Mother's rules. If I didn't, if I talked back, I would get cuffed to furniture or stuffed in a closet to contemplate my actions. She made Zander do it. If I was really bad, refusing to go out with my brother in search of wallets or cash to steal, then worse would happen. Like Zander would push me down the stairs.

I tried to run away. Went to the police and reported Mother's treatment of me. Her cop boyfriend said I was a troublemaker, smoothed it all over and made the authorities look the other way. He took me back to Mother.

And once again, Zander was in charge of punishment. That time, my foster brother closed my hand in a door.

When I healed, I did what Mother said. What else could I do? I learned to lie and steal. To run grifts with Mother and Zander. We moved around a lot to find new marks, used fake names. Mother's boyfriend helped with credentials and documents. Fake identities. Zander was always watching me, spying. Waiting for the chance to punish me again. Waiting for me to run so he could lock me up.

But every moment, I was searching for my chance to get out.

Little by little, I sought out independence. It felt like ages for me to find it. But as I got older, it was harder and harder for Mother and Zander to control me. I got my job at the plant nursery. That turned into a job designing flower arrangements for a local restauranteur. Just like Travis told me. Within a few years, I was taking courses at the local community college. I started dating Cam and moved in with him as quickly as possible. I thought Mother and Zander couldn't touch me anymore. Mother's cop-boyfriend had drifted off, so he was out of the picture, much to my relief. I thought I'd finally found my own life.

Of course, they ruined it.

Zander got me fired from my job and threatened to tell my school that *Lark Richards* wasn't my real name. But instead of coming home like they wanted, I ran again. Farther away than ever before. I ran to Santa Barbara County, and I took Cam with me.

We settled down in Solvang and started again. It wasn't easy because Mother had my birth certificate and anything tied to my real identity. I had to work under the table, free-lancing and taking whatever gigs I could get. Even then, I hid the worst parts of my history from my boyfriend. I told him I was estranged from my family and that they wouldn't approve of our relationship. I just wanted my past to disappear. I wanted my foster family to forget me.

But my past came for me. Like it always has.

Zander and Mother tracked me down, and I realized I'd been a fool to ever think they'd let me go free.

After they found out where I was living, they were more

than happy to relocate to Southern California. A fresh pool of opportunities. Wealthy people to con. Zander showed up at my door, making threats and bullying me and Cam. I pushed back at first. That worked for a while. But my family has a way of wearing me down. A thousand relentless jabs and cuts, until I was once again desperate to escape from the pressure.

A business proposition. That was what Zander called it. One last con, and then they'd leave me alone.

Mother was the one who found Travis Bradley.

"*You*," I say. "You're the reason I started volunteering at the clinic. You wanted me to meet Travis. Wanted me to get close to him."

Starla is still looking down at me with her vicious, predatory smirk. "So you're remembering. Good for you."

Mother had certain roles she liked to play to gain people's trust. Nurse was one of them. She didn't have a nursing degree, of course, but she'd picked up enough knowledge over the years to fake it, and she had enough falsified credentials and charisma to talk her way into places. Clinics, retirement communities, hospice centers. Anywhere she could find vulnerable, lonely people who might have money to grift.

Mother got a part-time gig at the clinic where Travis was sometimes a patient. She never met him, but she heard the other nurses gossiping about his wealthy, estranged family. A brother in London who was practically a billionaire, he was so loaded. And a mom who Travis hadn't seen in years.

Starla plays with the clasp on her messenger bag. "Travis should've been more careful about sharing his history with a bunch of gossipy nurse's aides. He was a perfect mark."

Zander instructed me to get personal information from Travis that we could use. It's called social engineering. I would get personal details that only Travis would know, and Mother would turn around and contact Travis's family, pretending to be him. Fake-Travis would beg for money, and his distraught, estranged mom would pay up in the hopes of seeing her son again. A classic con. Given how rich Travis's brother is, Mother thought the plan could be worth millions.

"I needed you to bat your eyelashes and do that sweet, innocent routine you're so good at," Starla says. "Men love it. Worked on Travis, and it worked on his nephew, too."

"Travis was my *friend*," I spit out. "And I never intended to help you trick him. Or his family. I was always working against you."

When Zander made his business proposition, his promise of *one last con*, I knew better than to believe him. He and Mother had turned me into a cynic. I didn't see a way out—reporting them to the police was never an option I considered —but I knew I could ruin their plans.

And if I got lucky, they'd somehow mess up and screw *themselves* over in the process. Not sure how I imagined that would happen. But desperation breeds desperate hopes.

I got to know Travis, having no real plan of my own but to ruin theirs. But something happened that I hadn't expected. I truly liked Travis. We bonded in all the ways he described to me earlier. Clicked, like a long-lost father and daughter. I wanted to help him reunite with his family.

And I was all the more determined not to let Mother or Zander do anything to hurt the Bradleys.

I looked up Nina's email address, and I contacted her. At first, I just wanted her to know her son was alive, and that he missed her. Then I tried to warn her in case Mother and Zander got in touch with her.

But Mother had been busy, too. She suspected I wasn't being as compliant as I claimed. She insisted I meet with her.

"You thought you could double-cross me. But you were so far out of your depth, Lark."

"I did well enough."

"Only because your brother is a fool when it comes to you. The moment I talked to you, I realized you were never going to deliver what we needed on Travis. You needed to be punished. My mistake was trusting Zander to handle you."

"You had Zander get me fired from volunteering for the clinic! He convinced my boyfriend to spy on me. He beat me up, left me covered in bruises."

She leans over me. "If Zander had been smart, he would've locked you up while he was at it. And he wouldn't have given away what else we were doing."

After Cam and I had our huge fight and I broke up with him, I ran to Travis. He was the only person in the world I could trust. I shared more about my past than I ever had with anyone, though I didn't tell him everything.

I recall what Travis said earlier. *You showed up at my door with all your belongings. Bruises on you and hellfire in your eyes. You were furious, damn near dejected, and you wouldn't tell me what was really going on. But you kept mentioning my family.*

Because I knew, at least in vague terms, what Mother and Zander were planning.

While I was getting close to Travis for all those months, Mother had discovered another path to get her hands on the Bradleys' money. Going after Nina directly. Mother had been poking around the Bradleys' affairs, learning all about Nina that she could. She discovered that Nina was sick.

"How did you manage to get the job as Nina's hospice nurse?" I ask. "I couldn't figure that out."

She scoffs. "Never underestimate me. It took me months of learning Nina's schedule, turning up in the right places where she'd be. Helped that she's overly friendly and *loves* to chat. I was her new bestie. What luck that her new friend turned out to be a nurse, and one experienced with hospice care at that. Nina's the one who insisted the hospice service hire me. She has the kind of money that they were more than happy to make it all work out. And it *did* work out for me, Lark." She pats her messenger bag. "Our original con, convincing Nina to send money to Travis, would've been a one-time payoff. But as her nurse, I've turned Nina into my personal piggy bank. I've been bleeding her little by little since I got here. Gathering up her bank passwords, finding the places she stashed money and jewelry around the house. My only problem was *you*."

I glance around the garage, wondering how long we've been here. While my brain has been time-traveling through my memories, it can't be more than a few minutes in reality. Ryan is still wheezing slightly on the ground, though his sounds are getting ever fainter.

The Bradleys are my family now. The only real one I've had since my mom died. This is my *home*.

I have to defend it. But how?

My gaze hits on something underneath the workbench. A tool of some kind. Can I reach it?

"I already knew about your emails to Nina," Starla says. "I saw them on her iPad, and I discreetly blocked your sending address so you couldn't tell her anything else. I didn't think you'd be brave enough to come all the way to West Oaks, but then one of your little friends told Zander you were heading out of town."

"Another spy? But who—"

My eyes sink closed as I realize who knew. Denise, the barista from Sugar & Yeast Café. That morning, I left Travis's camper before he woke up and took the bus into Solvang. I stopped by the café, hoping to see Cam and ask if I could borrow his car. I thought he'd feel bad enough about our breakup to say yes. Not very nice of me, but like I said—I was all kinds of desperate.

Cam wasn't at work. But Denise was. And I was dumb

enough to let slip that I was traveling that day. Denise wouldn't let me borrow her car, so I took the bus.

Denise probably called Zander when Danny and I showed up later in Solvang, too. *Unbelievable.* No wonder he was able to follow us to the beach. Denise was full of sympathy, giving us freaking cookies, while planning to call my evil brother and snitch on me.

"Your friend called Zander," Starla explains, enjoying every minute of this, "and he told me. Took me all of two seconds to guess your destination. If you'd reached this house, you would've ruined everything for me. So I told Zander to stop you."

"You sent him to kill me."

"I had him wait in a car on Nina's street, just in case you showed up. And you did." Her smile falters, and her grip on the strap of her bag tightens. "Then imagine my shock and concern when I heard the dramatic story about Danny saving a woman's life. That, combined with Zander calling me in a panic. I was about ready to grab my cash and run. But apparently, you'd lost your memories. You showed up at the house —I *really* was nervous then—but you had no clue who I was."

My stomach burns as I think about that day. I shook Starla's hand, oblivious to the fact that she had ordered my death. She was the villain hiding in plain sight.

And now she's trapped me. How the heck am I going to get out of this?

38

Danny

I never thought I'd see the day. But Nina and Travis are hugging, and I'm grinning and tearing up.

This is really happening.

The moment I told her that someone was here to see her, Nina looked at me with wide, shocked eyes. Like she knew. Then I waved him in, and immediately she started to cry. For a minute there I was nervous, given how weak she was from her ordeal earlier today. But then she opened up with the biggest smile I've seen from her in ages.

"Travis, come here and hug your momma," she said, and then it was all over for the three of us. Laughing and sobbing and grinning ear to ear.

It's impossible to describe. How the years seem to be melting away, even though all three of us are a hell of a lot older and worn down by the time that's passed. Hopefully wiser too. Because now that it's happening, I realize how foolish I was to question it.

Travis sits on the stool by Nina's bed, while I stand on her other side. He holds her hand as they talk about what they've missed in each other's lives. Travis keeps wiping his eyes as he explains why he stayed away.

It would be easy to blame my dad for interfering when Travis wanted to come home before. But after everything, I don't want to be angry, and Nina certainly doesn't. We're focusing on the good memories instead.

"And what about this guy?" Travis says, gesturing at me. "All grown up. I bet you're proud of him."

Nina reaches for my hand. "Danny makes me proud every day."

I tell Travis about my Army days. Joining WOFD. Nina shares about her exchange students, her adventures in retirement. Then she gets to her diagnosis. Cancer, and deciding not to have further treatment. Travis gives us an explanation about his car accident—his lowest point—and the winemaker he works for, a woman I suspect he's smitten with. Laughter mixes with tears.

I don't know how much time passes in what feels like the blink of an eye. But then Travis is asking me about Lark. How we ended up falling in love. And I can't rein in my smile.

"I think I fell for her that first day in the hospital. She'd lost her memory, but she had so much personality. Making me laugh. I'd never met anyone like her."

"Sounds like the Lark I know," Travis says.

"From that very first day, Lark was—" I look around, realizing she's not here.

Did she leave? Or did she not come in? She probably intended to give us a minute to ourselves, even though I would've loved to have her stay the whole time. This is where she belongs. Just shows how overwhelmed I've been that I didn't notice her absence before.

A glance at my watch tells me it's been half an hour at least that we've been here, reminiscing.

Where is she? We're practically having a party, and she's missing out.

Then Nina says the same thing I was just thinking. "Lark should be here with us." Her words are slightly slurred. She's getting worn down, but no way am I going to tell my grandmother to go to bed. I'll wait for the nurse to do that.

And speaking of, where is Ryan?

A thread of worry winds around my heart.

39

Lark

"Your amnesia bought me time," Starla says. "But I knew your memories could come back. I had to find a way to get rid of you before that happened."

I glance over at the tool beneath the bench. A set of pliers. I bring my eyes to Starla again, but I slowly move my hands back, trying to grab the pliers with my fingers.

"You hired Kathy Sullivan."

"I had Zander arrange it. I was a little *busy* doing my *job* here. I actually had to care for Nina." She sounds annoyed, like Nina was being petty and demanding by having terminal cancer.

My fingertip catches on the pliers. They move an inch closer. A little more, and I'll be able to grab them.

"Kathy was an old friend of mine from NorCal. Before I brought her in, I had no idea how easily you might regain your memories. I just wanted you out of West Oaks, away from me. That turned out to be a disaster, but at least I'd figured out that your memory truly was gone. You were a lot more interested in Nina's grandson than you were in your past."

My fingertips brush the pliers. Almost... *Almost...*

I clamp my jaw tight, hiding my smile.

"If you had focused on Danny and your happy little fairy tale, we could've coexisted. But you had to look for Travis. You had to go back to Solvang and start digging it all up again."

It takes me a couple tries, but I get the tapered end of the pliers in between my wrist and the zip tie. And I start to push the metal against the plastic. Twisting it.

"Nina's overdose today?" I ask. "Was that you?"

She sneers. "I'm not that stupid. You think it's easy to mess around with someone's prescriptions without getting caught? That's the sort of shit the investigators like to look for these days, after true-crime documentaries about killer nurses. It's too obvious. No, that was Ryan and his incompetence. But I'm the first person Ryan called when Nina's oxygen levels fell, begging me for help, and I told Zander we had an opportunity. It was his job to take it. But he screwed that up, too. Got himself arrested instead of reining you in, like he was supposed to."

The pliers slip, scraping hard into the skin of my forearm, and I fight to cover up my flinch. "Aren't you afraid Zander will snitch on you?"

"To the cops? Never. He'll never turn his back on his mother. He knows it's his fault he got caught. But once I'm out of here, I'll hire a lawyer for him."

Come on, I think, tugging the pliers against the plastic. The thin strap of the cuff digs into my wrist, cutting off my circulation. *Come on.*

"I've made mistakes too. Who knew a little carelessness with my caller ID would give me away?" Starla walks over to

Ryan. She pushes his body with her toe. He's not moving. I can't hear him breathing.

My arms are shaking as I lever the pliers, harder and harder. I hold my breath.

"Now, I've got this mess to clean up." Her hand sticks into her bag, coming out with another syringe. "And that includes you, Lark."

Shit, I'm out of time.

Starla strides toward me, holding the syringe.

The plastic cuff breaks.

My ankles are still tied, but I launch forward, sweeping my arms and grabbing Starla around the legs. She crashes to the ground. I'm grabbing for the syringe, but I only succeed in knocking it away. It rolls beneath the workbench and out of sight.

"You *brat!*"

Starla rolls, grappling with me. But she manages to kick me in the stomach and wriggles away. In a second, she's got her hand in her bag and comes out with the gun. Her usually perfect hair is a crazed mess around her face, matching the feral shine in her eyes. "I warned you. But you know what? I have an even better idea."

Starla kicks me again, this time in the head. Pain explodes. There's a high-pitched whine in my ears.

I feel her pulling my arm. Something tight around my wrist. I blink, my vision clearing enough for me to see that she's zip-tied my wrist to a set of metal shelves, which are bolted to the wall.

Starla grabs a rag from the workbench and stuffs it into my mouth, so deep I think I'll choke.

She leans in and whispers, "I'll leave you here and let you burn with the rest of them."

Burn?

She takes something from the shelf above me.

The room spins as my eyes try to follow what Starla's doing. She's gone to the other side of the garage, the storage area. She's dumping something liquid all over the boxes there. I hear it splashing. The smell reaches me, sharp and chemically.

"Maybe the police will blame you," she says. "They'll think you snapped and killed Ryan, set the fire. Couldn't handle the mental pressure you were under. Assuming the fire melts the plastic on your cuffs... But it doesn't matter what they believe. You'll be dead, and I'll be long gone."

Holding her bag against her side, she walks to the exit door that leads onto the driveway.

The last thing she does is strike a match and toss it.

Danny

"I'll figure out where everybody is," I say, standing up from where I was sitting on Nina's bed. "I'll be right back." I walk down the hallway toward Lark's room.

"Lark?" I pop my head in, but the room is empty.

I try the kitchen next. I guess Matteo, Aiden, and Quinn left a while ago. I check my phone and find a few text messages from them, saying goodbye and sharing well wishes. Thank goodness they were here earlier today, because I couldn't have handled everything without them. Before we got word that Zander had been arrested, there's no way I would've felt safe leaving Lark and Nina here if my friends hadn't been around to keep my loved ones safe.

But now, the house feels way too quiet. Eerie even.

"Lark?" I call out again. "Babe, where are you?"

She hasn't texted. Is it possible she went in the backyard? I'm about to step in the direction of the back door to check.

But then my entire body goes still. A scent just reached my brain, calling up a primal response inside of me before I've even processed it into words and logic.

Smoke.

I smell smoke.

"Fire!" I shout, just as the smoke detector siren wails.

Travis runs out of Nina's room and down the hall. "What's happening?"

I wave my arms at him. "Just get Nina out of here, then call 911! Go. Get Nina away from the house. I have to find Lark!"

I see smoke coming from the hallway that leads to the garage. Small tendrils just beginning to form. Not much heat yet. I have to find Lark and get her to safety.

I run to the garage door. When I press my hand against it, there's heat, but not much yet. I try the knob, and it's not opening. Something's blocking it. "Lark!" My fist bangs on the door.

If she's in there, I don't hear anything. "Get away from the door! I'm coming in!"

I raise my boot and slam it against the door. Wood splinters. The door flies inward. Smoke pours out.

I sprint into the garage.

The entire far wall is in flames.

I nearly trip over a prone figure on the ground, and my heart clenches. But it's not Lark. It's Ryan. I check his vitals. Shit, I don't feel a pulse.

Then I spot Lark. She's got a gag in her mouth, her hands and feet bound. Her eyes are closed and she's not moving. My heart, guts, lungs, everything rises into my throat. *No, no no no.* I race over to her, dropping to my knees. I feel for her pulse, and it's there, but weak. My eyes sting from the smoke, and I'm nearly out of my mind with fear and adrenaline.

"Lark, baby, hold on. I'm getting you out of here."

I slice the zip tie with a knife from my workbench, lift her up over my shoulder, and sprint out of there through the side door. I run across the driveway until I'm far enough from the house. As gently as I can, I lay her on the concrete. From the corner of my eye, I see Travis laying Nina over on the grass near the sidewalk.

All I want in the world is to stay here with Lark, help her, but Ryan is still inside the garage. If there's any possible chance he's still alive, I can't leave him in there. And I can't send my sixty-five-year-old uncle in to get him either.

Travis runs toward me. "I called the fire department. What do I do now? What do I do?"

Sirens in the distance. I don't have time to give him instructions. I launch myself at the garage instead, racing back into the growing inferno.

Keeping as low as I can, I race to where Ryan is lying on the ground. I heft him over my shoulder. I can't think about the fact that Nina's home is going up in flames. That the contents of this garage represent a lot more than just some cars and tools. These are memories of my grandmother, my granddad. And Lark. The days we spent here getting to know one another. Falling for each other.

I don't understand what happened out here, who is responsible for this. But I can't think about any of it.

I run outside to the street and lay Ryan next to Lark. Travis is bent over her. He looks up at me with sheer, terrified panic in his eyes. *My* eyes. A reflection of the same desperate terror that's overtaking my soul.

"She's not breathing!" Travis cries.

The sirens are getting louder. A truck is responding, but every split second counts. And I have two injured people in front of me.

"Do you know CPR?" I ask Travis.

"Yeah, kinda."

"Try to help Ryan," I tell Travis. "Do whatever you can."

Then I dive toward the woman I love. Because for me, there's no choice. I have to choose her. Every time.

As I start chest compressions, I murmur to her. Beg her. "Please, Lark. I love you. Stay with me. Stay here with me, please." My voice is shaking. Tears flood my eyes. I'm a medic, for fuck's sake, and I've been through crises much worse than this. I've been deployed in war zones. Treated my teammates who just lost their legs to an IED. This isn't how I react.

But I've never seen the woman I love dying in front of me.

We haven't had enough time together. Everything I want with Lark flashes in my mind. How much she means to me. Our future. Our *forever*.

It can't end like this.

Finally, Lark drags in a breath, coughing and choking. My heart starts beating again.

Paramedics suddenly surrounding us, working on Ryan. Barking questions at me. Firefighters are swarming too, guys I probably know, but I can't tear my focus from the woman I love.

I move out of the way for the medics to give her oxygen. But I stay close enough that my gaze doesn't waver from hers.

"I love you, Lark. I love you."

TWO DAYS LATER, I pull up to Nina's house. Lark tries to get out, but I put my hand over her middle. "Wait, let me come around for you."

"You don't have to. I'm fine." Her voice is still a little ragged from the smoke inhalation. Though it's much better than it was at first.

"I know you're fine, but I'm not. Let me take care of you."

She gives me a small eye roll, but she lets me come around to her side and help her up. The woman is lucky I'm not carrying her right now. I just want to spoil her in every possible way. Do anything I can to make her feel protected and loved.

She's told me over and over again that what happened wasn't my fault, just like it wasn't hers. I'm still working on getting it through my head. Used to be, I was the one reassuring her.

We get up to the porch, where Travis is waiting for us with a mega-watt grin. "Hey! Welcome home!" He crushes Lark into a hug, and I just barely hold back from scolding him to be careful. "Nina's so excited to have you back."

The past two days have been some of the most difficult I've ever spent. In the aftermath of the fire, Lark and Ryan were both rushed to the hospital. Lark had suffered smoke inhalation, as well as a concussion. Ryan was in far worse shape, with an overdose of morphine adding to the smoke that choked his lungs. But incredibly, he survived. He's still in the hospital with his family at his side.

Aiden, Quinn, and Cliff have been shuttling back-and-forth between Nina's house and the hospital, making sure we all had food and anything else we needed. My other friends from Station Two and West Oaks PD have been making appearances as well. Jess has been working overtime at the house helping Travis with Nina, and my uncle hasn't left his mom's bedside throughout this entire ordeal.

There were some really scary moments early on when the doctors were checking over the extent of her injuries. When I had no idea what had really happened.

And then, finding out that it was Starla. Realizing that the person responsible for Lark's suffering was right under our noses all that time. Had been alone with Nina countless times. That messed me up. Made me want to tear up my insides if it could somehow rewind the clock and change what that woman had put my family through.

My only consolation is that—for all her bravado, all the brazen things she did—Starla didn't get away with it.

Nina figured it out. In those initial moments of chaos, when the ambulance was roaring away and West Oaks FD was putting out the garage fire, Nina insisted on having her iPad. It took a few minutes to get clearance from the firefighters, but Travis was able to get back in the house for Nina's device. Immediately, she pulled up the app for our security system and checked the cameras. Then she told the police, who'd already arrived by then, that Starla must have done it. Nina had spotted her nurse fleeing the garage.

Nina had no clue then what was really going on, but it was her quick thinking that led to an APB going out. Highway patrol picked up Starla on the outskirts of town. She had the cash and jewelry she'd stolen over the course of many weeks from Nina, plus the info for an overseas account where she'd transferred a huge chunk of Nina's living trust.

Now, she's in jail like Zander, set to be arraigned in the next day or two. Quinn has been keeping us updated, and the case is being handled by District Attorney Lana Marchetti herself. Multiple counts of attempted murder for both of them, false imprisonment, arson, theft, computer fraud... I lost track of how many crimes those two are being charged with. Plus the murder of Kathy Sullivan, whose body was just found yesterday near Fresno.

Starla and Zander won't be seeing the outside of a prison for a long time, if ever.

While we were in the hospital, Lark told me and a West Oaks PD detective everything she now remembers about her life. Her damaged vocal cords kept getting tired, and she had to write some of it out instead. But she refused to stop until every last detail was out in the open.

She explained that she didn't tell Travis about her "Mother" because she was so ashamed. Though Lark had tried to run and fight back against her tormentor, she often complied as well, and it was too difficult for her to share those dark secrets even with someone she trusted. But when she told me and the detective, she kept her chin up and her eyes clear. It still hurt to tell the story, but there wasn't an ounce of shame anymore.

I'm so proud of her. Damn proud to call her mine.

"I can't wait to see Nina," Lark says, and Travis grins, rubbing her arm.

"Then let's go."

We follow Travis inside. There's a faint smell of charred wood. Matteo told me the garage is a mess, and it's blocked off from the rest of the house. I don't even want to think about the damage to the '71 Charger. But I guess that'll be a project for Lark, Travis, and me. Not to restore it to some imagined moment in the past, because that's not possible. But we'll build it into something new. Something better. *Together.*

In fact, I already have some ideas for that car for when it's finished.

Nina and Matteo look up from her iPad when we walk in. "Thank God you're here," Matteo says. "The Scrabble slaughter can end."

"We didn't finish our game yet," Nina complains.

"You just want to run up the score against me." Matteo comes over and gives us both hugs. "Welcome home, but I'm gonna run. I'm supposed to go to a birthing class with Angela in fifteen minutes, and I don't want to know what she'll do to me if I'm late." He gives Nina a kiss on the cheek and dashes off.

I pull over an upholstered chair for Lark to sit down. But Nina's frowning. "Well, *that* greeting was half-assed. I'm still waiting for my hug."

She opens her arms, and Lark jumps up into her embrace.

They hold on to each other fiercely, Lark hiding her face against Nina's shoulder, though I can tell she's trying not to put too much of her weight, small as it is, on Nina's frail frame.

Lark's shoulders are shaking. "I'm so sorry. If I'd known earlier…"

"It's all right," Nina murmurs. "It's all right. It's over, and you're home."

Nina and Lark hold one another for a long time, a silent understanding passing between them. The two people I love most in the entire world. Their spirits are so strong and vibrant that it shines out of them. Filling me with pride and gratitude.

Travis looks on, eyes filling with tears. He grabs me and hugs me to his side. "I love you, Danny. I'm so glad I'm here with you. You don't know what it means to me."

"Me too, Uncle Travis," I whisper. "Me too."

I don't know what exactly is ahead for our family. How much longer the four of us will have together like this. Nina's getting weaker every day, and I'm finally admitting to myself that there isn't going to be a miracle. Cancer is one fight that we aren't going to find our way out of.

But I intend to make every last moment count, and I know Lark will be right there with me. Through the soaring highs and the devastating lows. We'll make it to the other side together.

EPILOGUE

EIGHT MONTHS LATER

Lark

W e're driving along an unpaved road, trees hemming us in on either side. The SUV Danny rented shakes with every rock and divot.

"Almost there," he promises, grinning like a little kid, he's so excited. "You're going to love it."

"I know I am," I say. But mostly I just love seeing him so happy. Especially after what the last few months have been like.

The trees open up, and Danny pulls the SUV up to a small cabin. It's simple and rustic, just how he described it when he told me about this trip. We are totally off the grid here. No electricity or plumbing. We've been tent camping a few times together already, but Danny was excited to find this rental, which is on private land and completely secluded for miles around.

And the sky is wide open above us. When it's night, the view of the stars promises to be breathtaking.

Our own little piece of heaven.

"What do you think?" Danny asks as we're getting out.

"It's perfect. I do love it. So much."

He goes around to the trunk. "Just wait to see what else I brought."

This trip is our last hurrah before I start taking botany courses at West Oaks College. Quinn helped me work out my legal status, which was a lot easier once we figured out my real identity. My last name really is Swanson, and I was able to get a birth certificate, driver's license, and everything else I needed. In the past month, I started a job at the West Oaks Botanical Gardens, and even though I'm mostly pulling weeds and soaking up information like a sponge, I couldn't be happier. Every day feels so full of promise. And getting to go home to Danny at night is the perfect ending.

Danny's back at work too, which I don't always love, because it means that several times a week I don't see him much at all. But his shifts at the station give me plenty of time to spend at the Pink House with Quinn, laughing together and commiserating and learning to cook now that Aidan has left West Oaks and moved to Colorado. Didn't see *that* one coming, and it's a long story that will have to wait for another time.

I've met with my old friends in Solvang, too, even Cam. I told them what Denise did, how she ratted me out to Zander. But I'm not giving her any more of my thoughts or energy. I'm focusing on the present and future, while also making peace with my past.

While Travis still lives in Santa Barbara County near his winemaker, he visits us all the time. I text with him a lot too, especially when Danny's on shift. Now that I have all my memories, Travis and I have rediscovered our friendship and carried on as if it had never been interrupted.

Travis had a few legal issues of his own to sort out. Specifically, that DUI charge in Las Vegas. He sometimes still has bad days with his chronic migraines, and that's when I make the trip to him, bringing food and comfort and whatever else he needs. Travis loves spending time with his nephew too, but my relationship with Danny's uncle is something special and different. Travis fills the space in my life that was empty for a long time after losing my real mom.

And Nina...

Nina's absence echoes everywhere.

Losing her two months ago bound Travis, Danny, and me together in an entirely different way. While I only knew her for a short time compared to them, I loved her. Now that she's gone, I've lost a piece of the new family that I only got to enjoy for a short time. I just hope that my presence in her life was as meaningful as hers was in mine.

But it's been much harder for Danny. Losing his grandmother wounded him deeply. Even though he held himself together, I could see the pain sneaking through in his eyes when he looked off in the distance. For so much of his life, Nina was the one person he relied upon most. The only person he trusted to always have his back and choose him first.

The pain of losing her isn't something that I can fix or take away. I can only show him how much I love him every single day. Always choosing him. But it's not like that's a burden. Finding Danny, loving him, is the best thing that's ever happened to me.

This weekend is the first time that we've been away from West Oaks, just us, since she passed. Danny might have planned this trip, but I've got something special up my sleeve, too.

I just hope he likes it. That he's ready to take the next step with me toward our future.

～

Danny

NINA PASSED seven weeks and five days ago. Every one of the moments since feels like it's imprinted on my soul. A painful tattoo in indelible ink.

But each one comes a little easier. Thanks to Lark.

After Travis returned, Nina had a new surge of energy for a while. And again when my father finally got himself to West Oaks to say goodbye. She had her two sons by her side, plus me and Lark, and happiness radiated from her. I've rarely seen Nina smile so much for as long as I've known her.

She and Lark had some long conversations during that time too. I would wake up finding Lark gone from our room, and she would be asleep with her head on the mattress next to Nina, the two of them holding hands while both slept. Lark got so immersed in Nina's care that she sometimes took over for me and Jess.

But after the joy of having her family back together again, it was like everything went downhill even faster. Saying a last goodbye to both of her sons gave her permission to start letting go.

She was ready to rest.

The morning she died, Travis was sitting right beside her.

My dad stood behind him, a hand on Travis's shoulder. Lark and I huddled together on the opposite side. The people who loved her most, surrounding her. Nina's eyes were closed, but I knew she was awake. She felt us. She took her last breath, and when it was over, Lark put her arms around me and held me.

My uncle was sobbing quietly across from us. My dad stood utterly still.

Lark whispered that she loved me over and over again in my ear. And even though I couldn't return those words aloud, not with everything else bunched up inside my throat, I've never loved her so much.

The wild thing is, I felt Nina's love too. This bright sunlight had infused the room, the morning sun peeking in at just the right angle to make the place glow and sparkle. I've never felt so much love in my life as I did during those moments. My heart was so raw and exposed that the love hurt, yet it healed too. And I just pray that's exactly what Nina felt as she left us.

A few weeks after, we rented a boat with Travis and spread Nina's ashes over the ocean so she could travel to new and undiscovered places. Even though she's never going to leave the place where she lives in our hearts.

There have been ups and downs since. Some days, especially in the mornings when I'm drinking coffee and looking out at the willow in the garden, I feel my grandmother's memory surrounding me with light. And other times, the pain of losing her is so overwhelming that I struggle to get out of bed. But every time, no matter what I'm feeling, Lark is right there with me. Giving me someone to love and cherish, and cherishing me right back.

After I unload the SUV, we bring our things inside and make a simple dinner. As the sun is setting, I string an oversized hammock between two poles in the middle of the clearing. Lark and I cuddle up inside it, swinging back and forth as the sun disappears. A few stars are just beginning to peek out, though it'll be hours before they're really putting on a show.

"I brought a present for you," I say. I've been slightly uncomfortable lying on the small box that's in my back pocket. I sneak my fingers behind me and pull it out. "Something you'll need now that you're starting school."

"Heart-shaped erasers?" She presses her lips together, smiling. But her mouth opens in a shocked *O* once she removes the box lid and sees what's inside. "What…what is this?"

Using one finger, she lifts out a set of car keys.

"For the '71 Charger," I say.

"I know, but to borrow, right? So I don't have to take the bus?"

"No, it's a *gift*. I want you to have it." I kiss her jaw. "I already signed over the title. It's yours."

Lark wraps her arms around my neck. "I can't believe it. *Thank you.*"

In the past seven-plus weeks since Nina died, I've thrown myself into finishing the restoration. Travis helped a ton, and so did Lark. But what am I supposed to do with two classic cars? My red one is all fixed up, no trace of the scratches. And the midnight-black paint looks incredible with her hair. It's a gift for me, really. She's nuclear-reactor hot driving that car.

Also, I would give her anything and everything to see her smile like she is now.

But her lips twist, turning mischievous. "Actually, I have a present for you, too."

Lark tugs a folded piece of paper from her back pocket. I open it. The sky overhead is fading quickly to deep indigo, but there's still enough light for me to study the details on the paper.

It's a listing for a one-bedroom row house just a mile away from the beach. The place is situated at the north end of town, where the coast is more rocky and less popular with beachgoers, but stunning. The apartment itself is tiny and nowhere near modern. But it has lots of light. There's a rooftop deck that already has a container-garden growing, with vines creeping up trellises. And a garage, too, with space for a small workshop.

"You've talked about finding a new place," Lark says, rushing to fill the silence. "Since you don't want to be in Nina's house forever, and you gave up your room at the Pink House."

I nod. I've been trying to wrap up Nina's estate, and it made sense to keep living in her house for the time being, though Lark and I now share a single room. But the house still belongs to my father. Though we're doing better after he and Mom made the trip to say goodbye to Nina, I've been steadfast in wanting my independence. I don't want to be handed things just because of who my father is. Nina earned that house by taking care of her family for so many years, and I didn't.

So Lark is right. I do want a new place. It's been in the back of my mind for a while.

But this…it's unexpected.

"I crunched the numbers," Lark goes on. "I came up with a budget, and together we can afford this place as long as we're careful about what we spend. I talked the landlord into holding the listing for a few days until we decide. Okay, begged is more like it." She bites her lip, eyes round and expectant. "Assuming you'd want to move in with me? I know we already share a room, but I mean *really* move in. To our own place."

My insides are melting into a warm, gooey center. I'm such a mess of affection for this woman, so touched by her gesture, that I can't come up with any words to sum it all up.

"If you don't like this one, we can look for something else," she says. "Or separate apartments if you want. If this is too much too soon. I just wanted it to be a surprise, and you've been so busy lately, being back on shift at the station and handling Nina's estate and—"

I drop a soft kiss to her lips, cutting off her rambling. "Of course I want to move in with you. I love the place you found. It's absolutely amazing, and I couldn't imagine anything better for us."

"Yeah?"

I fold up the paper and let it flutter off the side of the hammock. Then I take the car keys and the box and drop those out too. We'll pick them up later.

"But I'd take anyplace if I get to be with you," I say. "The backseat of a car. A tent in the forest. Under a cozy tree."

Her brow arches. "That's because you're an exhibitionist."

"Only a little." I work open the buttons on her top, peppering her skin with soft kisses. "But I don't just mean sex. I love you. I love *being* with you. Hope you like me too, because I plan to hang on to you. Can't get rid of me now."

"Somehow I'll manage."

We slither out of our clothes, which is a lot harder to do in the hammock than I imagined it would be. We almost fall out half a dozen times, and we're cracking up by the time we're naked.

But then the sounds of heavy breathing and needy sighs fill the air, along with the chirping of crickets and wind ruffling leaves. When I slide my swollen, aching cock inside of her, Lark gives me one of those whimpers I can't get enough of. I kiss her to swallow up the sound.

"Stay with me?" she whispers against my lips. "Forever?"

"Always."

We get that hammock rocking under the open sky until the rest of the stars come out.

The End.

Aiden's story starts a brand new series in
HARD KNOCK HERO!

And don't miss THE ONE FOR FOREVER, Rex & Quinn's story and the final book in the West Oaks Heroes series.

ALSO BY HANNAH SHIELD

ABOUT THE AUTHOR

Hannah Shield once worked as an attorney. Now, she loves thrilling readers on the page—in every possible way.

She writes steamy, suspenseful romance with feisty heroines, brooding heroes, and heart-pounding action. Visit her website at www.hannahshield.com.

Made in United States
North Haven, CT
28 July 2023

39646209R00200